CODE NAME ANTARES

Grant Stevens
and
Team Alpha Tango

by

Jamie Fredric

D1304376

Other Books by Jamie Fredric:

Mission Critical
Black Ops 1

Warning Order
Black Ops 2

In the Mouth of the Wolf
Black Ops 3

Sacrifice of One
Black Ops 4

Last Op
Black Ops 5

Shanghai Mission

*

Visit: jfredric.blogspot.com

Dedication

For All Those Who Have Served

*

All Gave Some, Some Gave All

Team Alpha Tango
Home Base - "Eagle 8"

Grant Stevens - Captain, (Ret.); graduate U.S. Naval Academy; born in California; brown hair; brown eyes, 6'1"; fluent in Russian and Japanese; Code name "Panther"; Team call sign: "Yankee Zero-Niner"

Joe Adler - Lieutenant, (Ret.); born in Oklahoma; brown hair, blue eyes, 5'10"; fluent in German; Code name "Mustang"; "Yankee Two-Seven"

Frank Diaz - CPO; born in NY; black hair, brown eyes, 5'9"; EOD; fluent in Spanish, some Portuguese; "Yankee Three-Six"

Ken Slade - CPOS (Senior Chief), (Ret.); born in Alaska; bald; brown eyes; 5'10"; pointman/navigator; speaks the Inuit language, some Russian; "Yankee Four-One"

Cal "Doc" Stalley - Petty Officer 1st Class; born in Virginia; dark blond hair; blue eyes; 5'10"; corpsman; fluent in French, some Chinese; youngest of the Team; "Yankee Five-Two"

Darius "DJ" James - Petty Officer 1st Class; born in

Florida; dark brown hair; brown eyes; 5'9";
communications; speaks some Turkish, Arabic;
"Yankee Six-Eight"

Mike Novak - Petty Officer 1st Class; born in
Wisconsin; dark blond hair; hazel eyes; 6'0"; sniper;
speaks Hungarian and some German; "Yankee Seven-
Three"

Matt Garrett - Captain, (Ret.); graduate of U.S. Naval
Academy; born in Maryland; brown hair; brown eyes,
6'0"; fluent in French and German; "Yankee Eight-
Four"

Chapter 1

March
Palmer Road
Maryland
Monday - Day 1
0015 Hours

Petty Officer Sam Franklin drove the gray Navy truck along dark, winding, two-lane Palmer Road. He rolled down the window a couple of inches, flicked out the butt of a Lucky Strike cigarette, then exhaled a lungful of smoke from the side of his mouth.

Rolling up the window, he shot a quick glance toward Lieutenant Paul Wayne. "Sure will be glad when this cold snap is over, sir. I'm ready for warm weather."

Wayne had an M16 laying across his lap. Both he and Franklin had .45s holstered. "Can't do much about it, Sam, just keep the heater turned up. Maybe you'd rather be riding with Sid and Tom back there," he indicated with a thumb over his shoulder.

"No, sir. It's just fine here."

"That's what I thought."

"Say, lieutenant, do you have any idea what we're hauling in those crates?"

"Sam, you ask the same damn question whenever we make a pick up at the factory. What's my standard response?"

"Need to know, sir. We don't have the need."

Even with high beams on, Franklin failed to see a pothole and drove straight through it.

"Whoa! What the hell, Sam?!" Wayne shouted. A noise overhead diverted his attention. "Sounds like a chopper. You're not breaking the speed limit, are you? Might be cops."

Franklin glanced at the speedometer. "No, sir! Right on the money!"

Wayne rolled down the window and stuck his head out. Scanning the night sky, he finally spotted flashing navigation lights. "Yeah, it's a chopper, but it looks like it's moving on." He rolled up the window, then pounded the back of his fist on the rear divider. "You men stay on alert back there!" He reached for the M16, chambered a round with the charging handle, then flipped the selector lever to safe.

As the truck went around a curve, its high beams landed on two men standing in the middle of the road. Franklin hit the brakes. The truck went into a skid, but he over-compensated, and the rear tire caught the thick edge of blacktop. The sound was ear-piercing as the truck's undercarriage scraped across asphalt until the truck came to rest in a shallow ditch. Two guards in the bed were thrown around, their bodies rolling into the side of the truck.

Wayne's rifle landed on the floorboard. He and Franklin both drew their sidearms, but it was too late. Bullets shattered both side windows, killing the two instantly. Two attackers, dressed in cammies, with black one-hole masks pulled over their heads, cautiously walked closer, continuing to aim the Uzis toward the cab.

The two guards in the bed regained their balance, and scrambled for their M16s, when out of nowhere, two more attackers rushed from the woods. Both guards fired. A bullet struck one of the oncoming men. He yelped in pain, grabbed his side, and collapsed, as the other man fell to the ground near him. Everything went quiet. Both guards were breathing heavy, listening for any sound of movement. Anything could've happened up front.

The two attackers at the front of the truck couldn't take a chance and fire randomly into the bed, possibly damaging the "merchandise." Drawing weapons from side holsters, they eased their way along the truck, one on either side.

"Lieutenant!" one guard shouted. Silence. "Sam!" He started to lean forward, when weapons fired, killing him and the other guard.

Three attackers walked closer, peering into the bed. Blood oozed from under both guards, mingling into one pool.

Immediately, two of the men jumped up into the truck bed. The crates were still secured, intact, undamaged. Slicing through the restraining ropes, they shoved the crates toward the tailgate.

The lead man called in the chopper, as he swiveled his head, looking for navigation lights. He signaled with a flashlight as the chopper came into view, flying from the west. A bright landing light flashed on, and they heard the distinct *thump-thump* sounds of a Huey's rotors. Its skids touched blacktop no more than twenty-five feet from the truck.

Pulling one crate from the bed, the two men carried it to the chopper, while the injured man was helped into the cargo bay. Within a matter of minutes both crates had been loaded. The attackers hopped onboard, the rotors picked up speed, and skids lifted off the blacktop. The pilot set it on a southeast heading. Within minutes, its lights disappeared over the horizon, on its way to making the first delivery.

*

Bull Run Regional Park
Virginia
0500 Hours

A 1972 black Toyota pickup truck with a camper shell, was parked at the edge of a small clearing, facing toward a bumpy, narrow path, leading back to the main road.

The driver discovered this location months ago. He determined traffic entering and leaving the park during this time of year would be practically nil, and because of the time.

He was wearing nondescript clothes, all black: leather jacket, pullover sweater, jeans and Converse sneakers. He glanced at the clock on the dash, then pulled a black one-hole mask down over his face. The chopper should be getting close. The pilot had been given instructions to circle within close proximity of the clearing until spotting his signal.

A faint sound of rotors at his three o'clock. Grabbing a flashlight from under the seat, he got out, lowered the tailgate, then walked toward the center of the clearing. Holding the flashlight overhead, he pressed the switch on and off. The dark, clear night made the light seem brighter, acting like a beacon.

In less than a minute, a Huey was hovering overhead. Cold air swirled around him, with dirt, leaves and small debris caught up in it. The chopper's landing light came on as it began its decent.

He hustled back to the truck, started the engine, then backed up, getting it as close to the cargo bay as he could. There'd be no wasting time now. He jumped out of the cab and rushed toward the chopper. Three men stood in the cargo doorway.

He glanced at the wooden crate behind them, then noticed the injured man laying on the deck. Blood had soaked through his cammie jacket. "What happened?"

"Two of the guards opened up on us. Don't worry. We took care . . ."

"Did you have any problem offloading?"

The man who called himself "Python" asked with a scoffing tone, "Are you kidding?! Do you know how many times we've hadda do this kinda fuckin' shit?"

"I don't give a damn, just hurry up and get that loaded." When the crate was secured inside the truck, he pointed to the injured man. "See that he gets treatment. Since you've done this kinda fuckin' shit before, you probably know of someone who won't ask questions." He reached inside his jacket, then lobbed a thick envelope to "Python."

"That's half of what we agreed on, as promised. I

expect to get confirmation from the ship within a day. Then, I'll contact you to arrange final payment."

"Python" tossed the envelope up and down in his palm. "What are we supposed to do with the chopper?"

"Make sure it's clean, then leave it at the airfield. I'll take care of it from there. Now, go!" he shouted, pounding his fist against the side of the chopper.

The pilot checked his coordinates. The Huey slowly began its ascent then turned east and headed toward the coast again. But this time its destination was a small airfield just north of Rehoboth Beach, Delaware.

A couple of minutes later, before he reached the main road, the driver pulled onto the shoulder. Stripping off his mask, he tossed it on the floorboard, then reached under his seat. He grabbed a small black box, raised an antenna, and pressed the red button, setting a timer. Returning the box under his seat, he took a quick glance in his rear view mirror, seeing only darkness. There wasn't any need for him to wait. He didn't have any doubt the incident would be reported on the local news in the morning. He put the truck into gear and headed back to D.C.

*

The dead end side street he lived on had one flickering street light at the corner. He drove past the street, shut off the headlights, then turned left down the narrow alley, passing five homes. Each house had its own single car garage across the alley.

Driving just beyond his house at the end of the

street, he put the truck in neutral, set the brake, then got out. As he walked to the garage, he glanced at the other houses, each one dark, quiet. His car was parked on the west side of the garage, in the shadows, less noticeable.

He unlocked the garage door, then slowly raised it. As soon as he backed the truck in, he immediately killed the engine. As an extra precaution, he locked it, and took one more look through the canopy window, ensuring the crate was still covered with the tarp.

As he unlocked the dead bolt on the wood-paneled house door, he glanced around one last time before going inside.

A yellowing shade on the single kitchen window was always lowered, even though he didn't have too much concern about someone poking around outside. He knew every one of his neighbors, even if only by sight. He'd rented the small, furnished, two bedroom home five years ago, talking the landlord into leasing it on a month-to-month basis, after he paid a hefty deposit.

He dropped his keys on the counter, then hung his jacket on a nail by the door, before getting a can of ginger ale from the fridge. Sipping on his drink, he went into the living room, going directly to the front bay window. One house on the corner had a light on. His neighbor, Glen, was getting ready for his shift at the plant. Every other house was dark. He slowly drew the dark curtains together.

Sitting on an upholstered, high-backed chair by the window, he took a long drink, then leaned back. He focused his eyes on the opposite wall, not looking at anything in particular, but reviewing the evening's events. It turned out precisely as planned. . . except for the killing of the Navy guards. But he had no control over the incident, and had to take the word of the men he'd hired. At least they managed to leave the scene before being discovered.

He rolled the cold can between his palms remembering the anticipation he experienced months ago when he, Nicolai Kalinin, was about to begin his mission in the United States.

*

He first saw the American at Dupont Circle Metro station. Located below Connecticut Avenue NW, the station's north entrance escalators were 188 feet long. The station had two tracks, with two side platforms, and two entrances: one to the north on Q Street NW and one to the south on the southern edge of Dupont Circle. It was one of the busiest stations in D.C. and that was the reason the American chose it.

Misha Zelesky, assigned to the Russian Embassy, was to meet the American at 2000 hours near the bottom of the north escalator, where the hustle and bustle would keep attention away from them. As a means of recognition, Zelesky wore a black raincoat, black hat, and carried a brown leather briefcase. The American would be wearing a brown leather jacket, jeans, and a Baltimore Orioles orange baseball cap with black brim.

Zelesky usually picked up messages the American left at drop sites, and with a possibility the American had been watching, the decision was made. Zelesky would meet him.

Why the American decided on a face-to-face for delivering the instructions and not leave them at a drop site, was still unclear. Unless the instructions were of the utmost importance.

Maybe out of pure curiosity, and without the knowledge of his "handler," Kalinin wanted an up close and personal look at this American, who for reasons yet unknown, had decided to become a traitor to his country. Arriving twenty minutes early, Kalinin positioned himself twenty feet away from the bottom of the escalator, trying to blend in with commuters.

For nearly fifteen minutes he waited for Zelesky to arrive, finally spotting him on the escalator, wearing the clothes agreed upon. Kalinin moved farther away, getting behind one of the route maps, keeping his eyes on the Russian.

Zelesky waited near the escalator, constantly looking at his watch. At 1955 hours, he spotted him coming down the escalator, wearing the Orioles baseball cap.

The American gave an almost imperceptible nod in his direction. A sound of an approaching train, and a sudden rush of wind being pushed ahead of it, didn't draw their attention away from the task at hand.

Backing up, moving farther away from the tracks, both Zelesky and the American continued watching passengers hurrying closer to the edge of the platform as the sound of a train increased in intensity.

From his angle and from passengers constantly passing by, Kalinin wasn't able to get a clear look at the American's facial features, especially with the baseball cap pulled down to his eyes. All he noticed was a clean shaven face, hair cut very short, possibly dark brown or black, height just under 5'10", weight about one sixty.

The American reached inside his jacket, took out a plain white envelope, and handed it to Zelesky. No words passed between the two men. And as passengers exited from the train, hurrying toward the "up" escalator, the American immediately walked away from Zelesky, mingling with the crowd. He removed his baseball cap, and soon disappeared within a sea of people.

Zelesky slid the envelope into his pocket, waited until another train pulled into the station, then he left, heading for a specific drop site where Kalinin would pick it up.

It wasn't until he returned home that Kalinin opened the envelope. The details on the paper inside were very specific. From those details, "Antares" set in motion his plan to steal top secret weapons from the U.S.

Chapter 2

December
Three Months Earlier
Residence of the Russian Ambassador
Washington, D.C.
1400 Hours

A spotless, black four-door Mercedes pulled into the U-shaped driveway at 1125 Sixteenth Street, NW. Parked behind a seven-foot high wrought iron fence lined with low bushes, its view of the street was unimpeded.

The driver got out and hurried around to the passenger side, opening the rear door. A stocky-framed man in his early sixties, stepped out, folding his dark gray coat over his arm. These colder days were much more reminiscent of his homeland. Russian Ambassador Anton Vazov glanced at gray clouds rolling across the sky. The local weather forecasted possible snow flurries.

As he walked toward the building, he reflected on the lunch he just finished at the Monocle. Only a half mile from the Capitol, the restaurant was a popular spot for all politicians. While Vazov didn't have much hope in picking up the slightest tidbit of information, there was always a possibility. But it was the food that made him a regular patron. The flavors from today's lunch still lingered on his tongue: a green salad topped with a mound of fresh crabmeat and a small sirloin steak, cooked rare, and for dessert, a slice of New York-style cheesecake.

Taking a quick look over his shoulder, he walked to the main entrance of his residence, a residence that also served as the Embassy of the Soviet Union. The building was four stories, with the first two used as office space, the third was his residence, and the fourth, so-called attic space.

After the building became the USSR's Embassy, rumors spread within the higher echelons of the U.S. government, that concealed in diplomatic pouches were materials to build an atomic bomb. Every piece was rumored to be stored and assembled in the attic.

"Good afternoon, Mr. Ambassador." Dasha Yudin smiled as she stood behind her desk, smoothing down her beige skirt. Yudin was new to the embassy staff, having arrived from Russia three weeks earlier. Her requirement for the position was to be fluent in English. A plain looking twenty-six year old, she always wore her long brown hair tied into a tight "bun" (coil) at the back of her head.

Vazov nodded quickly at the young woman, as he saw his aide approaching.

"Mr. Ambassador," Oleg Duboff said. "Let me take your coat, sir." Duboff folded the coat over his arm. A small, thin man, barely 5'7", Duboff had been at the embassy two years, serving as aide to the previous ambassador.

"Come with me to my office, Oleg," Vazov said, smoothing his hair back.

Miss Dasha Yudin sat down again, folding her

hands on top of her desk, waiting for a phone call. . . any phone call.

Stopping at an elevator, Duboff pressed the button. The doors immediately parted, and the two men stepped in, with Vazov entering ahead of his aide.

At the end of the second floor, facing Sixteenth Street, was the ambassador's office. Duboff scurried in front of Vazov in order to open the door.

The ambassador immediately went to his desk, looking for any new folders or envelopes. Even though he had his office "swept" everyday for listening devices, Vazov remained cautious.

"Anything new today, Oleg?" he asked as he pointed to a folder.

Duboff hung the coat on a brass coat tree then came closer to the desk. "No, sir. Nothing yet today."

Disappointed, Vazov jabbed his index finger against the folder. Inside was a white envelope. There wasn't any return address, but the postmark showed Baltimore, Maryland, and was addressed to him specifically. The letter inside had been typed and was brief, indicating the individual had top secret information. Below that were three numbered items, each indicating a different location for "dead drops." If he, Vazov, was interested, an envelope would be at drop number one in two days. If the envelope was not picked up at the end of that day, it would be assumed Russia had no interest.

Vazov turned and went to one of the front windows. A steady stream of traffic flowed in both directions along Northwest Sixteenth Street. Four blocks south was Pennsylvania Avenue and the White House.

A sharp rapping at the door made him swing

around. "Mr. Ambassador!" a man shouted. Duboff immediately hurried to the door, but it opened before he reached it.

Two men entered. They needed no introduction. Misha Zelesky and Petya Vikulin, both assigned to the embassy as security, both KGB.

Zelesky put a finger to his lips, then pointed to a cabinet.

"You can go, Oleg," Vazov said as he waved his aide away. As soon as he left, Vazov came around the desk and walked to a six-foot high, antique wooden cabinet. Behind two doors were six shelves on the left, two on the right, with a reel-to-reel tape recorder on the right lower shelf. He turned the recorder on then adjusted the sound. Music from the opera "Aleko" by Rachmaninov began playing.

Vazov slid his hands into his trouser pockets, as he turned to face the two men. Even with the music playing, he spoke softly. "What do you have to report?" His eyes went from one man then to the other.

Vikulin removed an envelope from his jacket pocket, handing it to Vazov. "It was taped under the bench in the park."

As Vazov opened the envelope, he asked Zelesky, "You still haven't seen the individual?"

"No. Unless we set up surveillance twenty-four hours a day, it is not likely we will. It is even possible he has someone else make the 'drop.'"

Vazov put the envelope on a shelf and pulled out one black and white photo and two pieces of paper. The photo and first page were stamped top and bottom in red ink: "Top Secret."

Laying the papers down, he held the photo closer, trying to determine what he was looking at. It appeared to be part of a device attached to possibly a rifle barrel. He switched the photo to his left hand then picked up the first page. It was an official-looking copy of specifications of a weapon, but again, it wasn't complete, only portions were detailed, the remainder blacked out.

Vazov scanned the page. The Department of Defense logo was on the top left. Down the left side were places listing the title of the document and its classification. Closer to the bottom were spaces for signing off on the program. In the lower right was the program date. All signatures and dates had been blacked out.

Laying down that page, he picked up another, but this was a plain piece of white paper. The message had been prepared the same as the first two, hand printed in black ink:

"If you have further interest, mark a black X on the light pole at 'drop' number one, no later than 2200 hours tomorrow. You will be contacted."

At the bottom right was a name printed in red ink. It had been printed very clearly, at a slight upward angle: "Primex."

Vazov slid the papers and photo into the envelope. He tapped the envelope against a shelf as he wondered why this "Primex" had not yet asked for any money in exchange for this information. Perhaps Moscow must first make an offer. Or, there was the possibility political asylum would be all that was required.

Vazov had already dismissed the notion that this was a setup orchestrated by the CIA or FBI.

"I will contact Moscow," he said looking at the two men. "Once I have an answer, I will know how to proceed."

As the two men left the office, Vazov secured the cabinet doors. Whenever a meeting of importance took place in this office, the music would play.

Chapter 3

December
Point Lookout State Park
Maryland
0040 Hours

Point Lookout State Park, at the tip of the peninsula, was where the Potomac River met the Chesapeake Bay. The park was popular during daylight hours from spring through fall. Fishermen, boaters, and families enjoyed the facilities, no longer remembering it was once one of the worst, harshest prisons ever established during the Civil War.

Kalinin arrived early, driving his dark blue, 1973 Z28 Camaro along the last mile of Point Lookout Road. He chose this out of the way destination for the upcoming meeting.

He shut off the headlights, then dropped the speed down to twenty mph. The car rolled past a small building on the left. He tried to spot any sign of movement around the darkened entrance to the visitors' restrooms, but there was nothing to see.

Barely pressing the gas, he continued along the road leading into a cul-de-sac that looped back around. A three-story house, with the tower of a lighthouse protruding through a red-shingled roof was just beyond a tall chain link fence. The lighthouse was no longer in operation, its lantern dark for years. A single pole light, near a locked gate, was just bright enough to light up the entrance walkway.

He came around the loop, spotted a parking area on the left side, backed up, then shut off the engine. Reaching under his seat, he felt for the cold steel of his Makarov, then laid it on the dash.

Leaning back, he reviewed every minute detail, pulling names, incidents and dates from his mind. He knew there'd be questions, each one testing him.

Letting out a long breath, he glanced up the road. Still no sign of a vehicle approaching. He leaned across the center console and popped open the glove box, took out an envelope, then turned on the overhead light. Inside the envelope were the car's registration and ownership papers. A brief smile crossed his face, as he put them back in the envelope then closed the glove box. His license was tucked inside his wallet. Earlier that day he'd put both passports in an envelope then taped it under the glove box, not wanting to take a chance if he was stopped by local cops.

There wasn't any doubt that he and the vehicle would be searched. He'd be surprised if it didn't happen. Taking his Makarov from the dash, he thought it best to make himself seem less threatening, so he put the weapon under the seat.

Satisfied everything was in order, he glanced at his watch. Exactly 0100 hours. He got out, closed the door, then walked to the front of the car, just as he saw headlights.

Taking a couple paces away from the Camaro, he faced the oncoming vehicle, its headlights settling on him. Keeping his arms by his side, with his gloved hands in full view, he took a deep breath.

He was about to have his first, and long-awaited meeting with his "handler."

*

Darkened windows prevented him from seeing how many people were inside the Mercedes, even as the vehicle stopped in front of him, then backed into a space two away from the Camaro.

Just before the driver backed up, Kalinin got a quick look at the license plate: Nation's Capital, DPL 48. A small sticker indicated the date and year the vehicle was registered as a diplomatic vehicle. Verification complete.

Headlights remained on, as the two front doors opened, and an overhead light came on. He shielded his eyes, finally able to see inside. Three men: driver, one passenger up front, one in the rear. Driver and front passenger got out and closed the doors.

Kalinin stood his ground and waited. The driver, Misha Zelesky, approached the front of the Mercedes. He was close to six feet tall, barrel chested, thinning dark hair. His black coat was intentionally left unbuttoned, exposing a weapon in a shoulder holster. Taking up a position by the front bumper, he folded his thick hands in front of him, keeping his eyes on Kalinin, without so much as a nod.

Kalinin returned Zelesky's stare, until the second man came around the vehicle. From a description Kalinin had, the man had to be Petya Vikulin. He was not quite 5'10" with black hair, and broad shoulders.

Zelesky walked in front of Kalinin, motioning for him to raise his arms, then he expertly patted him down, only finding his wallet. He asked in Russian, "Weapon? Identification?"

Kalinin tilted his head toward the Camaro, responding in Russian. "Weapon is under the seat. Identification papers are in the glovebox."

"What about a passport?" Zelesky asked. He'd been ordered to be thorough, to search for any type of ID.

"Taped under the glove box."

Zelesky searched inside the car, pulling the Makarov from under the seat, then he removed both envelopes. He handed everything to the man sitting in the rear.

A few moments passed. Finally, the man in the car got out. Ambassador Anton Vazov gave the envelopes to Zelesky, directing him to return them to the car. Then carrying the Makarov with him, he walked slowly toward Kalinin, and handed him his weapon.

Kalinin put the Makarov in his waistband. At 6'2" he seemed to tower over the shorter Vazov who was motioning with an index finger for him to lean closer. Kalinin complied, allowing Vazov to study his features more closely in the headlights. It wasn't so much the brown hair the ambassador seemed interested in, but more a half-inch scar on the chin and hazel-colored eyes.

Vazov finally extended a hand. "Nicolai, at last we meet."

Kalinin returned the handshake. "Yes, sir, at last."

"I must say, Nicolai, your American name, 'James

Broyce' suits you very well. Shall I call you 'James?'"

"I like the sound of 'Nicolai' for now, Mr. Ambassador. I have not heard it spoken for a long time."

Vazov smiled briefly then questioned, "And would you prefer speaking in our 'Mother' tongue, or have you forgotten much of the language after spending so many years in America? How old were you when you came here? Three? Four? That would be about thirty-two years you have been away from Russia."

Responding to a test question, Kalinin answered in Russian, "I was three, sir. And it has nearly been thirty-six years, but I can assure you, Mr. Ambassador, I have not forgotten our language, nor have I forgotten what my parents told me about Russia. I will speak in whatever language that you feel most comfortable with."

Vazov laughed a short, deep laugh. "Then we will speak in Russian." He pointed to the scar. "How did that happen?"

"During a ballgame when I slid into third base. Do you follow baseball?"

"No, I am not interested. Now, come. Walk with me." He turned to the two security men. "Wait here. Keep watch."

Zelesky and Vikulin backed away, both of them drawing their weapons. Zelesky shut off the headlights, leaving on the parking lights. He stayed near the two vehicles. The Mercedes' keys were on the dash, just in case they had to move fast.

Vikulin went across the road, then walked slowly toward the restroom building. He positioned himself at the corner on the south side giving him an unobstructed view of the road.

Ambassador Vazov motioned toward the rocks, as he rubbed his arthritic right hip. "I must sit for a moment, Nicolai."

"Of course, sir." Kalinin brushed sand from the rock wall, nearly one foot in height, then he motioned for Vazov to sit. "You have not been in America very long, Mr. Ambassador. I am sure former Ambassador Balicov's death came as a shock."

"Yes, it was a shock for everyone. It has taken me a long time to review papers, surveillance tapes and videos, dossiers." He folded his hands on his lap. "While I did not know your parents, Nicolai, I read their dossier. It said they died instantly in the auto accident. You were away at the time?"

Kalinin lowered his head. "Yes, sir. The ship I was stationed on in Norfolk was going through sea trials."

"From what I've read, and now meeting you, they did a remarkable job in raising you. They were dedicated to you and Russia."

"I know, sir." Kalinin took a deep breath, briefly picturing his mother and father.

"How old were you when you found out you were Russian?"

"Fourteen. My parents explained everything to me."

"Were you shocked?"

Kalinin shook his head. "No, not shocked. They said things over the years that made me wonder. I began to question them as I got older."

"And you were ready to serve Mother Russia, just

as they had?"

"More than ready then, and now."

Vazov lightly slapped the top of his thighs as he said, "I would like to talk more about your years in America, Nicolai, but now is not the time."

Kalinin put a foot on top of the rocks, resting his arms on his knee. "One day soon perhaps we will have the opportunity."

"If and when that day finally comes, both of us may be back in Russia."

"Yes. That is possible. But actually, I look forward to returning to Kursk, sir, to see where I was born."

"Much has changed in Russia, Nicolai."

Kalinin slid his foot off the rock, hearing a quiet sound of water slapping against the sandy shore. He stared ahead into the darkness momentarily before looking down at Vazov. "Much has changed here as well, sir."

Silence between the two men lasted a couple of moments until Vazov said, "All your years living here have led you to this moment. Are you prepared to do everything we might ask of you, even if that means 'eliminating' someone?"

Kalinin didn't hesitate in responding. He locked onto Vazov's dark eyes. "Mr. Ambassador, anything you ask of me, no matter what that might entail, I will complete without question."

Vazov pointed over his shoulder then lowered his voice. "And if I ask you to use your weapon--here, now?"

Kalinin glanced quickly at the two security men, then drew his weapon. Keeping it out of view, holding it low in front of him, he questioned, "One or both, sir?"

"You are confident enough to take out both?"

"I am, sir, except I probably do not need to remind you that you are going to need a ride back to the embassy."

Vazov finally cracked a smile. "Never mind. I trust your ability."

Kalinin slid the weapon back into his waistband. "Sir, I will do anything you ask of me, but I have a request, and suggestions."

Vazov tilted his head. "Go ahead."

"Mr. Ambassador, you know I only rent the house I am currently living in. I do not want any devices installed."

"I assume you mean a scrambler or shortwave?"

"Yes, sir. I cannot take the chance that my landlord will inspect the property. And if I must leave in an emergency, it might take too long to disassemble and remove the equipment."

"But what if you need to use the safe house? You realize both those devices are installed."

"If circumstances dictate that I go there, then those would undoubtedly become a necessity. But I hope that will not happen."

Vazov was beginning to feel less and less like Kalinin's handler. On the other hand, he was impressed by the younger man's forward-thinking and ability to take charge. From this first meeting, Vazov realized Russia's newest "sleeper" would serve her well.

Vazov struggled slightly trying to stand. Kalinin held his arm, assisting him. "Let us go to my car,

Nicolai. This evening is not treating me well."

The two men settled into the leather back seat of the Mercedes. Vazov reached overhead and turned on a reading light, then removed a large envelope from the front seat pocket, and a folded piece of paper from his jacket. "The paper lists our established 'dead drop' sites."

Kalinin glanced at the list. "I will familiarize myself with these." He refolded the paper, slipping it into his leather jacket.

Vazov handed him the envelope. "This will be your first assignment."

Kalinin nodded. He removed the papers from the envelope. Three sets, each set stapled. "Were these left at the same location?"

"No. Each set of papers was retrieved from different 'drop' sites."

Kalinin examined photos and every page. As far as specifications, very little was listed.

All the while Vazov kept his eyes on him, watching to see if there was any form of emotion. But there was none. The younger man was completely in control.

"Well, Nicolai, do you have an idea on what that weapon could be? Why have the Americans labeled it 'Top Secret'?"

Kalinin dropped the envelope on the seat. He turned slightly, looking at Vazov. "There is not much to go on, but I would say it has to do with some type of laser technology. But since it is classified as top secret, there is obviously something very special about it. Do you know exactly how many weapons are being 'offered'?"

"Not yet."

"And has a meeting been set up with the individual, 'Primex'?"

"Moscow has just approved our request to proceed. Misha will meet him at whatever location and time he has chosen. I can only assume that is when details will be given about the 'transfer' of the weapon. At least that is what I am anticipating. He indicated there may be another meeting afterward. Why he is insisting on separate meetings, I do not know.

"As soon as I return to the embassy, I will have Misha go to the location and make the mark. Then we must wait until we are contacted."

"Am I correct in assuming that once the meeting takes place, I will be in control of the mission?"

Vazov smiled slightly. "You will still report to me while you are here in the U.S., but yes, the plan for the mission is entirely in your hands."

"And what about funds, sir? Equipment will be needed, payoffs will . . ."

"I will give you enough cash that should see you through this assignment. Remember, when it is time for you to move the weapon or weapons, you will have access to Russia's jet at Dulles International Airport."

"From what I understand, sir, in order to give the 'merchandise' diplomatic immunity, official papers must be filled out."

"That is correct. I will give you a seal and a special stamp. You must remember that each package must be clearly marked 'diplomatic pouch.'"

"I understand," Kalinin nodded. "And once I have secured the weapons, will you contact our comrades in

Moscow?"

"The decision was already made that you will deliver them to Moscow. Then, once in Moscow, arrangements will be made for transferring half to the Afghans, however many that may be. My contact in Kabul is Major Zubarev. He is dealing with the Afghans." Vazov detected something in the face of the younger Russian. "What is it?"

"You mentioned our aircraft at Dulles, and I realize at this point we do not know how many weapons will be made available, nor do we have an exact date when this will happen, but. . ."

"What is your concern?"

"My concern only pertains to multiple weapons, perhaps ten or more, and if that is the case, I believe we should not put all the weapons aboard the aircraft. If anything happened. . ."

"I understand. And your suggestion is?"

Kalinin hesitated, letting the idea roll around his brain, confident that it was plausible. "We have cargo ships traveling up and down the American coast, do we not?" Vazov nodded. "Do we have any carriers operating in or close to the Mediterranean?"

"Two. Why?"

"As soon as we learn of a date for the 'transfer' of the weapons, would you be able to put the captain of a cargo vessel on alert?"

"You want to deliver the weapons to that ship? But how?"

"I will find a way. Then, once the cargo ship is within range of the carrier's helicopters, the weapons can be picked up and delivered to Kabul. I will personally make the delivery to Moscow."

Vazov could only wonder how Kalinin was able to put this plan together in only a matter of minutes. "I will see what I can do." He reached inside his jacket. "You may need this. Do you know what it is?"

Kalinin took the envelope then removed a small book, barely two by three inches. He flipped through the tiny code book. "Yes, sir. I remember my parents using one. It is a 'one-time pad.'" A one-time pad is a type of encryption almost impossible to crack. Characters from plain text are encrypted by the use of a character from a secret random key (pad) of the same length as the plain text. This results in a cipher text. Each code page is used one time. The code is printed on sheets of chemically treated paper called "flash paper." Once heated it converts to nitrocellulose, then burns almost instantly, leaving no ash. The two men had exactly the same book.

He put the book in his pocket. "Once I have the weapons that are going to Moscow, I will write a coded message on page eight of the Washington Post, and leave it under the embassy gate. You can have the seal and documents left at one of our drop sites."

"Why not leave the message at a drop site, Nicolai?"

"I believe this would be the fastest way, without your men having to make several trips looking for a message."

"It appears you have thought of everything, Nicolai."

"I hope so, Mr. Ambassador."

Vazov indicated with a thumb over his shoulder. "I

have large canvas pouches in the trunk. I am hoping you will be able to use them for the weapons."

"If they are not large enough, I am sure I can 'break' down the weapons."

"Oh, I kept your Russian passport." He patted his inside pocket. "I will see that it shows you are a diplomatic courier and ensure it has proper date stamps, coinciding with countries you have 'visited.' One of the men will leave it our drop site.

"Remember, Nicolai, unless there is an absolute emergency, do not phone the embassy."

Kalinin got out, then leaned in. "Of course, sir. I will only use the means discussed."

"Good night, Nicolai."

"Good night, Mr. Ambassador." He closed the door, went to the Camaro, and slid behind the wheel. He started the engine, but waited until the Mercedes was out of sight before he turned on headlights.

As he drove through the park, he remembered his parents. He hadn't thought much about them over the last several years. But talking about them briefly with the ambassador made him remember the years he had with them. Maybe for the first time in his life, he was grateful they had been his parents.

*

Nicolai Kalinin was born one month prior to his parents leaving Kursk, Russia. Traveling under false American documents with the last name "Broyce," they were smuggled into Geneva, Switzerland. For the next three years the Kalinins worked at the International

School of Geneva. The jobs were menial, but they established themselves as reliable, compassionate people. When he was three, they moved to the U.S., settling in a small town outside Charlottesville, Virginia. They were welcomed into an up-and-coming community, being treated like any other young American family. The mother and father held decent jobs, the family attended church on Sundays, and they supported their young son in his endeavors. They were devoted parents, preparing their son for his future in America.

Attending public schools with the name "James Broyce," he excelled in math and science, participated in sports, and developed a love of baseball. After graduating high school, he joined the Navy, and served five years as an Interior Communications electrician. ICs directed and coordinated the installation, maintenance and repair of interior communications systems on ships and at shore facilities, including communication systems, indicating and navigation systems, visual landing aids for aircraft, and alarm, safety, and warning systems. After his final tour of duty, he moved back to Charlottesville. Taking advantage of the GI bill, he attended the University of Virginia, earning a B.S. in Electrical Engineering.

With the deep level of his cover, and a 4.0 grade point average, he was confident he'd be hired by a defense contractor. He applied for a college internship program with ZXR Corporation, and began the program one week after graduation. Over time he was promoted to different grade levels, and was always willing to take assignments aboard Navy ships, training, repairing, upgrading systems.

He worked day after day, year after year, never knowing when he'd be called upon to serve Russia, or what he'd be asked to do. His day and time had finally come.

Chapter 4

March
Iwo Jima Memorial
Monday - Day 1
1950 Hours

The temperature hovered just above forty-one degrees, as familiar March winds blew across Virginia and D.C. at thirteen knots, gusting to twenty. As usual, traffic along N. Mead Street was still heavy, but most occupants inside cars hardly took notice of the Memorial.

A door to the Chevy SUV closed. Grant screwed down his baseball cap, and zipped up his black windbreaker. Shoving his hands into the pockets, he started pacing back and forth along the lighted walkway behind the SUV. The call had come in on the special phone earlier in the day. No specifics had been given, only that he and Adler were to be at the Memorial by 2000 hours. More than one possibility ran through his mind.

Adler sat in the rear passenger seat, drinking a last mouthful of warm black coffee. He crushed the empty paper cup then stuck it in the door pocket. "There's more coffee in the thermos, Ken, Mike, and a couple bologna sandwiches in the bag."

"Thanks, LT," Ken Slade responded.

Sipping on his coffee, Novak looked in the rearview

mirror watching Grant pace. Slade kept an eye out for any approaching vehicles.

Adler zipped up his old Navy khaki jacket before opening the door. He caught up to Grant. "Well, Skipper, has that brain of yours come up with any reasonable explanation why we've been 'invited' here?"

Grant stopped then leaned against the tailgate, and shook his head. "I can come up with plenty, Joe, but . . ."

"Boss," Slade interrupted, as he poked his head out the window. "There's a car comin'."

Grant and Adler walked along the side of the SUV, seeing headlights swing around the curve, lighting up them and the SUV.

The tan, 1978 Dodge Aspen was an unmarked vehicle previously owned by the Maryland State Police. The driver pulled into a parking space and shifted into "Park." He switched on an overhead light, then made a notation on a clipboard. Laying the clipboard on the seat, he got out and walked to the Chevy.

He approached Grant and Adler. "Captain Stevens?" he asked with his eyes going from one to the other.

"I'm Grant Stevens," Grant responded, extending a hand.

"I'm Staff Sergeant Stu Reilly, sir, your driver for the evening." Reilly returned Grant's handshake. Even though he was active duty, as a member of the White House motor pool, and on standby twenty-four/seven, Reilly wore civilian clothes. He was about 5'8", with a slim build, and short, thick brown hair.

He turned to Adler. "Lieutenant Adler?"

"That's me," Adler nodded, offering his hand.

"It's routine for me to ask for your IDs, sirs."

Both Grant and Adler took out their wallets, then flipped them open. Grant noticed the staff sergeant had a weapon in a side holster. He and Adler left their .45s in the SUV.

Reilly took each wallet, and shined the light from a small flashlight on each State Department and retired military ID. "All right, sirs. It looks like we're ready for departure." He opened the rear passenger door. Adler slid in.

"Would you mind if I rode up front?" Grant asked.

"Not at all, sir." He opened the front door.

"Wait one," Grant said, as he turned around. "Mike, Ken, head back to Eagle 8. Contact the rest of the team and put them on standby as a 'just in case.' Matt should be on his way back from California. Make sure you contact him. I'll call you when we're ready for retrieval, which I assume will be somewhere in D.C."

"Roger that, boss," Novak responded, before starting the engine.

Grant got in the Dodge. "Okay. Let's go."

Reilly unhooked a mike from the Motorola Micor Radio attached under the dash. In the trunk was a multi-band transmitter, with two whip antennas attached outside.

"Reilly calling guard house. Over."

"Go ahead. Over."

"Departing with two guests. ETA ninety-minutes. Out."

*

Traffic leaving D.C. was still heavy. Oncoming headlights remained constant, while in front of the Dodge, red taillights became a blur. Once Reilly turned on Highway 270, traffic thinned. He pressed the accelerator and picked up speed, but was mindful of staying within the posted speed limit.

The three men kept up a steady conversation, talking military most of the time. Grant noticed that not once did Reilly take his eyes from the road, except to glance in the rear- and side view mirrors, nor did he question the purpose of this evening's trip.

"Excuse me a minute, sirs." He reached for the mike again, reporting ETA in forty-five minutes. He'd make the same call three more times.

Thirty-five minutes later, they were on Park Central Road, a dark, winding blacktop, leading deeper into Catoctin Mountain Park. Posted at the entrance was a sign: Closed December - March. Official Vehicles Only.

With high beams lighting the way, the vehicle eventually turned right onto an unmarked road. Signs warned they were entering a U.S. military installation with restricted access.

Turning off the high beams, Reilly left parking lights on and slowed down. Bright overhead spotlights provided enough light at the guard house, where two Marines waited at the entrance, with one stationed at the exit. All had rifle straps slung over their shoulders, and weapons in side holsters.

Two guards stepped closer as Reilly rolled down his window. He was a familiar figure, having made this same trip many times over the past six months.

Grant and Adler handed over their IDs. The Marine leaned toward the open windows, comparing the two faces to the IDs. As he did, the second guard casually walked around the vehicle looking in windows. The inspection was made only in a cursory manner, since all details had been delivered earlier in the day. The guards knew who and how many to expect.

Returning the IDs, the guard gave a quick salute, then waved them through.

No more than fifty yards past the guardhouse was a perimeter road that circled the entire property, with a chain link fence outside it. Just beyond was a sign: Camp David.

Chapter 5

The Dodge started up a slight incline, leading to the front of Holly Cabin. Nestled in the trees, the one story, gray-colored building was once the original Laurel Lodge where presidents held conferences and greeted dignitaries from throughout the world. Small pole lamps lit up a blacktop path leading to a screened porch. Interior lights glowed from every window. Smoke, rising from a brick chimney, permeated the air.

A Secret Service agent, wearing a black raincoat, came from inside the screened porch. He spoke softly into his wrist mike. "Visitors have arrived." Posting himself on the path, he stood with his hands folded in front of him.

Reilly got out, nodded toward the agent, then hurried around to the passenger side, opening both front and rear doors. "The agent will escort you from here, sirs. I'll be waiting whenever you're ready to leave."

"Thanks, Staff Sergeant," Grant said. "C'mon, Joe."

The two walked up the path, both curious and anxious about the upcoming meeting with President Andrew Carr.

With only a brief nod, the agent led them onto the porch, knocked, then opened the cabin door. Once Grant and Adler had entered, he posted himself directly outside the door.

The President greeted them from across the room. "Captain! Lieutenant! Great to see you both!" He walked toward them with his arm extended.

"Mr. President," Grant said, smiling, as he shook Carr's hand, returning the firm grip.

"Mr. President," Adler said.

"Take off your jackets. Just hang them in that closet, then join me," Carr said, motioning with a hand toward a couch. Normally dressed in a suit, this evening the President wore a pair of dark blue slacks, an open-collar white shirt, and a dark, red cardigan sweater.

A wood fire blazed in the stone fireplace opposite the couch. A brass, three-panel folding screen was on the brick hearth, keeping burning embers at bay.

As Grant and Adler walked to the couch, Carr said, "Sit, please." The two men complied. "'Captain' and 'lieutenant' are pretty formal, gentlemen. Would you mind if I called you 'Grant' and 'Joe'?"

Grant nodded. "We wouldn't mind at all, sir."

Carr pointed to a tray on the coffee table that held a pitcher of water, glasses, and a bucket of ice. "How about something to drink? Maybe some coffee."

"Not for me, but thanks," Grant responded.

Adler followed Grant's lead. "No thanks, sir."

Carr sat on a wooden, hand-made rocker. His eyes went from Grant to Adler as he spoke. "Gentlemen, let me thank you again for the remarkable job you did with the China incident. God only knows how many lives you saved, including the Vice President's. By the way, have you talked with or do you know how those two SEALs are doing?"

Grant responded. "We haven't spoken to them personally, but understand they're with their Team, ready for another mission."

"Typical for you SEALs, right?" Carr laughed.

"Yes, sir. Always ready," Grant responded.

Carr rocked back and forth slowly, with an expression that changed almost immediately. "I'm sorry you had to come out here, but I felt this was the safest place for us to discuss a . . . situation."

"Fewer 'eyes and ears'?" Grant asked, now more concerned than ever. If the President didn't feel comfortable talking in the White House, something very "heavy" must be going down.

"Exactly," Carr responded. "What we're about to discuss is top secret."

"Excuse me, sir, but before you begin, will we be able to bring in the rest of the Team, or will only Joe and I be involved?"

"Why don't I tell you first, then you decide what's best."

"Very well, sir."

Carr's worry was evident. "First let me say that there are only two other people who are aware that I'm talking with you tonight. NSA General Prescott and SECDEF Daniels."

He let out a breath, then started rocking. "Gentlemen, we are confident there's a traitor within the DoD."

Grant and Adler gave each other a quick look. How many times during their Navy careers did they wonder if their involvement in finding and capturing a traitor-- or foreign mole--would be their last time? But it was happening again, this time on U.S. soil.

Carr continued. "What we are dealing with has to do with a laser guided weapon developed by the Navy."

He held up a hand, palm facing the two men. "Now I know what you're thinking. Laser guided weapons aren't anything new. And you'd be correct. They've been around for years. Several countries already have them, even Russia. But this particular weapon is special." He reached for a folder on the coffee table, stamped with red letters TOP SECRET, then handed the folder to Grant. "Take a look at those photos and drawings."

Adler scooted closer to Grant as Grant opened the folder. The photograph showed a weapon, similar to a rifle, slightly more compact, but unlike any rifle either one of them had ever seen.

As they examined the black and white photos, Carr explained, "That's a laser guided rifle, completely computerized."

"Computerized?" Grant asked with wrinkled brow.

"That's right. The developers were able to use the same computer technology designed for the Apollo spacecraft. There's a lot in that report," he pointed toward the folder, "that I don't completely understand. But think about it. A rifle that can be programmed, controlled by computer, has its own GPS. Just set it and forget it--or so I've been told." He gave a half smile, then added, "If you read further into that report, you'll see there's the possibility the design could be altered into almost any size for mounting on ships, planes, or any military vehicle."

"This is fantastic," Adler said, holding two of the photos. "Mike would eat dirt for one of these," he laughed quietly.

"Mike?" Carr asked.

"Uh, yes, Mr. President," Adler answered. "Mike Novak is the Team's sniper."

"I'll keep that in mind."

Grant processed the information, then asked, "Mr. President, when was the prototype completed?"

"Two prototypes, Grant, and that was nearly a year ago. After successful testing, a limited number went into production. The factory was to begin production on another order in about a month."

And that's why we're here, Grant thought. "Has something happened to those production models?"

"Those first ten were stolen."

"Wow," Adler said under his breath.

Grant asked, "When?"

"Last night, around midnight."

"Anything else to go on, Mr. President? I mean, did it happen at the manufacturing plant or during transport?"

"During transport to Indian Head. As SOP, they were secured in special crates, five to a crate. The crates were loaded on a military truck, with a driver, a guard up front, and two riding with the crates. Those guards were well armed.

"About twenty miles from the base, along a deserted stretch of Palmer Road, the truck was attacked. The driver and guards were killed."

"Jesus," Grant said quietly. "Any indication how they made off with the weapons?"

"NIS (Naval Investigative Service) hasn't come up with anything yet. I've been told there wasn't any evidence indicating the crates were opened. No wood remnants, no screws, nothing. Whoever took them, took them completely intact."

"I'm assuming, Mr. President, that whoever was in charge has been questioned?"

"Correct. At the plant and Indian Head." Carr took the lid off the ice bucket, used tongs to put ice into a tall glass, then started pouring water. "You sure I can't get you something?" The two men declined.

Carr swallowed some water. "Not everyone's been questioned, though. I'm sure NIS will continue interviewing and weeding out individuals who may have had more knowledge of the weapon design. There isn't much I can do to slow down the investigation without causing suspicion. Now, I know you boys worked for Admiral Torrinson at NIS not long ago, so you should know how those folks operate."

"Yes, sir." Grant's eyes narrowed as he began interpreting Carr's statement. "Mr. President, I'm getting the impression you want us to 'fly under the radar' on this one."

"You're right, Grant. You'll be conducting a, shall we say, private investigation. I don't want any departments to think I'm stepping on toes, but I also don't want that many involved at this point. We are sure of one traitor, but who's to say there aren't more involved, and from possibly different departments." Carr sipped on some water. "So, have you decided if you'll need your whole Team?"

"I think it'll be best, Mr. President. And I'd like to bring in Agent Mullins. As in the last operation, Scott will have responsibility for lining up refueling, transportation needs, and equipment that might be necessary. He's an invaluable asset to the Team, sir."

Carr rolled the glass between his palms. "Understand, and you ask for anything you deem necessary." He put the glass on the coffee table. "I know you'd like your man to get familiar with one of those, but I don't know if there'll be time for training."

"Mike's a smart guy, Mr. President. With your approval, I could send him to Indian Head for a day of training while we begin our investigation."

"I'll start the ball rolling tonight. Have him go directly to Indian Head in the morning. He'll report to Captain Ramsay." Carr stood, with Grant and Adler immediately following. The meeting was just about over.

"Mr. President, who should I contact with any further questions or if I have updates?" Grant asked.

"Have Agent Mullins contact me directly. A call from the State Department will less likely be questioned."

"Very well, sir."

"Anything else, Grant?"

"No, sir. Joe and I will start immediately when we meet the Team."

"Speaking of which. . . you should probably give one of your men a call from here. The staff sergeant will drive you back to the Memorial." Carr pointed to a door. "There's a phone in my office."

Five minutes later Grant joined Carr and Adler near the front door.

Adler had his hand on the knob, when the Secret Service agent opened it, then stepped aside.

"Grant, Joe," Carr said, "this isn't the first time the country will be depending on you."

Grant returned Carr's firm handshake. "We'll do our very best, Mr. President, and as quickly as possible."

Chapter 6

Palmer Road
Near the accident scene
Tuesday - Day 2
0030 Hours

Two Chevy SUVs drove along Palmer Road, slowing down as they approached where the attack occurred. Grant had the entire Team with him, knowing he'd need every pair of eyes to search for clues, especially in the dark. They couldn't hold off and wait until daylight. Time was of the essence.

As soon as the SUVs stopped, the seven men jumped out. Stalley and Diaz grabbed a couple of emergency flares, setting them in front and behind the vehicles.

Grant turned on a flashlight, the beam settling on an area just off the shoulder. "Looks like that's where the truck ended up," he commented, before turning toward his men. "I don't know what the hell we're looking for, but there's gotta be something that'll give us a clue on who pulled this off and maybe how. Spread out." With flashlight beams leading their way, the men began scouring the area.

Novak moved the light back and forth along blacktop. "Anybody find any casings?!"

Six responses came back: "Negative!"

"NIS probably confiscated all the physical evidence

they could carry," Grant commented.

"Looks like this was where NIS may have 'planted' at least one flare!" Slade shouted as he continued walking along the asphalt.

Suddenly, a set of high beams came around a curve. Slade swung his flashlight back and forth, aiming it low. The distinctive staccato sound of "jake brakes" warned them a big rig was approaching. The truck slowed, then rolled to a stop. The driver leaned his head out the window. "Everything okay here?!"

Slade walked closer to the cab. "Yeah. Everything's under control. Thanks."

The trucker shifted into gear, but kept looking in his large, side view mirror. Slade stood in the middle of the road, watching until lights were no longer visible. "Hey, boss, think that guy might call the cops?"

"Can't worry about him, Ken."

"Skipper!" Adler called. "Take a look at this!"

Grant jogged to where Adler was standing, just along the shoulder, about twenty yards away from where the truck ended up in the ditch. "Whatcha got, Joe?" he asked, with his eyes following the flashlight beam toward trees.

Adler moved the light in a circle on the ground. "See that?" Without waiting for Grant to answer, he directed the light up toward the top of the trees, then made an arc with it until it pointed to the opposite side.

"Yeah, but I still . . . Oh, shit!" Grant finally realized they were looking at debris from pine trees-- pine needles, pine cones, small branches, most scattered along both sides of the road. But mounds of debris, dirt and small stones indicated NIS probably swept the road clean.

"Right, Skipper! A chopper!" Adler said, continuing to move the light.

"Good work, 'Sherlock'!" Grant said, slapping Adler's shoulder. "Now, where'd they go?"

"Beats the shit out of me!"

"Boss!" Stalley yelled. "Found something over here!"

As Grant approached, Stalley got down on a knee, pointing to a dark spot on the asphalt. "I wouldn't swear to it, but I'm bettin' that's blood."

Grant aimed his flashlight beam on the spot, then he turned toward the ditch. "I doubt the guards would've left their vehicle, Doc. You're thinking one of the attackers took a bullet, right?"

"Yes, sir. I sure do," Stalley answered as he stood.

"**You** wouldn't know where they went, would you?"

"Uh, no, sir."

"That's okay, Doc. You're not the only one." Grant turned and started following the broken white centerline. Just as he was about to give up, his flashlight beam landed on something. He knelt on a knee, then his eyes followed the light further down the line about eight feet away. "Joe!"

Adler came rushing across the road. "What'd you find?"

"What do these look like to you?" Grant aimed the light.

"Black scrape marks?"

Grant stood and punched Adler's shoulder, grinning as he said, "You know damn well what they are. You were right. A chopper." The two black marks were left by the skids of the Huey.

It wasn't likely they'd find any more evidence. Grant at least had something to go on--a chopper was definitely part of the attack. "Hey, guys! Let's get outta here and head back to 'Eagle 8.'"

*

Eagle 8
Virginia
0345 Hours

Three empty pizza boxes, two nearly empty buckets of fried chicken, an empty bag of chocolate chip cookies, bottles of beer and soda were scattered on top of the kitchen counter. A fresh pot of coffee percolated near the stove, with the smell of the strong brew drifting throughout the room.

National news was being broadcast on NBC, but sounds from the TV faded into the background. With rumpled clothes, unshaven, in need of showers, Team A.T. sat at the dining room table, each man in his own thoughts, trying to put together a means for locating the traitor--and missing weapons. Newspapers from the past two days were strewn around the table and floor.

Slade and Diaz each had a paper open, scanning every page, looking at articles, pictures.

Grant rocked his chair back and forth, balancing on the two back legs, when he heard the door at the end of the hallway close. "Hey, Matt!"

Garrett took off his coat as he came toward the

living room. "Sorry I'm late. Rough weather coming across country."

"No problem. Get yourself something to eat and drink then join the party."

Garrett draped his coat on the back of the couch, then went to the kitchen. He poured a cup of coffee, then took a chicken leg from the bucket.

Adler was slouched in the chair, with his legs stretched out in front of him, his fingers locked behind his head. "Time for a break," he said, as he got up. "I'm gonna get some coffee." As he walked by the bucket of chicken, he snatched a wing. While he ate, he waited for the second pot of coffee to finish perking. Tossing the chicken bones in the trash, he licked his fingers, then poured the steaming black brew into his cup. "Anybody want a refill?" he said loudly, holding up the pot. Three hands went up. He unplugged the pot and carried it to the table.

Grant pushed his chair back and stood, while rubbing his fingers in small circles on his temples. The little information they had was getting them nowhere fast.

Jamming his hands into his back pockets, he started walking around the table. *Four dead men because of two crates. How many more are gonna die? What the fuck are we missing?*

"Hey, boss?"

"Yeah, Doc?"

"You feelin' okay?"

"Just frustrated and angry as all hell, Doc. Thinking about those four guards who probably didn't have a chance."

"Yeah. I know what you mean," Stalley responded, running his fingers through his dark blond hair. He tried changing the subject, if only briefly. "How about some cold chicken? LT's left a few pieces," he laughed, tilting his head toward Adler.

"Yeah, sure. Sounds, good." Grant watched the youngest team member walking toward the kitchen. The two of them had a bond of sorts, in part because Stalley helped save his life, but as a corpsman, Stalley reminded Grant of his father, Mike Stevens, HMCS, killed in Korea. (Hospital Corpsman, Senior Chief)

Words from the TV newscaster finally started registering with Grant: ". . . have brought more troops into Afghanistan." He swung around, picked up the remote, and turned up the sound.

With his arms folded tightly across his chest, he began taking in every word being reported. The news reporter reviewed events that occurred three months prior on December 27:

"Seven hundred Soviet troops landed in Afghanistan disguised as Afghan military. Within these troops were KGB and GRU special forces officers from the Alpha and Zenith Groups, who took control of major governmental, military and media buildings in Kabul. Simultaneously, other objectives were occupied. The operation was fully completed by the following morning. But the overthrow of the old government seems to be causing more opposition to the Soviets being in Afghanistan."

Chairs scraped across the wood floor as Novak and James got up. They walked toward the TV and stood next to Grant, listening to the report, and watching the video being shown.

The news reporter continued: "Soviet troops are finding themselves drawn into guerilla warfare, fighting against urban uprisings, tribal armies, and sometimes against mutinying Afghan Army units. Soviet-led Afghan forces are fighting against multi-national insurgent groups, the Mujahideen."

The more Grant heard, the more he found himself putting small pieces together. "Sonofabitch!"

"What's happening, Skipper?" Adler shouted from across the room.

But before Grant responded, Slade called, "Boss, you need to read this!" He folded the paper in half and laid it down. As Grant got to the table, Slade pointed to an article.

Grant read the caption: Wreckage Discovered Off Coast.

"Jesus Christ!" he said under his breath.

The article stated the previous night an explosion had been seen off the Delaware coast. The following morning debris had been spotted by the Coast Guard but bodies had yet to be found. Examination of debris indicated it was a Huey. Efforts to find the registered owner had so far failed. The investigation was still underway.

"Well, boss, you think the weapons went down with the chopper?" Slade asked, rubbing a hand briskly over his shiny, bald head.

"What I think, Ken, is somebody's tying up loose ends."

Adler handed him a cup of coffee. "And you know this to be how? That gut of yours?"

Grant remained quiet, rolling around different scenarios, coming up with two possibilities, neither of which gave him a "warm and fuzzy."

"Well?" Adler asked.

"Gotta call Scott," Grant said, turning to go to the phone, acting as if he didn't even hear Adler.

"Hold it!" Adler said, grabbing his arm. "No secrets allowed!"

Grant put his head down, slowly shaking it. When he raised it, seven pairs of eyes were staring at him, waiting for an explanation. "If I'm correct, our mission will encompass more than just tracking down a traitor." He shifted his eyes to Adler, who returned a look through narrowing blue eyes.

"Are you saying we've got another mole on our hands?!"

"There's more going on here than just meets the eye. Somebody sold those weapons to somebody else who plans on using them, or at least use the technology." He tilted his head toward the TV. "And Afghanistan seems the perfect place." Setting his eyes on his men, he finally said, "Look, why don't you all get some shut-eye. We've got work to do tomorrow. DJ and Frank, plan on setting up surveillance at the Russian Embassy."

"Are we lookin' for anything or anybody in particular?" Diaz asked.

"Good question, Frank, but you guys have plenty of 'know how' to pick out anything suspicious. Take glasses, scopes, and maybe one of the cameras with a long-range lens."

"Roger," James answered.

Grant happened to glance at a large security monitor above the fireplace. "DJ, check camera number four," he said pointing to the screen. "Seems to have some interference."

"On it, boss." The screen was divided into six smaller pictures, each in black and white, focused on sections of the property. Every five seconds the pictures would automatically change.

"Hey, Mike!" Grant called.

"Yeah, boss?" Novak answered, leaning around the corner as he was pulling a skivvy shirt over his head.

"Sorry I didn't mention it sooner, but the President's given his okay for you to try out one of those prototypes."

Novak's eyes lit up, as he came into the living room. "No shit?!"

"Yeah. No shit. You're to report to Captain Ramsay at Indian Head. I want you to leave at first light."

"I'm guessing I'm taking my car?"

Grant nodded. "Yeah. We've gotta make sure the SUVs are ready."

"Okay, boss."

Novak turned to leave, when Grant called, "And, Mike. In case you've got any ideas. . . that weapon is **not** to leave the base." Novak kept walking. "Do you copy, mister?!"

"Aye, sir! Copy that!" Novak said over his shoulder, as he continued grumbling, "Guess I'll have to be satisfied with our new issues."

Grant couldn't help but smile as he put his hand on the phone.

The new issues were the HK MP5SDs. The weapon featured a integral but detachable aluminum sound suppressor and a lightweight bolt. A bullet would leave the muzzle at subsonic velocity so it didn't generate a sonic shock wave in flight. The MP5SD was designed to be used with standard supersonic ammo with the suppressor on at all times. With the design of the suppressor, the weapon could be fired with water inside.

Grant stood by the side table. "Matt, I'll fill you in as soon as I call Scott."

Garrett sat on the couch, swallowing a mouthful of warm coffee. "Whenever you're ready."

"First tell me. Do you feel comfortable turning over the business to your employees?"

"They've been basically running it for a while now. I'm confident they can handle it. Besides, I'll be checking in every now and then. Of course, they'll never know exactly when."

"You've had a helluva responsibility since your dad died, Matt."

"Life throws curves sometimes, but. . . hey! If it weren't for dad and his friends, there may not be Team Alpha Tango, right?"

"It still amazes me they planned all this," Grant responded. "Have you seen or talked with them?"

"We talk on the phone, but they still want to keep a low profile when it comes to our 'little' group."

"Sure wish the guys could meet them."

"It could happen," Garrett answered.

Adler came back into the living room, wiping his face with a towel. "Hey, Skipper, are you considering bringing Grigori in on this?"

"If this is a Russian mole, Joe, maybe he can pull some info from his brain that might give us something to go on." He glanced at his watch. "I'm gonna call Scott at home. I'm hoping he'll be able to patch me through to the President in a couple of hours."

*

"C'mon, Scott! Pick up!"

"Yeah," Mullins answered in a gruff, sleepy voice.

"Scott, it's Grant."

"Grant? What's wrong?" He rubbed a hand over the top of his brown hair, then threw off the covers. Stifling a yawn, he sat on the side of the bed, trying to get his eyes to focus on the clock.

"Your phone's not secure, so I'll explain fully when I see you. In the meantime, as soon as you get to the office, I'd like. . . Wait! Never mind. I'll . . ."

"What the hell?! You wake me up and then say 'never mind'?!"

"Just hold your shorts! What I started to say was I'll meet you at your office at 0700. I assume you'll be there, right?"

"Yeah. I'll be there. But you'd better bring strong coffee. And donuts!"

Chapter 7

Near Russian Embassy
Tuesday - Day 2
0620 Hours

Winds were blowing anywhere from ten to fifteen knots, carrying on them a smell of rain. Sunrise was still a half hour away. Street lamps illuminated sidewalks. Lights in front of building entrances cast shadows across driveways. A few pedestrians hustled down sidewalks along both sides of the street, most wearing raincoats or windbreakers. Some were more prepared and carried umbrellas.

Across the street, and a half block north of the Russian Embassy, DJ James and Frank Diaz sat in Diaz's green Ford F-150. James had his window rolled down half way, trying to prevent windows from fogging.

Two large thermos bottles of hot coffee leaned against the backrest. Between the two men was an open paper bag with four unwrapped McDonald's Egg McMuffins, and two crumbled wrappers.

Diaz took a sip of coffee from the thermos' plastic cup. He pressed binoculars against his eyes. While he scanned the embassy grounds, he asked James, "Think boss knows something we don't, DJ?"

James chewed a last mouthful of muffin, then

washed it down with coffee. "You know LT always jokes about his 'gut instinct.' Me personally? I'd rely on it every time, Frank." He tossed the wrapper in the bag, then pulled out another, tapping Diaz's shoulder. "Here. I'll keep watch."

While James used the glasses, he asked, "Have you heard from your kid lately?"

Diaz bit into a McMuffin, then swiped the back of his hand over his mouth. "Got a letter from him last month. He and his mom were visiting her dad in Upstate New York."

"How old is he? Ten? Twelve?"

"Goin' on thirteen."

"Jesus! He was just a baby yesterday."

"Yeah. And I missed half his life," Diaz responded, with a touch of regret in his voice.

Traffic started picking up. Diaz scanned the area across the street in front of the embassy. James watched pedestrians, moving his eyes from the side mirror to the windshield.

"Eleven o'clock, coming this way, black leather jacket," Diaz announced.

James swung the binoculars just past the embassy, focusing on a tall man. "Whoa! He looks just like. . ."

"Yeah! Get the camera!"

James picked up the camera from the floorboard, adjusted the telephoto lens, then snapped two quick pictures.

Already surprised by what they saw, they were even more surprised as they watched him remove a rolled up newspaper from under his arm. He slowed his pace, letting a few pedestrians pass him before stopping in front of the embassy. Easing closer to the wrought iron gate, he bent down, quickly slid the newspaper underneath, and immediately started heading back the way he came.

"Boss and his instincts!" Diaz said. "DJ, you stick with him. I'll follow in the truck in case he's got a vehicle parked somewhere and we need to haul ass."

James checked his weapon, adjusted his earpiece, and quickly got out. He closed the door quietly, then stayed hidden behind the truck. Once the "target" was far enough ahead, James crossed the street, keeping his eyes focused on the man, who was walking at a steady pace, continuing toward L Street, where he turned. L Street was one-way going east.

James crossed to the opposite side of L, then started following the man. He pressed the PTT. "Still in sight, walking east."

Diaz started the engine, checked his side mirror, then pulled out into traffic, easing into the left lane. The light at L Street turned red.

"C'mon! C'mon," he mumbled, growing impatient. Finally it turned green, and he swung a left, shooting across oncoming traffic, getting into the left lane of L. Brakes squealed, horns sounded. He ignored them as he slowed down, seeing James coming back across the road.

Traffic on L was deadlocked. Diaz lowered the power window. James stood close to the door, prepared to take off if the man kept walking. "He's straight ahead on the left." Diaz leaned toward the windshield.

The man stopped next to a dark blue Camaro about six cars ahead of them. He appeared to be unlocking the door, all the while constantly watching people and vehicles, but for one brief second, his eyes seemed to lock onto James.

"Fuck!" James said under his breath, as he jumped into the truck. "Think he just 'made' me, Frank!" Both he and Diaz anticipated they were about to go on a chase through the streets of D.C.--once they were out of the gridlock.

The next block, Fifteenth Street, was five hundred feet away. The traffic light turned red. Diaz and James tried to stay focused on the Camaro. It was still parked, but they could see its brake lights and a right turn signal flashing. The light turned green, and traffic started moving slowly.

"Shit! Somebody let him in!" James spat out, seeing the Camaro easing in front of a red VW beetle.

Slowly the traffic moved and finally, the Camaro was second at the light. No flashing signal from the Camaro, only brake lights.

"He's going straight!" James said.

The light turned green and the Camaro went straight toward Vermont.

"Don't you turn red, you fuckin' bastard!" Diaz swore.

The Ford was five vehicles back, a little too close for Diaz's liking, but they couldn't take a chance and possibly lose the Camaro.

The light at Vermont turned green. Every car had its left turn signal flashing.

"Where the fuck's he goin'?" James said, as Diaz made the turn.

Soon they were entering Thomas Circle. The

Camaro stayed in the right lane, taking the exit for Massachusetts Avenue.

"He's gotta know we're here!"

Diaz didn't respond, but kept his full attention on the blue car. "Shit! He's heading for DuPont Circle! That's a fucking mess anytime! Stay on alert, DJ! Try and get a license number!"

James was using the glasses off and on, but whoever was driving the Camaro, always managed to make certain at least one or two vehicles were behind him.

At DuPont Circle a narrow, concrete divider, the height of a sidewalk, separated the four lanes into two. Traffic lights controlled each two lanes. The Camaro slowed as it approached the red light from the left-hand side of the divider, staying in the right lane. The car was at least twenty feet from the crosswalk, moving forward slowly. Diaz and James were four cars back. The instant the light turned green, the Camaro's tires burned rubber as it shot over the divider, narrowly missing being T-boned by a Cadillac. Sparks flew out from under the rear end of the Camaro as the muffler struck concrete. The driver maintained complete control as the car flew down Connecticut Avenue.

"Fuck! Fuck! Fuck!" Diaz shouted, pounding his fist against the steering wheel. He swiveled his head, trying to see a way to break through the traffic. He didn't stand a chance.

"Goddammit!" James said through clenched teeth, continuing to watch the Camaro as it became just a blue dot in the distance.

Horns were blaring behind them. Diaz had no

choice but to drive on. "Hope you're ready," he said, shaking his head.

James' heavy eyebrows nearly knitted together. "What the fuck for?"

"For the ass reamin' boss is gonna give us," Diaz responded, as he sped around the circle practically on two wheels, before exiting at Connecticut. He pressed the accelerator, attempting to maneuver in and out of traffic.

"You honestly think we've got any chance in hell of finding that bastard?" James said, using the binoculars, searching up and down side streets.

Diaz continued pounding his fist against the steering wheel.

*

State Department
Office of Scott Mullins

Grant turned the corner then continued down the hallway, walking under a continuous row of florescent lights. With a large thermos of strong, Navy-type coffee in one hand, and a box of freshly made, still warm donuts in the other, he stopped in the open doorway. Mullins was sitting behind his desk with his fingers linked behind his head, his eyes closed.

"Permission to enter, **sir**!" Grant called loudly.

Startled, Mullins' eyelids popped open, and he shook his head. "Jesus, Grant!"

Grant closed the door, then put the thermos and donuts on the desk. "Coffee and donuts as ordered." He dropped his baseball cap on one of the wooden chairs, then unzipped his windbreaker.

He unscrewed the thermos top, and removed the cork. "Got any cups?"

Mullins was still rubbing his eyes, as he swung his chair around and took out two mugs from a credenza drawer.

"Made the coffee myself," Grant commented as he poured the steaming brew into each mug. "Oh, and the donuts are from Joe's favorite bakery, made fresh this morning."

Mullins leaned back, inhaling the strong aroma. He took two continuous sips, then cleared his throat. "Good stuff."

"The key to making good coffee is never measure, just dump," Grant responded with a slight grin. "You drink and eat. I'll talk." He filled Mullins in on the meeting with President Carr."

"Jesus! That must be one helluva weapon," Mullins commented.

Grant nodded. "Mike went to Indian Head earlier to test it. It'll be interesting to hear what he has to say." He reached for the thermos. "Ready?" Mullins shook his head while he bit into a jelly donut, ignoring powdered sugar floating down on his black tie.

As Grant refilled his mug, he continued talking about the Team's inspection of the site where the attack occurred. "Did you see the newspaper report about a chopper going down?"

Mullins nodded as he wiped his mouth. "You think

that's 'your' chopper?!"

"Think it's too much of a coincidence for it not to be," Grant responded, as he leaned forward. "Listen, Scott, as requested by the President, we've gotta keep this 'close to the vest' for now. Will you be able to help without going through your chain of command?"

Mullins swallowed a mouthful of coffee and started reaching for the thermos, instead, he leaned back, hesitating briefly. "The President, huh?" Grant nodded. "Guess that's all the approval I need. Any idea on where you'll be going on this next 'vacation'?"

Grant put his coffee mug on the edge of the desk, then walked to a wall map. Leaning close, he tapped his finger on Russia then continued sliding it along a route leading to Afghanistan. "Still not sure, but something's telling me this might be the place."

Mullins squinted, trying to focus on the country Grant was pointing to. "Whoa! Christ, Grant! That's a hotbed of real bad shit!"

Grant went back to the desk. "I know, Scott, but like I said, I just suspect right now. Hope I'm wrong."

Mullins shook his head slowly. "And you thought your trip to China was a bitch! At least the whole country wasn't shootin'."

"You're right. Only half of it was." Grant thought briefly about the rescue mission to China.

The phone rang. "You expecting any calls?" Mullins asked.

"No, but Frank and DJ were on surveillance. Might be them."

Mullins picked up the receiver. "Mullins. Yeah, he's here." He handed the receiver to Grant. "It's

Frank."

"Yeah, Frank."

"Boss, uh. . ."

"Lay it on me, Frank."

"You were right about having us set up surveillance at the embassy. We spotted some guy shoving a rolled up newspaper under the gate. He wasn't your typical newspaper boy, boss. We decided to follow him and. . ."

"Frank, don't tell me you lost him."

Diaz cleared his throat. "Okay, I won't."

"Goddammit, Frank!"

"The guy was good, boss. Even with all the pedestrians and traffic, somehow he 'made' us."

Grant flopped down on the chair. "Where'd you lose him?"

"DuPont Circle. He high-tailed it up Connecticut Avenue. By the time we made it around the circle, his ass was long gone." Grant was silent. "Sorry, boss, but I can give you a description of the car and him."

"Not even a plate number?" Grant asked, shaking his head.

"He was too fuckin' clever. Always managed to have somebody right behind him, hiding it. DJ couldn't even make it out with glasses." Diaz thought it best to continue, considering Grant went silent again. "He was driving a dark blue, '73 Z28 Camaro. And, boss, we snapped a couple of pictures of him. You're. . ."

"Where are you now?"

"Eagle 8."

"See you in about an hour." End of conversation.

Diaz dropped the phone in its cradle, as James

asked, "Well?"

"Well?! He's fuckin' pissed, DJ! He's saving the ass reamin' till he gets here!"

*

Grant clenched his jaw, as he leaned forward and began rubbing his palms briskly together in frustration.

Mullins finally asked, "You planning on starting a fire with those hands, or you wanna tell me what happened?"

"They spotted a guy who they think was passing a message to somebody in the Russian Embassy. They lost him in traffic."

Mullins opened the desk center drawer and took out a yellow lined pad and a pencil from the tray. "What kinda car was it?"

"A '73 Z28 Camaro, dark blue," Grant answered, but he was already preparing to move forward in another direction. "Scott, how long would it take to confirm whether or not the Russians have a plane at Dulles."

"Would they use a major airport to move those weapons?"

Grant shrugged his shoulders. "Why not? Especially if they claim diplomatic privilege. Besides, we've gotta start somewhere. But whether it's Dulles or not, I can't see them using a slower mode of transportation."

"Like a boat?"

Grant nodded, with his words coming slowly. "Right. Like a boat."

"You're not seriously thinking that, are you?!"

"With both Russian carriers operational in the Med, yeah, that's what I'm thinking."

"But they still have to get the weapons. . ."

Grant waved a hand. "I know. I know. Give me time to work that out." He got up abruptly. "I've gotta go. Hope you can get something on that Camaro."

"I'll let you know asap. Hey, do you have enough cash on hand?"

"Should be plenty in the safe, but I'll verify there's a good 'mix.'" Grant put on his baseball cap. "You can reach me on the car phone or at the house."

"Here," Mullins said, as he put the cover on the thermos. "And take the donuts."

"I'll take the coffee. You keep the donuts."

"What about Joe and the guys?"

"I've got another three dozen in the Vette."

Grant extended his hand, and Mullins grasped it firmly. "Talk to you soon."

Chapter 8

Building of the First Directorate
Darulaman Road
Kabul, Afghanistan
1400 Hours Local Time

The KhAD, the Afghan secret police, officially known as the State Intelligence Agency, was headquartered in one of the most well protected areas in Kabul. Work never stopped, whether inside or outside the building.

Under the firm control of the KGB, the KhAD was used by the Soviets to gather intelligence, infiltrate the Mujahideen, spread false information, and bribe tribal militias into fighting. KhAD's system of informers and operatives extended into virtually every aspect of Afghan life. It assumed responsibility for training young Afghans to be loyal to the Soviet Union, but a good deal of money and the promise of better weapons to recruit new members was a necessity.

Farhad Hashimi, head of the KhAD, a graduate of Colgate University in New York, was considered to be very intelligent and very powerful in all aspects of the organization. His close association with the KGB was purely political, enabling him to bolster his own self image, remain in power, and obtain modern day weapons--weapons he might one day use against the Soviet Union.

*

Hashimi's footsteps echoed as he walked along a passageway in the headquarters building. This day he wore a typical outfit known as a perahon tunban, consisting of a knee length light-colored shirt and dark, baggy trousers, along with a vest. As a government official, he also wore a cap made of sheepskin.

Stopping just outside the doorway of the main entrance, he looked toward the mountains where snow had already begun to melt, but along with spring rain, many roads were washed out, making passage difficult. He put his arms behind his back, as he perused the inner courtyard. Guards walked the perimeter and meandered through the entire grounds, either carrying AK47s or RPG launchers.

A sound of far-off gunfire and explosions made him retreat further from the doorway, just as an MI-24 attack helicopter flew overhead, called in by a Russian patrol coming under fire outside a small village. Fighting between Soviets, Afghans, Mujahideen had not improved; if anything, it had worsened. Hashimi needed weapons desperately, and not used or weapons confiscated from other wars. He wanted modern weapons.

An all-terrain vehicle, a UAZ-469, similar to a Jeep, drove into the courtyard then stopped close to the building. Two men got out, both wearing Soviet Union army uniforms. Major Viktor Zubarev, KGB, and his security guard and interpreter, Sergeant Tresinsky.

Zubarev was about 5'11" and slim. His uniform,

shoes, cap were impeccable. The way he carried himself and his dark brooding eyes evoked authority. He took long, slow strides as he walked toward Hashimi.

Today the Afghan was to learn whether the Soviets would deliver the weapons as promised. No one, including the Soviets, seemed to have complete knowledge or details of the weapons, just that they were developed by the Americans and considered top secret.

What he suspected, though, was the Soviets weren't going to hand them over without some form of payment. He assumed that was one reason why Zubarev was meeting with him. It would be interesting to learn what kind of price Russia would put on five top secret American weapons.

As the Russians approached Hashimi, two Afghan guards took their places closer to the entrance. Hashimi motioned for Zubarev to follow him. They would conduct their business as they walked along the passageway, staying out of perimeter rooms as a precaution in case of attack.

Hashimi wanted to keep the meeting as short as possible and got right to the point. "Do you have word on the weapons?"

A low-flying chopper made them go quiet, while they followed the sound with their eyes.

Zubarev rested a hand on his Makarov in his side holster. "I am expecting them in several days."

"What about the type of weapons? What makes them top secret?"

Zubarev shook his head. "That I still do not know. But with that classification, you can be assured they will be like nothing either one of us has ever seen."

"And when will you tell me the price, Major?"

"As soon as we receive word they are safely aboard our ship. The weapons must be inspected and tested before we turn them over to you. You understand, of course."

Hashimi's distrust in the Russians had steadily increased, but he was willing to do anything necessary to obtain the weapons. All he could do was wait, and not cause a rift between himself and Zubarev.

Chapter 9

Somewhere in D.C.
0750 Hours

Driving around for nearly thirty minutes, trying to ensure he wasn't being followed, Nicolai Kalinin had time to reflect on the incident. Where the hell did he go wrong? What mistake did he make? How'd the Americans find him? Maybe he shouldn't have left the message in the newspaper. But that had been the plan, confirmed by Vazov. When it came to options for leaving messages, there weren't many. And he sure as hell couldn't just walk into the embassy.

He had to put his thoughts in order. His first task was to wipe down everything inside the house and Camaro, removing any evidence that could lead to him--or the embassy. He wasn't concerned about the name on the car's registration. But fingerprints were a different matter altogether.

Once the task was accomplished, he'd park the car in the garage, then take the truck and head to the safe house. *The safe house.* He gritted his teeth. Having to use the place was something he hadn't planned on. It was too soon for his strategy to turn to shit.

He pounded the steering wheel in anger, until a sudden thought flashed through his mind. Was it possible? Could it have been the American, the traitor, who had turned against the U.S. and now Russia? Was he a double agent?

Very little was known about him--only what he wanted Russia to know. He told them just enough to confirm he had legitimate top secret information. Kalinin surmised he must be working somewhere in the Pentagon for the Department of the Navy, considering the document had a DoD logo.

If the American was a double agent, would it mean plans had to be altered? Would flying the weapons to Moscow be out of the question? He couldn't think of how the American would know about the plane, but assumptions were always possible.

Working under diplomatic cover, Kalinin felt confident he could handle it. Moscow was anxious for those weapons to arrive.

He glanced at his watch. He'd stalled enough. Whether it was daylight or not, he had work to do. He made a snap decision and decided to hold off on moving the last of the weapons for at least another day or two. Even though the Americans didn't know who he was, they'd be watching airports and probably the embassy.

Weaving in and out of traffic, he glanced in the rearview mirror. Calming down, he eased off the accelerator, chastising himself for losing control. He couldn't afford to call attention to himself.

Thinking clearly again, a picture of the American traitor came to mind. But what if it wasn't him? What if there was someone else who had the ability to process information, no matter how little there might be? Someone who, like himself, had the intelligence, natural instinct. . . He cut himself off. The idea was remote. The odds were pointing toward the traitor.

*

He turned down the alley behind his house, then parked by the garage. As he unlocked the garage door, he glanced down the alleyway. All clear. He got in the truck and backed up close to the house.

Once the Camaro had been parked inside the garage, he tucked his Makarov in his waistband, removed all papers, then wiped down everything, inside and out, then locked it, taking the keys with him. With the car and garage locked, he hurried to the house.

Ever since he met with the ambassador, he was ready to evacuate hastily. Two suitcases were always packed. Clothes he needed for a week were in drawers and hanging in the closet.

He put the suitcases and clothes by the kitchen door, then started a wipe-down of light switches, light bulbs, faucets, door knobs, toilet seat cover--everything he could have touched. He was thorough. He had to be.

After everything was loaded in the truck, he did one more walk-through of each room, letting his eyes settle on every object, confirming each had been cleaned.

Stepping slowly backwards out of the living room, he continued looking around, until he was in the kitchen. Using a corner of his jacket to grab the door knob, he went outside, locked the door then wiped the knob. He kept the key. His rent was paid for the month. He'd contact the landlord to let him know he was leaving the area. A new job offer in Houston seemed as good a reason as any. ZXR would confirm he had resigned.

Driving back downtown, he remained vigilant of his speed and all traffic laws. Every once in a while he'd glance in the rearview mirror, not looking for vehicles that might be following, but at one crate stashed in the bed containing top secret weapons. His misstep this morning was a thing of the past, a mere blip in the road.

Driving along Nineteenth, he slowed then turned on L Street. About five blocks later he was at the parking garage, had a ticket stamped, and drove to the second level. Spotting the silver Pontiac at the end of the row, he pulled behind the car, ensured no one was around, then got out. As he dug a key from his pocket, he confirmed there was a black check mark on the pillar.

As he raised the trunk lid, he saw a tag hanging from the rearview mirror. Ambassador Vazov paid a monthly parking fee.

Not wasting any time, he grabbed the cardboard box from the trunk, slammed the lid, then wiped the edge with the bottom of his jacket. A second later he was driving out.

*

Safe House
Alexandria

The two-story house, barely twelve hundred square feet, was in need of maintenance, inside and out. Paint was peeling off clapboard siding, shingles were old, tree roots had lifted and cracked a section of sidewalk. The house was perfect for a Russian mole to lie low.

Kalinin drove the truck along the grass- and dirt-covered driveway, then stopped in front of the single car garage at the back of the lot. Unkempt boxwood shrubs were growing on three sides, two small windows had been blacked out. The structure was in worse shape than the house.

He got out of the truck, unlocked the padlock, then pulled the doors open. As he returned to the truck, he stopped momentarily, listening for any unusual sounds. All he heard was the heavy traffic on the main road, and a commercial jet flying low, making its approach to Washington National Airport.

Once he parked in the garage, he checked the contents inside the cardboard box: official documents, an official seal, a rubber stamp and ink pad. Under cover of darkness, he'd come back and prepare the pouches. Each pouch was made of heavy, plain canvas, with two leather handles and two zippers that met in the middle. The zipper pulls and handles would be secured together with a length of wire. A metal seal would then be crimped around the ends of the wire.

Securing the garage doors, he carried one suitcase and his jacket to the house, trying to absorb everything about the building and property. He didn't plan on staying long, but being familiar with his surroundings could be critical to his survival if it came down to that.

He unlocked the back door with a skeleton key, then shoved the suitcase across the worn, gray vinyl kitchen floor. Once he was inside, he relocked the door, then left the key in the lock. He laid his jacket on the small wooden table, as he scanned the room. Plain white cabinets, older white appliances, and a white enamel sink made him wonder how many times this place had been used.

He didn't expect to find much food, if any. He was right. The fridge was empty, but some canned and packaged goods were in a small pantry. Enough to sustain life, but not very appetizing.

Wood floors creaked as he walked through the living room to the front window. Spreading the blinds apart with his fingers, he took a moment to look across the property. Seeing nothing of immediate concern, he turned and finally spotted the telephone on a small table by a dark brown upholstered couch. The KGB was efficient at installing scrambler equipment. Behind the couch a connector cord went from a block on the baseboard to the scrambler, with a similar cord going from the box to the phone. He picked up the receiver. Dial tone.

Now he had to find the other important piece of equipment. Stairs opposite the front door led to the second level. Taking two steps at a time, he hurried up the narrow staircase.

Straight ahead was a small bathroom. To the right was an unfurnished bedroom. He went to the main bedroom. It had simple furnishings: a single bed, dresser, nightstand with a lamp. Blinds were closed on both windows. He opened a closet nearest the room's entry door. A single light bulb, with a cord hanging from its base, was overhead. He turned on the light.

The back wall was covered in thin, six-inch vertical wood planks. Running his fingers down the middle section, he felt an indentation. Hooking his fingers in it, he pulled carefully. A panel swung open. On a shelf was a shortwave radio. He had the frequency memorized, and was an expert at Morse Code, but more importantly, he had the one-time pad. He removed the small book from his trouser pocket. Tapping it against his hand, he debated whether to keep it with him or conceal it in the house. If the Americans found this place. . . He put it back in his pocket, then closed the panel.

As he started to leave the room, he hesitated by the bed. As much as he needed sleep, he needed food more. There was no telling when he'd get another opportunity. He decided to pass on the canned goods. A rundown diner he drove by would have to do. Besides, the fewer objects he touched, the fewer he'd have to worry about wiping down.

He had one more task before leaving. Notify the ambassador he was at the safe house. And since he now had access to the radio, he'd assume responsibility for contacting the cargo ship, confirming weapons were onboard. Vazov would notify Kabul the weapons were on their way.

With the scrambler activated, he dialed the embassy.

Chapter 10

Eagle 8
Virginia
0930 Hours

Diaz stood by the large picture window with one hand resting on the wood frame, the other holding a can of Pepsi. Any minute now Grant should be arriving, driving his black Vette. Diaz thought as menacing as that Vette looked, it wouldn't compare to Grant's expression. The meeting wasn't going to be pretty.

"Hey, Frank!" Adler called from the kitchen.

Diaz turned around, took a gulp of his drink, then walked to the kitchen. "Yeah, LT?"

Adler rested his elbows on the counter, as he balled up a wad of napkins. "You've been worried shitless since you walked in the door." Diaz sucked on more Pepsi, then just shrugged his shoulders. "Hey!" Adler called, as he threw the crumpled napkins, hitting Diaz square in the face. "C'mon! Get your mind on track and remember every minute detail from this morning. Did you have glasses on that newspaper? Was there anything that made that car stand out?"

Diaz's head started bobbing up and down. "I got ya, LT." He hustled over the the table. Sliding a pad and pencil toward him, he grabbed the pencil and started jotting down notes.

"Need some help?" James asked dragging a chair closer.

"You're in this just as deep as me!" Diaz replied, jabbing James' ribs with an elbow.

Ten minutes later, they heard the deep rumble of the Vette's engine. Within seconds, the door leading from the garage slammed. Grant ignored the two men and went right to the kitchen, dropping three boxes of donuts on the counter, then the thermos.

"You look like you need some fresh, hot java," Adler said, reaching for the coffee pot. Grant slid a mug toward him, as Adler asked quietly, "You still pissed?"

"I can't believe they lost him, Joe." He picked up the mug and blew some breath into the hot brew, as he noticed Diaz and James hunched over the table. "What's with them?"

"Besides trying to avoid you? They're scrounging through their brains, trying to dig out details from this morning." He leaned over the white boxes, opened all three, and finally selected a jelly donut with powdered sugar. "Speaking of this morning. . . let me show you something." He headed for the dining room.

Grant followed him. "Have you heard from Mike?"

"He should be back by thirteen hundred. Sounded pretty giddy," Adler laughed.

"I'll bet." Grant swiveled his head. "Seems like we're missing three more."

"Oh, that reminds me! Doc, Matt and Ken are at the airfield checking out our most recently acquired piece of equipment."

"What the hell are you talking about?"

"You're gonna love it. A Seasprite chopper."

Grant nearly choked on his coffee. "Where

the. . .?"

"Our most kind and illustrious benefactors! Apparently, Matt's been trying to work a deal to get us one. Now, just to let you know, he said it's used, but it's been extensively overhauled and it's the one with twin engines. It's supposed to reach airspeeds up to a hundred thirty knots with a range of four hundred eleven nautical miles. Certain modifications were made just for us!"

The Seasprite was a conventional type of turbine-powered helicopter, with a four-blade main rotor and three-blade anti-torque rotor, retractable tailwheel landing gear and a streamlined fuselage.

"That's the one that can float, right? Sealed hull?"

"Usually floats like a boat!" Adler laughed. "Except with the modifications made, we may not want to try it!"

Grant just shook his head, unbelieving. The generosity of the gentlemen who made Team Alpha Tango possible was still overwhelming. "Like to take a look, but too much going on right now. Didn't you say you had something to show me?"

"Oh, yeah." Adler shoved the last piece of donut into his mouth as he walked to the opposite side of the table and spread out two photographs. "Look at these."

Grant leaned toward the photos, then picked up one. He snapped his head up, staring almost dumfounded at Adler.

Adler pointed at the picture. "The guy looks like he could be your brother!"

"Is this the guy they lost?!" Grant asked, tilting his head toward Diaz and James.

"Yeah. He was in front of the Russian Embassy."

"This is very . . ."

"Creepy?" Diaz asked, without looking up from the writing tablet.

"Not exactly what I was going for, Frank," Grant responded. "But close enough."

He dropped the photo on the table, while Adler watched him, wondering why there hadn't been more of a reaction.

Grant sipped the coffee, then went near the two men. "Well, what've you got for me?"

"Besides an apology, boss?" James asked.

The phone rang. "That might be Scott," Grant said, walking to the side table. "Stevens."

"Grant, got some info for the Camaro, but don't know if it's gonna help."

"I'm listening."

"I eliminated anything registered outside D.C., or owned by females. I came up with eight. Any idea on how to get that figure down?"

"Eliminate any registered to drivers under the age of twenty."

"Hold on." Mullins slid his finger down the page. "We're down to five. Now what?"

"Wait a minute. I know I may be reaching here, but if those weapons weren't aboard that chopper when it went down, that means they were brought someplace or . . ."

"Or what?!"

"Listen, can you do a cross-reference?"

"Depends."

"Cross-reference that Camaro with another

vehicle."

"So you're thinking two vehicles, same owner?"

"Yeah. But here's the thing. We--I mean you need to check SSNs and see if that 'owner' is still alive."

Mullins dropped his pen on the desk and rocked back in his chair. "Some day I want you to explain how you come up with this shit!"

"Practice, my friend. Practice!"

"Do you want me to fax what I've got in the meantime?"

"Do it."

Mullins rolled his chair near the end of the credenza, put the paper in the fax machine, and punched in the phone number. "Okay. It's on its way. Anything else?"

"Two things."

"Why do I ask?" Mullins said shaking his head.

"Check with the Coast Guard; see if any more debris was found from that chopper--any debris. Before you do that, I'd like you to contact the President. I want to bring Grigori in on this."

"Whoa, Grant! This is top secret shit! You promised the President. . ."

"I know what I promised! I have no intention of telling Grigori everything unless the President gives the okay. But Grigori could be our best shot at tracking down this guy. Maybe he has 'insider' details, since he used to be KGB. The Russians have gotta have at least one safe house here. Grigori might know where it is."

"Do you want to speak with the President directly?"

"If he has the time. Oh, one more thing. Did you check on a Russian plane at Dulles?"

"There's an *Antonov* registered to the embassy."

"That's all I need for now."

"Hang close to the phone, Grant" Mullins said. "It shouldn't take me long to touch base with the President."

Grant hung up, then reached for the fax Adler was handing him, as Adler asked, "Don't you think the odds are pretty remote that one of those names belongs to our guy?"

"Gotta start somewhere, Joe." He took the fax to Diaz. "Frank, you and DJ take a look at these. Maybe you can plan the best and shortest routes to each of those addresses. Scott's supposed to call back with info that might shorten your trip. And you'd better take DJ's car."

"Copy that, boss," Diaz said, taking the paper. "How long before you want us to leave?"

Grant checked his watch. "I'll give Scott a half hour."

Diaz nodded, then said, "C'mon, DJ. I'll treat ya to a cup of coffee and donut."

As the two started to walk around Grant, he blocked their path, pacing back and forth, rubbing the back of his neck. Should he take a chance, whether it was legal or not? Desperate times call for desperate measures. "Listen, get the shotgun mike. Once you're through looking for the Camaro, set up somewhere close to the embassy again."

Diaz and James shot glances at each other, before James responded, "Whoa, boss! You sure?!"

Grant leaned closer, nearly coming toe to toe with James. "Are you having a hard time hearing. . . or just understanding?!"

James threw his hands up. "Okay! Okay! I copy!" The two turned away, mumbling as they walked down the hall, going to the garage.

"Dammit!" Grant said through gritted teeth, as he started toward the kitchen.

Adler followed him. "Now do you want to talk about that picture?"

Grant refilled the mug then shoved a box of donuts across the counter toward Adler. "I've seen him before."

"Well, of course you have! Every time you look in the damn mirror!"

"Joe! I said I've seen him before! Why am I not being understood?!"

"Jesus! What the hell's your problem?!" Adler shot back.

"My problem?! Oh, let's see. There's a traitor and mole on the loose. We're missing top secret weapons. Now I have to inform the President about the mole. And I don't have a fuckin' clue which direction to go! Is that problem enough, Joe?!"

Time to defuse the tension. Adler shoved the box of donuts back at Grant. "Here! How about some extra sugar to turbocharge your brain even more!"

Grant kept staring at his good friend, slowly getting himself back under control. With an almost indiscernible smile, he asked, "Where were we?"

"You said you've seen that guy before. Where?"

Grant leaned back against the counter, crossing one foot over the other. "Can't remember, but it's been awhile. We were a lot younger."

"So this guy's been a 'sleeper' all that time."

Grant tilted his head back, squeezing his eyes shut. "Jesus! I wish I could remember!"

"You don't suppose he knows about you, do you?"

"Hard to say. And, no. None of those names Scott found were familiar. For some reason I don't think we met formally anyway."

The secured phone rang. Adler rushed to answer it. "Adler."

"Joe! Scott here. I've got the President."

"Wait one," Adler said. Grant was already walking toward him.

"I'm here, Scott."

There was a brief moment of silence, then, "Grant?"

"Yes, Mr. President."

"Can you tell me how you're progressing with the operation?"

"We may have a lead, sir. Two of my men got a picture of someone at the Russian Embassy, who we're almost certain was making a drop. But I don't believe it was our traitor. Hate to say it, sir, but I think we've also got a mole on our hands."

Carr's 6'4" frame slumped in his chair, not believing what was being suggested. "A goddamn mole," he repeated quietly.

"It's just a theory, but somebody else has to be involved. This guy was probably a 'sleeper.'" Carr remained silent, so Grant continued. "Agent Mullins has been trying to trace a car the individual was seen driving." He hoped he didn't have to get into the ugly details. "Be assured, Mr. President, the Team is prepared to leave immediately if it comes down to that."

"And if it does come to that, Grant, where would that be?"

Grant took a deep breath. "With the current situation, it might be Afghanistan."

"And your reason?"

"I'm sure you know the Russians are having a tough time getting the situation under control. It would seem those weapons might give them or the Afghans an edge, even if it were a small edge. And if not Afghanistan, those weapons will end up in Russia. No doubt about it."

"A place you're quite familiar with, right?"

"Yes, sir, very familiar."

"And what about the DoD problem?"

"Still nothing, sir. I'm sorry. But if we can find this mole, there's always the possibility he could lead us to him."

Carr swung his chair around, disappointed with the answer. "Agent Mullins said you had a question."

"Grigori may be a valuable asset in determining certain factors in this op. I'd like your permission to bring him in on this."

Carr was quiet while he thought about Colonel Grigori Moshenko, former officer with the KGB. Colonel Moshenko who was instrumental in helping bring home five American POWs. Grigori Moshenko, personal friend of Grant Stevens and Joe Adler. Grigori Moshenko--Russian defector. Carr had issued an order that "misinformation" be leaked indicating the colonel and his wife had been relocated to the Midwest under assumed names. The only other way to protect them was to put them into the Witness Protection Program, something that was offered, but refused by the Moshenkos.

"Do you plan on bringing Colonel Moshenko fully onboard?"

"Only with your permission, Mr. President. Otherwise, I'll only request details from him of KGB activities that could help in this op. Grigori won't ask any questions once he understands this is top secret. I can assure you of that."

"All right, Grant. I'll trust your judgement. You do whatever you deem necessary. Anything else?"

"Sir, do you know if the NSA has picked up any transmissions that might give us some direction?"

"Nothing's been reported, but I have a feeling you've got something in mind."

"This guy's going to stay quiet right now, but he's got to make a move soon. My first thought was he'd try and get the weapons out by plane, the Russian Embassy plane. But now I'm not so sure."

Carr wondered if he should make his own suggestion. "Grant, you know we can't inspect in any way, shape or form, anything marked as a 'diplomatic pouch.' But I can have the plane put under surveillance, keeping an eye out for unusual packages. We can't stop it from leaving, though."

"Anything will help, sir. We'll have to depend on getting accurate intel on a flight plan."

"I can take care of that, too."

"Mr. President, may I suggest you ask NSA to flag any unusual traffic, especially if it's coming out of the Med?"

"Will do. Anything it picks up, I'll make certain it gets to the analysts as soon as possible."

"And our own ships should listen especially for ship-to-ship and ship-to-shore transmissions. I understand the *Minsk* and *Kiev* have been operating together in the Atlantic and Med before being assigned to permanent ports. They both carry KA-27 choppers which could be used for . . ."

"Wait a minute, Grant. Refresh my memory. Wasn't that the same type chopper you brought the POWs out of Russia with?"

"Uh, yes, sir. It was."

"You were saying?"

"A chopper could be used to pick up the weapons from another craft like. . ." Grant went quiet.

"Grant?"

"Sorry, sir. I had a thought that I'll need to discuss with Agent Mullins."

"How do you keep track of all those ideas?"

"With great difficulty, Mr. President."

Carr smiled. "Can you tell me what you plan on discussing with Agent Mullins?"

"Of course. The other craft I was thinking of might be a Russian cargo ship. Maybe that's where the weapons were flown that night." Grant started pacing, wondering if his idea was plausible. "But . . ."

"Yes, Grant?"

"I was just wondering if the thieves would put all their 'eggs in one basket.' Maybe they'd separate those crates, loading each one on different modes of transportation."

"So, you're thinking a plane and a boat?"

"I'm just trying to cover all bases, Mr. President."

"Do you have anything to substantiate your request regarding the NSA?"

"No, sir, but those folks may need to listen for traffic from here, also."

"I'll call General Prescott, and I'd better let Secretary Daniels in on this conversation. SECNAV will have to be briefed."

"One final question, sir."

"Go ahead."

"I know you want the weapons returned to the States, but what if we don't have any option and . . ."

"Grant, we have no way to tell whether blueprints or specific instructions for their use were included. But I don't want those ten falling into the wrong hands again, so you do anything you have to so that doesn't happen."

"Yes, sir. We'll take care of it either way."

"If that's all, Grant, I'll let you get back to work."

Grant detected a smile in Carr's voice, and he responded, "Thank you, Mr. President."

Carr hung up. Swiveling his chair side to side, he considered everything Grant reported, everything he asked for. The situation had taken a turn for the worse. A mole. A 'sleeper.' "Jesus," Carr mumbled, as he loosened his tie.

It was a known fact that spies worked out of the Russian Embassy. But how long had this guy been in the States, waiting to act? Where was he working, living? A chill ran up the President's back, as he wondered how many more 'sleepers' could be in the U.S.

It was time to make those phone calls.

*

As soon as Grant ended the call, he phoned Moshenko. "Hey, Grigori. It's me."

"My friend, how are you?!"

"I'm good. Listen, Grigori, don't want to talk on the phone. Can we meet someplace, say in an hour?"

"Of course." Moshenko walked to the front window, checking the weather. Blue sky was beginning to break through fast moving clouds. "The park at the end of my street is a good place. There is a gazebo on the south side."

"Sounds good. See you later."

Moshenko hung up. Standing by the window, he rolled the Davidoff Grand Cru cigar between his fingers, wondering about the upcoming meeting. Since he and Alexandra had been in America, he and his good friend never had any secretive meetings. If the meeting concerned Alexandra and him, Grant would have been more specific.

Noises and aromas from the kitchen told him Alexandra was preparing their upcoming meal, beef stroganoff and noodles. As he walked to the kitchen, he continued wondering about the meeting.

*

Eagle 8
Virginia

Diaz, James and Adler stood near the sofa. Grant was on the phone with Mullins. "Fax that to me, Scott," Grant said, as he motioned Adler toward the machine.

"Before you ask," Mullins said, "I made contact with the Coast Guard's Command Senior Chief Phil Borrman in Baltimore. That command handles the Chesapeake Bay region. He and Tony were acquaintances, so I took a chance to see if he could offer up some info not already published in the news. But he couldn't tell me much more. They still had their chopper and a boat searching off the coast. Heavier sections of that Huey sunk, and any pieces that hadn't already been collected had probably drifted away in the Gulf Stream. They're almost positive, though, that some type of explosive took it out."

"Bodies? Weapons?" Grant asked, hoping he'd get some positive feedback.

"Some body parts, but identification won't be easy. There's a possibility something, or pieces of something, might eventually wash up on the eastern seaboard, but don't count on it."

"Shit!" Grant said, rubbing a hand briskly over the top of his head.

"Look, I asked Borrman to contact me if they find anything. Okay?"

"Yeah. By the way, NSA is gonna start flagging all unusual or suspicious transmissions. The President will most likely be contacted first. See what you can do to get on that contact list."

"I'll make a call right now."

"One more request."

"Gotta sharpen my pencil," Mullins laughed.

"Find out if any Russian cargo ships were steamin' that day between Maryland and North Carolina, maybe no more than a hundred miles off the coast. There had to be something going or coming out of Cuba."

"Loaded or empty?"

"Could be either."

"Will do."

"Gotta go. And thanks, Scott. I know you're doing your best."

"I'll be here if you need anything else." End of conversation.

Adler held the fax toward Grant, who felt as if he finally had something to go on. He perused it briefly before handing it to Diaz. "Looks like we know what those bastards transferred the weapons to."

"A damn Toyota pickup?" Diaz asked with surprise.

"Look at the owner information, Frank. Both the Camaro and Toyota were registered to 'William Goldman' who died five years ago."

"Should we still check out this address, boss?" James asked, pointing to the paper.

"That's the first one on your list, DJ. I have my doubts you'll find anybody home. So. . ."

"We'll do a thorough search, boss," Diaz said, motioning with his hand as if he was unlocking a door. Both he and James headed for the garage.

"Wait!" Grant called. "Leave the shotgun mike. You two have enough on your 'plate.'"

"Roger that!" James responded, with obvious relief in his voice.

Grant picked up one of the photo's, then folded it. As he slipped it in his pocket, he started having one of his "go quiet, ignore everything" moments. He grabbed a pen and notepad from the table and started writing.

Adler stood by, waiting. Finally, Grant handed him the paper. "Joe, contact Matt and the other guys. Give them this."

Adler read it quickly. His expression showed he was in complete agreement. "I like it!"

"Yeah. We'll talk later." Grant dug his keys out of his Levis' pocket. "Scott may call, and when the guys get back, you'll need to fill them in." He walked to the hall closet for his jacket. "I'm assuming the Gulfstream and chopper are ready to go."

Adler gave a thumb's up. "Fueled and 'froggy.'" As Grant slung his jacket over his shoulder, Adler asked, "Do you want Ken and Mike to cover the embassy?"

"Yeah. I know there's a car phone, but make sure they have a radio just in case they end up 'hoofing' it. Oh, and check the money in the safe. There should be enough."

"Any particular 'brand'?"

"Pounds, deutsche marks, rubles for now." He turned toward the door, waving a hand overhead. "I'm outta here."

*

As he drove through D.C., Grant couldn't get the picture of the Russian out of his mind. Who the hell was he? Why couldn't he remember where he saw him? Even though the photo hadn't been completely in focus, he couldn't deny the fact the two of them appeared to be similar in looks, height, close in age. *Come on, Stevens! Think!* He was positive it wasn't at the Academy. And more than positive the guy wasn't with the Teams. So where? One of the many ships he'd been aboard? The encounter had to have been brief. And probably from a distance. *Time for direction change,* he told himself, preparing to meet Moshenko.

A half hour later he turned into Moshenko's neighborhood, drove to the dead end then turned around, parking on the shoulder. Looking out the passenger side window, he spotted his good friend standing on the steps of the gazebo, a white, wooden octagonal structure.

At 5'10" Moshenko was easy to spot, with his muscular build, short, jet black hair that had some grey streaks at the temples, and the ever present cigar.

Once Grant locked the car, he took off jogging across the grass, noticing several small children playing in a sandbox at the opposite end of the park. Two women sat on a bench, keeping a close watch on them.

As Grant got closer to the gazebo, Moshenko blew cigar smoke from the side of his mouth just as he stepped on the pebble walkway. "My friend!"

"Hey, Grigori!" Grant said with a wide smile. The two friends grabbed each other's hand, then slapped each other on the back.

"Come," Moshenko said, as he walked up the three steps and motioned to the curved bench seat. "You are looking well," he said as he sat down.

"You just saw me last week!"

"And you are still looking well!"

"How's Alexandra?"

"She is fine, and hoping you will share some food with us. She is preparing beef stroganoff."

"Wish I could."

Moshenko noticed Grant's expression had changed. He watched him briefly before laying a hand on his shoulder. "You are troubled. What is it?"

"The Team's involved in another mission. It's been classified top secret."

Moshenko nodded. "I understand."

"No, no! It's okay. The President gave me the go-ahead to discuss this with you, so don't worry."

"All right, Grant. Is there something you want me to do?"

Grant gave somewhat of a grin. "No flying choppers this time, but I'm hoping you can reach into your brain and pull out some information that might help us."

"I will try," Moshenko responded, flicking an ash over the railing, before scooting forward on the seat.

Grant unfolded the photo. "This is a photo Frank and DJ took in front of the Russian Embassy." He handed it to Moshenko.

"You could be brothers!" Moshenko said with surprise, as he stared at the photo.

"That seems to be the consensus."

"Who is he?!"

"Don't know. I was hoping you could tell me."

Moshenko studied the man's face more closely, but

then shook his head. "I would surely remember him, my friend. I am sorry." He handed the photo to Grant. "But why did they take his picture?"

"My suspicion is he may be a 'sleeper,' Grigori," Grant responded, smacking the paper against his hand.

Moshenko stood, walked a couple steps away, then turned around. "So he has been in your country since he was a child?"

"Yeah, if I'm right. Why?"

"I had access to files at KGB that listed all such people."

Grant leaned back against the railing. "Something tells me that list was several pages long."

Moshenko sat down. "Yes. I am afraid it was. The names were listed according to the country they were assigned to. I just cannot remember right now."

"Well, it was worth a shot," Grant responded, folding the paper, then putting it in his jacket pocket.

"I will continue to. . . what did you say? 'Reach into my brain.'"

"In the meantime, let's try this. Do you know where the safe house is located, either in D.C. or at least someplace close? Or if there's more than one?"

Moshenko rubbed his chin in thought. "There was one only. But the location . . ."

"Wait one," Grant said. "I've got a map." He hurried to his car.

While he did, Moshenko got up and walked the inside perimeter of the gazebo, trying to remember. He wondered if the KGB had the forethought to make changes since he defected. For Grant's sake, he hoped not. He would help his friend in any way possible.

"Okay, here's a map of the metropolitan area," Grant said, spreading the map open on the bench. He remained quiet as Moshenko leaned over, looking at town and city names.

"Here!" he finally said, jabbing his thick index finger on Alexandria, Virginia.

"You sure, Grigori?!"

"Yes. I remember associating 'Alexandria' with Alexandra's name. Yes. I am sure!"

"Good. That's a start." As Grant folded the map, he asked, "Any street address to go along with that by any chance?"

"You must give me some time, my friend. It has been awhile. You have never needed the information before. But. . . I can tell you something about those at the embassy."

"I'm listening."

"Before I left Russia, I assigned two KGB officers to the embassy. It is more than likely they are still there."

"Do I hug you now or later?!"

"You can hug Alexandra!"

"And you know I'll take you up on it! Now, who are they?"

"Misha Zelesky and Petya Vikulin." For the next several minutes, Moshenko revealed descriptions, and all he could remember concerning the two KGB men. As grateful as Grant was for Moshenko's help, he couldn't help but worry. As he stood, he held a hand toward Moshenko, helped him up, then continued to grasp his friend's hand. "Listen, Grigori, you need to be extra careful, now more than ever."

"But nothing has changed, Grant. Our conversation will not go beyond your men. . . and the President."

"I know. But now that you've told me you knew the KGB 'boys'. . ."

"Do not worry. I will be cautious."

"Keep an eye on Alexandra, and without arousing her suspicion, okay? I don't want her to worry." Moshenko nodded. "Once this is over, maybe the President can come up with some way to have those two sent home."

"That might be difficult, Grant, although proving them guilty of espionage or threatening your government might work."

Grant gave him a shit-eatin' grin through perfect white teeth. "You're scaring me, Grigori! Sounds like something I'd say!"

"Yes. Your way of thinking is smoothing off on me!"

Grant's brow wrinkled before he laughed. "I think you mean 'rubbing off.'"

"I will mark that off my list of sayings to learn!"

Grant put a hand on Moshenko's back. "C'mon. Walk with me to my car."

*

Grant was ten minutes out from Eagle 8, when the car phone rang. "Speak."

"Skipper! Are you anywhere close?"

"Ten minutes, Joe. What's up?" He turned on the windshield wipers as a car in front plowed through a puddle.

"Ken and Mike are on the move!"

"What the hell are you talking about?!"

"They called in when they saw someone driving out of the embassy in an older Mercedes. I gave them the go-ahead to pursue."

"It wasn't our suspect, was it?"

"No. Older guy."

"Did they give you a description?" When Adler finished, Grant said, "Sounds like Vikulin, KGB."

"What should I tell Ken and Mike?"

"Stick with him. Grigori said when Vikulin worked for him at KGB Moscow, he was someone who always stuck to a schedule and had favorite 'haunts' in town." Grant glanced quickly at his submariner. "Have them report to you every time that guy makes a stop. And warn them they'd better not fuckin' lose him!"

"Be happy to!"

"Any word from Frank and DJ?"

"They found the Camaro locked up in a garage, but not much else in the house."

"See you in five, Joe. I've got an idea." Connection broken.

"Why does that not surprise me?" Adler said laughing, as he hung up.

*

**Safe House
2120 Hours**

Kalinin tucked his Makarov in his back waistband,

shut off the living room light, then went out the back door. Once he was inside the garage, he closed the doors, waiting briefly until his eyes grew accustomed to the darkness. Then he went to the passenger side and removed the cardboard box and a small flashlight from under the seat.

He lowered the truck's tailgate, lifted the camper's window, then crawled inside the bed. Kneeling alongside the crate, he turned on the flashlight, and hung it from a hook directly overhead, before pulling the canvas pouches closer.

He ran a hand over the wooden crate, then touched a strip of thin, but strong aluminum, one of three. Spaced ten inches apart, they were wrapped around the crate then secured underneath. The wood cover was screwed on.

By the time he'd cut through the strips and removed screws, sweat covered his body. He swiped a hand across his forehead. Then he lifted the top and slid it toward the back. He checked the time. Depending on how long his task would take, he might have an opportunity to examine one of the weapons.

He started digging through foam packing peanuts, grabbing onto a section of heavy plastic. Pulling it out, he held the weapon with both hands, but the plastic was opaque and he couldn't get a good view. He laid the weapon down, then continued digging through foam, until the five wrapped, top secret weapons were laying next to him.

He began filling each of three pouches with the foam, then slid in one weapon at a time, ensuring they were protected from touching or hitting one another.

He checked his watch again. He decided against an inspection and would have to wait until he was in Moscow.

Once the weapons were secured inside the pouches, he removed the special seal and rubber stamp from the cardboard box, preparing to classify each pouch as "diplomatic." The metal seal, with a hammer and sickle on both sides, would act as the official signature for the Russian Embassy.

With the truck and garage locked, he rushed back to the house, grabbed a glass of water, then hurried upstairs.

The evening hours were the best time to broadcast. The "E region"--the Heaviside layer-- is one of several layers in the Earth's ionosphere. Medium-frequency radio waves reflect off it and can be propagated beyond the horizon. During evening hours the solar wind drags the ionosphere further away from the Earth, increasing the range radio waves can travel.

He had to work fast, knowing the U.S. had "ears" listening, especially now. Once he opened the panel, he set a wooden chair in front of the shelf, then sat down. He now regretted not having a shortwave in the leased house, but it was a chance he couldn't take. And he should have asked the ambassador to contact the cargo ship the night the weapons were stolen, instead of relying on the word of mercenaries. Another bump in the road, but not significant enough to compromise the mission.

It was impossible to use his one-time pad. He'd have to rely on sending the message in Morse Code, except he'd add another code within it. The ship's radioman and the captain would have knowledge of the code.

With his thoughts in order, knowing exactly the wording he would use, he began sending Morse Code. He authenticated the message with his code name: Antares.

*

Aboard the *Igor Brobov*

The cargo ship *Igor Brobov* was making her return trip to Russia, having picked up cargo in Cuba. She was a small ship with only four cargo holds. All four holds were filled to capacity with sugar, corn, coffee, rice. With a heavy load, she was riding low in the water, her deck a mere thirty feet above the waterline.

Nearly one month ago, Captain Sergei Ivanov received a coded message from the Russian Embassy in Washington, D.C. Once he left Cuba with his cargo, he was directed to travel up the coast of the U.S. He would stay within a hundred miles off the coast of Virginia, reduce speed to twelve knots (thirteen mph), then wait to be contacted.

The ship had been "steaming" within the designated range, when he finally received another message. He was to give the ship's coordinates to a man going by the name of "Python," who would deliver special cargo by chopper.

One more message would arrive, requesting final

confirmation the special cargo was onboard, showing no evidence of tampering.

His involvement in this operation would cost him valuable time. His schedule was completely screwed up. With over fifteen years experience in the shipping trade, this "incident" was a first for him. Hopefully, the ship's owners would not question the reason. He assumed the embassy in Washington would notify them of his involvement.

*

Ivanov stood near the magnetic compass, peering out across the bow. All activity on deck had ceased, returning to normal after the delivery. He brushed a hand over his short, salt and pepper hair.

The door of the radar room opened and Radioman Gremesky hurried to the bridge with a message in his hand. "Captain!"

Ivanov adjusted his wire-rimmed glasses and reached for the paper. He read the brief, decoded message, and confirmed the code name. He handed the paper back to the radioman. "Send reply the cargo is onboard, intact. Proceeding on course designated." Ivanov breathed a heavy sigh, relieved he finally had permission to continue the voyage.

Chapter 11

Washington, D.C.
2115 Hours

Glare of headlights from light traffic reflected off wet blacktop along D Street. Every forty-five minutes a city bus traveled the route. Pedestrians were few.

At the corner was a two-story, white brick building. On the lower level was a restaurant, serving traditional Russian food. Patrons entered through a wooden door, with a half moon-shaped canvas awning above.

The car phone rang in the dark blue, four door Ford Torino. "Yeah, Mike," Grant answered.

"Boss, we just saw you go by. We're parked at the top of the street at the corner."

"Is he still inside?"

"Affirmative. His Mercedes is parked our side of street, one block behind us."

"Be there in a minute."

Stalley drove slowly past the building, then stopped briefly as Adler got out of the back seat then hurried across the street.

Grant waited until Adler was at the corner. "Okay, Doc, get movin'."

Stalley continued driving to the next street, then turned left. He rolled through the stop sign, then made another left. As he got to the next corner, brake lights flashed from a parked Chevelle. He hit the brakes, then flashed his lights. Mike Novak raised his hand out the

Chevelle passenger window, as Slade pulled out of the parking space. Stalley parked the Ford.

Grant set the overhead light to "off." Leaning toward the window, he finally spotted Adler near the street lamp. Stalley flashed the headlights twice. Adler disappeared around the corner and went inside the restaurant.

No matter how long it took, and if everything played out as they anticipated, this might be their best chance, their only chance to get some answers.

Grant picked up his .45, released the clip, then shoved it back in. He put on his baseball cap, and as he got out, he slid the weapon into his back waistband, then closed the door. He leaned toward the open window. "Doc, I'm gonna check the main road in front of the restaurant, then take up a position near that basement entrance," he pointed. "Stay here and be prepared if it 'goes south.'"

"Okay, boss," Stalley nodded.

Grant started walking toward the corner, when he heard voices. Cigarette smoke drifted toward him. He turned the corner and kept walking. Three men glanced at him but continued talking and smoking. When he passed the restaurant, he glanced over his shoulder, seeing they had crossed the street. He hurried back to the corner, then heard three car doors slamming simultaneously, immediately followed by an engine starting. He glanced at his watch again. *So far so good,* he thought.

Hurrying up the side street, he ducked into the basement entrance, two steps below street level. He'd be less exposed from this spot, and in a good position to move quickly.

Five minutes later, Petya Vikulin came out of the restaurant and stood briefly by the door, putting on his black leather coat. He made frequent visits to the restaurant since he'd been assigned to the embassy a year ago. The food was traditional Russian fare. Tonight he treated himself to Sevruga black caviar, topped off with Rublevka Gold Vodka.

He breathed in deeply then started walking toward the corner. As he made the turn, he heard the restaurant door open. Continuing to walk uphill, he became leery as he heard footsteps. He turned around, and walked backwards. The street lamp didn't illuminate the person's face totally, but he recognized the man as the one who had been sitting at the bar.

Adler stopped, lit a cigarette with a lighter, then hurried across the street, pretending to wave to someone as he ran.

Satisfied he wasn't being followed, Vikulin shoved his hands into his coat pockets, then began taking long strides, heading for the used Mercedes parked three blocks away. Only the ambassador had the privilege of being driven in a newer vehicle, another Mercedes.

Adler ducked into a side alley, spit a piece of tobacco from his mouth, then flicked the cigarette against the building. Slowly he eased his way toward the corner, staying in the shadows.

Vikulin was about ten feet from where Grant was waiting. Grant clicked on the miniature recorder attached to his belt, then he suddenly came out of the shadows, and stopped. Vikulin reacted quickly, moving his hand to his weapon in the shoulder holster.

"There's no need for that, Comrade," Grant immediately said in Russian, raising his hands to show he didn't have a weapon.

Vikulin hesitated a brief moment. "Comrade Kalinin!" he said in a loud whisper, as he slowly moved his hand away from the holster. "What are you doing here? Is the ambassador aware you are talking with me?" He swiveled his head, looking to see if they were alone.

"Do not worry. We are completely alone, but I must talk with you. Come over here," Grant indicated, as he moved back into the shadows.

Vikulin followed, but cautiously. He kept a slight distance from Grant as he asked, "This is serious, Comrade?"

"Yes. What we are about to discuss is state secret." (State secret is Soviet term for 'top secret.')

"I understand," Vikulin nodded.

"I am here under the direction of the First Chief Directorate."

Even in the shadows, Vikulin's face couldn't hide his surprise. "The First Chief Directorate?! You know who he is?!" Grant simply nodded because in fact, he didn't have a damn clue. The FCD's real identity was known only to the ambassador.

The position of FCD was well known throughout the intelligence community. Russia's First Chief Directorate was the equivalent of the CIA's Chief of Station. He was a so-called *legal resident* but who, in fact, was a spy, operating under diplomatic cover, with full immunity from prosecution. While the FCD was responsible for the collection of political, scientific and technical intelligence, Vazov was put in charge of managing covert agents.

Grant's pulse raced. He had to pull this off. "Can we continue now?" he asked, trying to sound annoyed.

"Yes. Of course, Comrade."

They both turned, hearing the restaurant door open, and then a sound of voices, belonging to a man and a woman. "Perhaps we should walk," Grant said, looking over his shoulder at a couple crossing the street. He continued the conversation. "You know my position here, and that I have a mission to complete."

"Yes, an important mission."

"First of all, in case we must meet again in secrecy, we will meet at the safe house. I want you to verify the location."

"I know where it is."

"When I said verify, I meant verify! That means confirm the address!" Grant spoke just above a loud, gruff whisper.

"It is 6289 Aless Court in Alexandria. I have been there. I installed the scrambler and shortwave."

"Good. Then you are very familiar with it. Now, I assume you realize the importance of my request?" Vikulin merely nodded. Grant took a deep breath. Under any other circumstances KGB Vikulin would never let anyone get away with this line of questioning and in this tone of voice. "My reason for meeting you tonight is evidence has revealed a possible traitor within the embassy."

Vikulin stopped short, unbelieving. "This cannot be true. I would surely know!"

"Not necessarily, Comrade. That is why I have

been brought in by the FCD. I might add that you had also been under surveillance for. . ."

"No! I am loyal to the Soviet Union!"

"Yes, I realize you are. That is why you are here tonight." As they walked past the Ford, Grant noticed Stalley had ducked out of view.

"Can you tell me what evidence you have or who the traitor is?" Vikulin was still overwhelmed by the news because as a KGB officer, he should have known.

"No. The investigation is ongoing at this time. Everyone is under suspicion. I need your help."

"Can you at least tell me what this person is being accused of?"

Headlights from an approaching vehicle made Grant step farther away from the street, trying to keep himself in the shadows. Once the car turned at the next street, he continued. "I assume you know about the American who has supplied us information."

"Yes. The man who calls himself 'Primex.'"

"That is correct," Grant answered, but his brain was saying, *Holy shit!*

"But I am sure I don't know any more about him than you."

"Have you personally seen or talked with him?"

"I have not, but Comrade Zelesky met him very briefly when information was handed over."

"Describe him." Vikulin gave Grant a description that Zelesky had relayed to the ambassador. It wasn't much help. The guy sounded pretty average looking. "It is believed our Russian comrade is making his own deal with this 'Primex.'"

Grant was a couple of paces ahead, when he turned

to see the Russian standing stone still, finally getting the words out, "I cannot, I will not believe this!"

Grant maintained his distance, as he slowly reached behind his back. "Perhaps it will help you believe when I tell you I have full authority to send you back to Moscow, tonight if necessary, because you now have knowledge about the investigation."

Vikulin's broad shoulders went slack. "You have my word, I will not reveal what you have told me. What can I do to assist?"

Grant brought his hand from around his back, motioning to Vikulin to continue walking. Grant spoke with authority. "Do your job. Keep your eyes open, listen for anything out of the ordinary. I still have a difficult task ahead."

"You mean with your mission? The weapons?"

Grant merely nodded. "I have had difficulty communicating with my contact."

"Yes. I understand. Ambassador Vazov often has problems contacting Major Zubarev. Kabul has seen increased rebel activity lately."

Grant couldn't believe Vikulin was giving up information so easily, so unknowingly. Maybe it was time to end this meeting. He couldn't push his luck. "I think we have discussed enough, Comrade."

Vikulin stepped near a Mercedes, digging his keys from his pocket. "Where or how should I contact you if I find anything of significance?"

"Use one of the drop sites, whichever is convenient for you."

Vikulin thought briefly. "That will be the garage off L Street. It is close enough to the embassy and busy enough to avoid attracting attention."

Grant quickly rethought that. "That may not be good, in case someone else from the embassy checks. I will find a way to contact you in a couple of days. As a reminder, just be sure to go about your daily routine normally. That is most important."

Grant backed farther away from the car, indicating to Vikulin the meeting had ended.

As soon as the Mercedes was out of sight, Grant let out a long, relieved breath. He turned off the recorder, then hustled to the Ford. Withdrawing the .45 from his waistband, he stretched out in the back seat, staying out of sight as a precaution.

Adler, who'd been across the street in an alley watching the whole scene, ensured the area was clear, then hurried to the car, getting into the front passenger seat. He rested an arm on the backrest and turned slightly. "Well? Any luck?"

Grant unhooked the recorder from his belt. "For KGB, he sure was a chatty bastard!"

"Lucky for us!" Adler said.

"Grigori probably would've shot him on the spot!"

Stalley checked for cars and pedestrians in the mirrors. "Think we're in the clear, boss. Wanna head for Eagle 8?"

"Go," Grant answered. He sat up and scooted near the edge of the seat. He started playing the tape, then laid the recorder on the center console in order for Adler and Stalley to listen.

When it finished, Adler said, "So, now we know half the weapons are going to Moscow. And I'll bet you're still thinking about the cargo ship."

"Affirmative, Joe. Hope Scott gets some news from NSA."

Adler asked, "Does the name 'Kalinin' ring any bells?"

Grant flopped back against the seat. "Complete blank. Dial Grigori's number for me, Joe." Adler complied then handed the phone to Grant.

"Hey, Grigori!"

Moshenko blew out a stream of cigar smoke. "Yes, my friend!"

"Listen, I had a meeting with 'Comrade Vikulin.'"

Moshenko couldn't stifle a laugh. "And did he cooperate?"

"More than he realized. Just like I'd hoped, he thought I was the guy in the photo and called me 'Comrade Kalinin.' Sound familiar?"

"'Kalinin,'" Moshenko repeated. He laid his cigar on the edge of the sink then reached for a bottle of Stolichnaya Vodka and poured a shot glass full.

"Think about it, Grigori, then call me at the house. Oh, I got an address for the safe house, so let your mind relax on that one."

Moshenko downed the vodka. "Very good news, Grant! I assume you will be making a visit soon?"

"Thinking about it."

"Be careful, my friend."

"Talk to you later." Grant started to put the phone down, when he decided to call Mullins. "Scott, it's Grant."

"Whatcha need?" Mullins laughed, sticking his fork in a container of Chinese pork fried rice.

"I'll explain later how I got this info, but see if you

can find the name 'Kalinin' anywhere in our intel."

"Assume that's a last name?"

"Yeah. Also got a code name for our DoD guy. He's calling himself 'Primex.' That could stand for 'primary explosive,' or a shitload of other stuff. See what you can find."

"Will do."

"Have you heard from NSA or anything about a cargo ship?"

"Nothing yet."

"Damn! Listen, we got an address for the safe house. It's 6289 Aless Court, Alexandria, but keep it 'under your hat.'"

"Jesus, Grant! You're really gonna have to fill me in on how the hell you. . ."

"Hate to cut you off, but gotta go."

*

Grant disconnected the call, then continued holding the phone, tapping it against the center console. Adler turned in his seat. "You've got something running around in that brain of yours, don't ya?"

Without responding, Grant said to Stalley, "Doc, pull into that gas station for a minute. I want to run something by you both before we're outta D.C."

"Sure, boss." Stalley glanced quickly at the gas gauge as he made a right-hand turn into the station. Close to the sidewalk, set atop a fifteen foot pole, was a lighted, round orange and white sign with blue letters: "Gulf."

Grant pointed. "Back into the space on the far side

of the garage."

Headlights from another vehicle showed in the rearview mirror as it pulled into the station right behind them. Stalley and Adler glanced in the side mirrors, watching as the driver parked a Plymouth station wagon alongside one of the pumps in the second island. A sign on the overhead awning showed: Full-Service. The driver, an older gentleman, rolled down his window and waited for the attendant.

Stalley backed the Ford up then killed the headlights and engine. He and Adler turned in their seats.

Adler finally said, "We're all ears."

Grant leaned back, linking his fingers behind his head. "You've got your weapons, right?"

"Primed and ready," Adler responded. "Wait a minute! The safe house?! You wanna go now, without the rest of the Team?!"

"Look, Joe, I don't think we've got a helluva lot of time before this guy moves the weapons. We've gotta take the chance, without prior surveillance, without knowing anything about that . . ."

"Well, I'm in!" Adler interrupted. "How about you, Doc?" Stalley gave a thumb's up.

Grant picked up his weapon from the floorboard. "Anybody got extra ammo?"

"Got my rucksack, boss," Stalley answered, as he opened his door. Within a minute, he'd brought his rucksack back, then handed it to Grant.

The phone rang. "What've you got for me, Scott?" Grant asked.

"You are one lucky s.o.b., Grant!"

"So I've been told. What's up?"

"NSA picked up a Morse Code. It hasn't been decoded yet, because whoever was sending had 'inserted' another code. But what I can tell you is it originated from Alexandria. Sounds like it could be your 'boy.' It was signed with a code name 'Antares.'"

"'Antares,'" Grant said, with a mocking tone. "Seems appropriate--bright star, red supergiant."

"Where the hell do you pull that shit from?!"

Grant ignored the question. "Okay, now tell me they got the destination point."

"The ship they tracked it to was traveling along the azimuth of one of NSA's intercepting stations. It was about a hundred miles off the coast."

"And that ship was . . ."

"A cargo ship, Grant, out of Cuba. Just like you suspected."

"That's gotta be it," Grant finally said.

"Wait! There's more! One of NSA's geeks remembered intercepting a message just before the weapons were snatched. It went to the same ship, only that one came outta D.C. Care to venture a guess where that point was?"

"The Russian Embassy."

"Bingo!"

"Do you have any info on the ship?"

Mullins gave a brief description, then said, "She's the *Igor Brobov*, and she's fully loaded."

"What about crew? How many?" Grant tapped Adler's shoulder, motioning for a pen.

"Hold on." Mullins searched the paper. "Here it is. When she left Russia she had fifteen plus the captain.

She could've picked up more in Cuba, so don't hold me to that number."

"Coordinates?" Mullins rattled off the numbers, as Grant wrote them in the palm of his hand. "Scott, fax me all you've got on that ship. We should be at Eagle 8 in about twenty minutes."

"What about the President? Should I update him?"

"Told him I would, even though there aren't any definitive answers yet."

"I'll do it."

"I know this is all preliminary, Scott, but you might want to keep your Coast Guard contact's number handy. Depending on what happens, we'll try and reach you if we have an emergency."

"Will do. But don't let that emergency happen, Grant."

"Assume you'll call if that message is decoded."

"You're first on my list."

"Listen, Scott, we've got a shitload of work to do. Appreciate all you've done, buddy. Owe you big time."

"Stay safe, Grant." End of conversation.

"Well, Skipper, sounds like we'll be traveling."

Grant nodded. "Take us home, Doc. . . and step on it."

Traffic passing in front of the gas station was sporadic. As the light on the corner turned red, Stalley stomped on the gas, sending the Ford fishtailing.

"Joe, call the house. Tell the guys to start getting gear ready."

"What about the list you gave me?"

"Especially that. I wanna be outta there by twenty-three hundred--if not sooner."

While Adler made the call, Grant leaned back and closed his eyes, as he tried to think things out. He didn't have any proof the weapons were aboard the cargo ship, but it sure as hell seemed the most logical. He hoped NSA could decode the message before the Team departed.

Then there was the matter of the safe house. Was the mole still there, especially after sending the message? Or was he on his way to Moscow? He ruled that out. Mullins would've known.

The only guarantee about this whole op? There wasn't any. He made his decision, relying once again on his 'gut.'

Chapter 12

Over the Atlantic Ocean
175 Miles off East Coast
Wednesday - Day 3
0010 Hours

Prevailing twelve knot winds were blowing from the southeast, driving three foot waves with intermittent whitecaps. Weather forecasters predicted an increase in winds to possibly twenty knots by noon. The water temperature was forty-two degrees.

The Seasprite was flying close to maximum speed, staying two hundred feet above the Atlantic. Secured to the chopper's undercarriage was a Zodiac. The modifications to the chopper made it possible. Carrying it this distance and speed was risky, but a risk that had to be taken. Rappelling onto the ship would have been even riskier.

Matt Garrett kept the chopper on course, heading for the coordinates given by Mullins. Somewhere in the distance was the their target--the Russian cargo ship.

Grant scanned the blackness ahead. "Are we getting close, Matt?"

"Within twenty miles. You should be able to see her lights just about now. We still haven't been hailed."

"Let's hope it stays that way," Grant commented.

Garrett automatically brought the chopper lower, then kept it at seventy-five feet above the water. He doused the navigation/collision lights, keeping it in stealth mode as long as possible. "Keep an eye out for any aircraft."

Grant picked up NVGs. "How's the fuel?"

Garrett glanced at the gauge. "More than enough to get us there. It's the return trip when we might need a refill!"

"Shouldn't be a problem," Grant said, confidently. "Keep an eye out, men! We're getting close!" He resumed his search for aircraft.

"We didn't have much time to talk, Grant, but I'm curious about something. Now that Mullins confirmed one crate's aboard that ship, how are you gonna find it? There are a helluva lot of hiding places."

"Yeah. Tell me about it. But something tells me the captain was left in charge."

"Like the bridge?"

"Like the bridge."

"Mast head light!" Adler shouted, as he leaned away from the open cargo bay. "One o'clock!"

More of the ship started coming into view. Her superstructure was four levels, shaped like a compressed, wide T. Not every window had lights, just the bridge. Each of four winch housings had a light on top, one on the signal mast.

Grant turned to leave the cockpit. "You're on your own, Matt." He patted Garrett's shoulder before going to the cargo bay to join the Team.

Dressed out in wetsuits, with hoods and swim shoe boots, they slipped their face masks over their heads, letting them hang around their necks. Scuba tanks and swim fins wouldn't be needed this op. What they did have were waterproof throat mikes and utility pouches. Each pouch was about eleven inches wide, with a waterproof zipper and a Velcro flap. On the outside was an oral inflation tube for sucking out excess air, or for inflation to give extra flotation capability.

Adler and Diaz had det cord, a small block of C4 and chemical pencils, each with a three minute delay. Use depended on how "cooperative" the crew was or wasn't, and whether the ship had to be disabled. Doc Stalley had a few battle dressings, tape, syringes, morphine. His full medical bag would remain onboard the chopper. Everyone carried flares, utility knives, wraps of parachute cord, and duct tape.

Weapons were .45s with silencers, K-bars secured in leg straps, but instead of their usual Uzis, they were armed with MP5s.

Garrett started deceleration. Assuming a slight nose up attitude and lower collective, he brought the chopper to fifty feet above the water.

"At fifty feet! Target two miles!" he shouted over his shoulder. "Have not received any hailing from ship!"

The Team adjusted throat mikes and earpieces underneath their swim hoods, slung the submachine gun straps over their heads, and finally put on swim masks and adjusted the straps.

"One mile!" Garrett reported. "At ten feet!"

James checked the cables on the overhead double anchor bar, confirmed both floor panels were fully open, then he hit a switch, and the two cables started unwinding, lowering the Zodiac. Each cable split into a Y, with a coupling at the end of each intersection for attaching to port and starboard on the boat. Just as it hit the water, everyone but James slid out of the cargo bay, splashing into the water within a few feet of the boat, and each other.

Stalley was the first one in the boat, assuming the role of coxswain. He scooted around a rope and rope ladder laying in the bottom.

The remaining Team scrambled onboard. Adler was at the bow, starboard. He undid the bow couplings, Diaz, the stern. Stalley signaled James, who raised and secured the cables, then closed the two panels.

Garrett was looking over his shoulder at James, who gave a thumb's up, then he disappeared from the cargo bay. Garrett waited five seconds, then nudged the cyclic lever forward. As the chopper rose, he put it into a tight turn to port, kept it low, then flew a mile before ascending to an altitude of one hundred feet. All he could do was keep an eye on the fuel gauge, watch for other aircraft and ships, then wait.

Stalley put the throttle handle in neutral, set the gas button to on, then pulled the cord. The engine fired up. He adjusted the choke, then watched for Grant's signal.

Grant was near the bow, port side. He motioned with an arm. "Go!" Everyone leaned forward, with Grant and Adler aiming the MP5s straight ahead.

Keeping their heads slightly raised, they kept their eyes on the ship. The Zodiac's nose rose out of the water as Stalley "kicked" it into high, then it settled back down. Salt spray washed over them as the Zodiac met the waves head-on. The closer they got to the ship, the more Stalley reduced speed.

*

Aboard the *Igor Brobov*
Bridge

Seaman Boris Gilyov, quartermaster, stood near a window, taking another look aft through binoculars, focusing his attention on the horizon. "I do not see those lights anymore, Captain. They just. . . disappeared."

Captain Sergei Ivanov grabbed the binoculars from the young seaman. "When did you last see them?"

"Ten minutes ago, sir."

Ivanov rested his eyeglasses on top of his head, then looked through the binoculars, slowly swiveling his head. "I do not see anything."

Gilyov pointed, as he said, "I know, sir. They were approximately at one o'clock. It could have been a plane, but it did not alter course. The lights appeared to stay in one position."

"Hmm," Ivanov said quietly. "Perhaps one of the American coast guard helicopters."

"It could have been, sir. It may have gone over the horizon."

Ivanov tapped Gilyov's arm with the binoculars. "Here. I doubt we will see it again. . .whatever it was."

Gilyov nodded, then went back to the chart room. As quartermaster, he stood day-to-day watches and was in charge of navigation, but under the watchful eye of the captain.

Captain Ivanov put his arms behind his back, slapping one hand against the other, as he walked to the chart room, located between the bridge and radio room. He leaned forward just enough to see under the chart table. Pushed against the wall was the crate, covered by a tarp. He was not comfortable having it aboard. Although he didn't think it was anything of danger, he was not accustomed to having so-called cargo delivered to his ship in the middle of the Atlantic Ocean. He believed that whatever was sealed inside the crate had to do with the military.

The men who delivered it were definitely Americans. Even though one of the men attempted to speak Russian, he destroyed the language.

Ivanov turned away. He walked slowly to the bridge, then stood behind Seaman Yegorov, who was at the helm. Ivanov began analyzing the situation: Americans, delivering something from the United States, to a Russian ship, that was to be picked up by a Russian helicopter. And here he was, a civilian captain of a cargo vessel, put in charge of this unknown object.

The ship was only making fifteen knots, considered a "slow speed" in order to save on fuel. He would have plenty of time to wonder.

*

Aboard the Zodiac

The Zodiac was barely moving as it approached the

ship from port side aft, remaining far enough away so it was still shrouded in darkness. The sound of the ship's engines and turning screws helped mask any noise from the rubber boat. The men stored their face masks in the bottom of the boat, except for Stalley, who kept his hanging around his neck.

"Take it to midships, Doc, so we can get a better look, then circle around to starboard," Grant directed.

Novak and James were using binoculars, scanning the port side. A lifeboat was suspended between two davits halfway down the side of the superstructure. "Don't see anybody yet, boss," Novak said.

As Stalley swung the Zodiac around, heading back to the stern, James focused on the superstructure. "Someone's at the forward bridge window."

Novak moved the glasses. "I see him. No. Two of them."

"Just tell me we're okay," Grant said.

"We're okay, boss," Novak replied.

Stalley drove past the stern, before cutting back, holding the boat steady as it bounced over the wake. Passing behind the ship, they had a view of the helipad platform, raised above the deck about five feet.

As they headed down the starboard side, they still didn't see anyone. For this time of night it meant most of the crew was below deck, asleep. That's what Team A.T. was counting on. What they were preparing for was at least two or three men on the bridge, at least one in the radio room, and a couple down in engineering.

With the interior of the ship put to memory from a diagram Mullins had faxed, the Team knew exactly where they'd be going and how they'd get there: Grant and Adler would take the bridge. Slade and James, the radio room. Novak and Diaz would secure crew quarters and engineering. Stalley would man the Zodiac.

"Okay, Doc," Grant said. "Bring us alongside, close to the superstructure."

Stalley put the engine in neutral as the Zodiac drifted alongside the ship. The Team pulled their hoods back and readjusted the earpieces and throat mikes. Slade picked up a length of coiled rope laying in the bottom of the Zodiac, and slung it over his head, adjusting it so it hung off his shoulder.

Grant turned to Stalley. "Doc, try and stay close. Be prepared to haul ass if plan 'A' turns to shit. Keep the glasses and flares handy."

"Roger that, boss."

Novak balanced himself in the bottom of the Zodiac, separating a rope from a compact boarding ladder. Both were attached to the eye hook of a grapnel. Holding onto the rope, he watched for Grant to give the go ahead. Grant nodded.

Steadying themselves, the men knelt in the boat, aiming their weapons upward, keeping watch. As the Zodiac rose up on a wave, Novak tossed the grapnel hook high, with the boarding ladder unravelling behind it. Just as the hook went over the railing, he jerked down on the rope before the hook could hit the deck, then he pulled, securing the hook on the rail. Pulling on it again, he drew the Zodiac closer to the ship, then handed the end to Stalley.

The Team slid their MP5s around to their backs, making it easier to climb, then they drew their .45s.

Slade was the first man up, with the rest of the team close behind. When he was close to the railing, he slowly raised up, checking all was clear. Keeping his .45 ready, he climbed over the rail and rushed for cover against the superstructure. James, Novak and Diaz immediately followed, with Grant and Adler bringing up the rear. As Adler went over the rail, he unhooked the grapnel, grabbed the rope, then lowered the hook into the Zodiac. Finally, he tossed the rope to Stalley, then rushed to join the Team.

Stalley put the engine into gear, waited until the ship had pulled ahead, then he slowly increased speed. Turning to port, he headed beyond the stern.

*

Winds started picking up, blowing at fifteen knots. Seas were getting rougher. Wave height was now four feet with an increase in whitecaps.

Staying close to the superstructure, the Team eased its way aft until Slade held up a fist, bringing everyone to a halt. He peered around the corner. The aft deck was clear, but bright lights weren't going to make it easy for them.

Grant and Adler backed away from the superstructure, trying to get a better view overhead. Access to the bridge was by way of steel ladders, one on each of four levels, with the top one leading to a deck that passed in front of the bridge.

As Slade continued scanning the area, he pressed the PTT button. "Clear."

"Go," Grant responded. They all knew what to do, and where to go without further directions.

Novak and Diaz slipped around the corner, went through a watertight door, then started down a steel ladder to the next level.

Holding their .45s with both hands, they waited, listening for voices. Quiet. They immediately went down the second ladder, ending at a passageway. The sounds from the engine room were a constant rumble, directly beneath them.

Novak started forward, with Diaz right behind him. The first door led to the crew's quarters. No light showed from underneath.

Hurrying along the passageway, they checked other doors, ensuring they were locked. No voices. Nothing.

They returned to their target room. Novak went to the starboard side of the door. Diaz put an ear against it, then shook his head. They didn't have a clue how many men were inside. Slipping the .45s into the holsters, they pulled the MP5 straps over their heads.

Keeping his back close to the bulkhead, Novak carefully reached for the doorknob, and began turning it. Besides engine noises, now they heard snoring and grunts. They entered cautiously and quietly, immediately inhaling stale cigarette smoke and body odor. Leaving the door slightly ajar enabled them to see more clearly. Four rows of bunk beds, stacked in threes, were pushed against the far bulkhead. Four beds were empty.

Diaz found the light switch by the door, and nodded to Novak. As he sealed the door, he flipped the lights on and off, again and again.

Grumbles, moans, and what was probably swearing in Russian sounded throughout the room. Novak and

Diaz stood close to the door, the weapons aimed straight ahead. Finally, two of the Russians sat up, stunned by what they saw. They shouted, getting the remaining crew's attention. Confusion and surprise was obvious on each face. Novak tapped an index finger against his mouth. The noise quieted down.

Holding his weapon in his right hand, Novak motioned with his left for the men to get on the floor, on their stomachs. Some were in skivvies, others totally nude, but there wasn't any hesitation in the quick response, as feet hit the deck.

While Diaz stood guard, Novak quickly and expertly hogtied each man with parachute cord. Strips of duct tape were slapped across mouths.

Completing their task, they shut off the light, then locked the door.

Diaz pressed the PTT. "Zero-Niner. Three-six. Crew secured. Going to next target." They hustled down to the next level, on their way to engineering.

Grant pressed the PTT and responded, "Copy that. Report to bridge when secured."

"Roger," Diaz responded.

With most of the crew now secured, there wasn't a need to wait longer. Slade looked back at Grant, who gave a quick nod. Slade checked it was clear, then motioned everyone forward. They headed up the steel ladder, quietly but quickly. Three more levels to climb before reaching the bridge and radio room.

They stopped on every landing, checking it was clear. It was eerily quiet, except for engine noise and the usual sounds of a ship underway. An increase in wind, and waves splashing against the hull gave Grant some concern about Stalley in the Zodiac.

Finally, they climbed the last ladder and stepped onto the deck. Lights inside the bridge lit up the entire length of deck. Even though they couldn't hear voices, they counted on at least three men in the wheelhouse and at least one in the radio room.

Ducking below windows, they kept moving until reaching the bridge. The element of surprise might prove to be an issue. The door leading to the bridge was through a watertight door. Instead of having a door handle, it had a "wheel" similar to one on a submarine's hatch. The door swung outward when opened. But with the weather being fairly decent, Grant guessed it wasn't "dogged down" on the other side. He'd have to take a chance. The men nodded they were ready.

He banged the .45's handle against the door, as he called out in Russian, "Captain!"

Without any hesitation or inkling of danger, Ivanov responded, "Enter!"

Grant spun the wheel and pulled the door open. The four men burst into the room. Motioning with his weapon, Grant shouted orders in Russian. "Hands behind your head! Hands behind your head! Move! Move!" The three Russians moved closer together, with total surprise and shock on their faces.

Slade and James rushed past them, through the chart room and into the radio room. Gremesky barely made it out of his chair, when Slade grabbed his arm and slammed him to the deck. "Hands behind you!" Slade ordered in Russian.

The young seaman's eyes were wide like saucers and he immediately obeyed. James pulled parachute cord from his utility pouch, knelt down, and tied Gremesky's wrists and ankles.

Adler quickly searched the three men, checking for weapons. Finding none he backed away, letting his eyes roam the perimeter.

Grant shouted, "Where is the crate, Captain?!"

The two seaman on the bridge snapped their heads left, waiting for Ivanov to respond. Instead of answering, he demanded, "Who are you?! What are you doing . . . ?!"

Grant cut him off and asked again with his voice deep and low, "I know it is onboard. For the last time. . . where is the crate?!" He stepped closer to Ivanov, within an arm's length away.

Ivanov remained quiet. Grant balled up his fist and sunk it deep into the man's solar plexus, sending him to his knees, trying to get his breath back, wincing in pain.

Seaman Krupinski shouted, "Captain!" and started to move toward Ivanov, when Grant caught him on the chin with the back of his hand. Krupinski collapsed on the deck, blood oozing from a cut.

Ivanov was still on his knees, bent over, panting. Grant stood over him, until he heard Novak in his earpiece, "Seven-Three, Three-Six coming in!" Novak and Diaz rushed through the doorway, immediately moving behind Grant and Adler.

Slade called out in Russian, "Found it!"

Grant swung around, looking toward the radio room, as Slade and James were pulling the crate from under the chart table. James whipped the tarp off the box.

Grant turned to Novak and Diaz, motioning for

them to tie up the three men, as Adler stood guard. Grant went to the chart room. Staring at the crate, he could only shake his head, mostly from relief, but also from surprise. A quick inspection showed it hadn't been tampered with. He motioned to Slade, who immediately dragged Gremesky to the bridge.

Grant whispered to James, "Call in Matt. Then disable the radio--disable, DJ, not destroy."

James nodded, then Grant left the room, closing the door. James sat by the radio set, and dialed in the prearranged frequency. Even though the door was closed, he spoke softly. "Alpha Tango calling Seasprite. Come in Seasprite."

"Seasprite here. Go ahead, Alpha Tango."

"Package retrieved. Will signal with flare when ready for pickup on 'Lido' deck. Do you copy?"

Garrett laughed, then responded, "Copy that! Out!" He glanced at the fuel gauge. *Still more than enough,* he thought, *but a few extra gallons wouldn't hurt, especially with winds picking up.* He stayed focused on the ship, as he turned on the navigation/collision lights.

Captain Ivanov tried sitting up straighter, the pain in his chest barely subsiding. He adjusted his eyeglasses as he silently questioned who these strangers were. The Russian language being spoken by the two sounded perfect, especially by the one who seemed to be in charge. But he couldn't be certain they were Russians.

In the radio room James cut the microphone wire. The radio was equipped with a Morse key, so he unplugged it and stashed it in his utility pouch. Communication would still come in, but nothing could go out. He left the room, and gave Grant a thumb's up.

Grant pointed to Slade, James and Diaz, saying to Slade in Russian, "Ready it for pickup."

The three carried the crate from the bridge, heading for the starboard ladder. Setting it down, Slade lashed the roped around the crate while James and Diaz positioned themselves on a step below, ready to put their backs against it. Wrapping one end of the rope around his waist, Slade started lowering.

Four ladders, four levels later, they were on the deck. They carried the crate toward the helipad, putting it near the steps. They'd wait till the chopper touched down before lifting it to the pad.

Slade turned aft and pointed toward lights. "There's Matt." He pressed the PTT. "Zero-Niner. Four-One. Ready to signal." He wasn't expecting a reply. The three men moved in front of the crate, getting down on a knee in defensive positions.

On the bridge, Adler kept scanning his surroundings, when something caught his eye. He scrambled around the tied men, looking behind the radar indicator. An AK-47 propped up, leaning against the bulkhead. He snatched the weapon, holding it for Grant to see.

Grant's jaw tightened as he walked closer to Krupinski, who had a hand pressed against his chin, trying to stop the bleeding. Grant squatted in front of him, and asked in Russian, "Are there any more weapons?" No response. He grabbed Krupinski's forearm, squeezing until the Russian winced in pain. Grant jammed the barrel of his gun against the man's temple. "I asked you . . !"

"Yes! In engineering. There is one that I know of!"

Fuck! Grant thought. He motioned for Novak to follow him off the bridge. Adler automatically took a position a few paces from the prisoners, looking out of the corner of his eye, knowing Grant was more than just pissed.

Grant rested the barrel of his weapon against his shoulder, looking down at the deck, expecting Novak to explain without him even asking.

Novak leaned closer, talking softly. "Three men secured. We searched but didn't find weapon. Don't know where it could've been, boss."

"Any chance there's somebody roaming the 'bowels' with it?" Grant asked, with his stomach beginning to tighten.

"Fuck, boss! You know we didn't have time to search the whole fuckin' ship! Mullins gave us a count of souls on board and . . ."

Grant held up his hand. "No more excuses, Mike. Go tell Frank to get that fuel line ready." Novak took off, swearing to himself.

Grant looked toward the bow. Winds were stronger than when they boarded, but that was the least of his worries. He shook his head, thinking it'd been twice somebody from the Team fucked up during this op. They couldn't afford fuck ups. He was pissed.

He pressed the PTT. "Four-One. Zero-Niner."

"Go ahead Zero-Niner," Slade responded, looking toward the bridge.

"Signal Matt. Copy?"

"Copy that." Within seconds, Slade fired the flare.

Garrett was ready. With the lights of the ship in his sights, he nudged the cyclic lever forward. The nose dipped until the chopper reached just over fifteen knots, then it transitioned from hover to forward flight.

Before returning to the bridge, Grant had to advise Adler. He pressed the PTT, and spoke softly. "Joe, possible crew member with weapon; possibly more. I'm coming in. Want you to lash helmsman to wheel to allow steering."

As soon as Grant walked onto the bridge, Adler began his task. Checking the helmsman was secure, he backed up, saw Grant give a slight tilt of his head, and knew that was his cue to get the hell off the bridge.

Giving the Russians one last glance, Grant finally left the bridge. He slid his .45 into the holster, then lifted the MP5's strap over his head. He started walking along the deck, with his weapon ready, focusing on the bow and along the cargo holds. The sound of the chopper got his attention. Peering through the bridge windows, he saw it descending.

He took off, running along the deck, stopping every now and then to scan the main deck. He surmised that if there was anyone Novak and Diaz had missed, and probably with a weapon, everyone in engineering, crew's quarters and bridge would be turned loose before any counter-assault was attempted.

It was quiet. Too fucking quiet. But then he thought he heard something, possibly someone running. Slinging the weapon's strap over his head, he ran to the ladder. With an arm resting on each railing, he stretched his legs out in front of him, and slid down the ladder, just like he did when he was aboard ship. He used the same process three more times. Sliding off the last ladder, he hit the deck running, racing toward the helipad.

Four of the men were on the deck below the helipad. Garrett remained in the cockpit. With his hand on the "stick" and the rotors spinning, he was ready for liftoff. From the side window he could see Diaz, who was trying his damnedest to finish refueling.

Suddenly, everyone focused on Grant running toward them, pointing rapidly, motioning them into the chopper. They scrambled into the cargo bay, again taking defensive positions.

Diaz immediately shut off the valve, disconnected the nozzle, then closed the tank with its pressure cap. Not wasting any more time, he dropped the heavy nozzle, ignoring the sound it made when it *clanged* against the deck. He ran to the cargo bay. Just as the rotors started picking up speed, a shot rang out.

"Fuck!" Diaz shouted in pain, as he grabbed the outside of his thigh. Adler and James reached for him and dragged him aboard.

Grant dove into the chopper. "Get us outta here, Matt! Mike! Find that sonofabitch!"

Instantly, Novak had his rifle in his hands, then he crabbed his way on his belly, getting close to the open doorway. He moved the rifle quickly but smoothly, looking through the scope.

Garrett adjusted the collective pitch control lever, and the helo began its vertical climb.

"Got him!" Novak shouted. He refocused the scope, took a breath, and squeezed the trigger.

Brain matter and blood exploded from the back of the man's head, spraying across the bulkhead where he was standing below the bridge. His lifeless body caromed off the wall, struck the rail, then catapulted over the top. The body collided with the deck.

"Matt!" Grant shouted. "Head for Doc! At our six!"

As the chopper started its turn, more shots rang out from automatic weapons.

"What the fuck?!" Grant roared.

"Starboard side, second level! Eyes on deuce!" Adler called out, as he returned fire with his MP5. Slade joined in the shootout.

Novak started to take aim, but the chopper had finished making a one eighty and he no longer had a shot. "Goddammit!" he blurted out, smacking a fist against the deck. He missed a chance for another shot, but his guilt crept in. If he and Diaz had only searched more thoroughly.

Grant grabbed Stalley's medical bag, unzipped it, then took out a battle dressing. "Joe, hold his leg up while I slide the crate close!" He chucked a roll of gauze to Adler, then ripped open the outer waterproof cover, then the inner package holding the battle dressing. He knelt next to Diaz. "Hold this against your leg, Frank. Doc'll be here soon."

Adler wrapped a length of gauze tightly around the dressing then tied it off. "Your wetsuit should help control the bleeding, Frank. Hang in there."

Grant patted Diaz's shoulder as he stood, then he rushed to the cockpit.

Whoever was firing the weapons, wasn't about to give up so easily. A steady spray of bullets whizzed by the Seasprite. Garrett pushed the chopper to its limits, maneuvering it expertly, trying to stay out of the line of fire. He flipped on the landing light.

Grant pointed, "Flare! Two o'clock, hundred yards!" The chopper banked right. Grant headed to the cargo door. "Take us down!" Except for the sound of the chopper, it suddenly went quiet.

Standing in the doorway, Grant impatiently waited for the chopper to descend. Adler knelt on the opposite side, ready to toss out the ladder. The Zodiac was barely moving forward. Stalley kept it under control as the craft encountered wave after wave, along with the constant swirling wind from the chopper's blades. He signaled he was ready.

James lowered the cables enough in order to manually "thread" each cable through the open panels. "Ready, boss!" He kept an eye on Grant, waiting for him to give an okay.

"At ten feet!" Garrett shouted.

Grant signaled James to lower the cables. Stalley maneuvered the Zodiac under the chopper, put the engine into neutral, then grabbed both cables.

He balanced himself on his knees as the boat rocked back and forth getting caught in the trough. Working quickly he hooked the two couplings on the stern, then the same for the bow. Finally, he raised the engine props out of the water, then secured it to the bottom of the boat. Signaling he finished, he rolled out of the boat, then popped up to the surface with a fist held high. Waves washed over him as he treaded water, bobbing up and down.

Grant hung onto a safety line, as he leaned out, then signaled with a thumb's up. "Go!" The hydraulics whined as the boat slowly rose from the water. As soon as it was secured, Adler tossed out the climbing ladder. Stalley fought the waves, stroking hard, finally reaching the ladder. He grabbed hold, and started climbing.

As his head cleared the edge of the cargo bay, Grant reached for his hand, then hefted him aboard. "You okay?"

"Yes, sir!" Stalley grinned. "'A' okay!"

Grant called out, "Take us home, Matt!" Adler immediately hauled in the ladder. Air whistled into the cabin through the two open floor panels, as the chopper picked up speed.

Stalley pulled off his swim mask, pushed his hood back, then wiped seawater from his face. His smile disappeared when he saw Diaz on the deck. "Jesus! Frank!" He dropped to his knees and instinctively grabbed a pair of surgical gloves from his bag, then scissors. He cut open the leg of the wetsuit.

The chopper was being buffeted by stronger winds. Garrett called over his shoulder, "Hang on back there!"

Grant sat on the crate. "What do you think, Doc?"

"Bone isn't broken. Bullet went clear through." He cleaned the wound, put on another battle dressing, then wrapped the leg. "Need anything for pain, Frank?"

Diaz shook his head. "So far so good."

Stalley tried steadying himself as he filled a syringe with antibiotics. "Can we get him to Bethesda?"

"I'll contact Scott. He needs to tell us where we're supposed to drop this off," Grant answered rapping his knuckles on the crate, "then I'll ask him to call Bethesda and tell them we're bringing Frank. We'll deliver him first. Will he be okay?"

"Yeah," Stalley replied, "but I'll keep an eye out for

any increase in bleeding."

As Grant started to get up, Diaz grabbed his arm. "Sorry, boss."

Grant arched an eyebrow. "For getting shot?"

"Yeah, that too. But mostly because we fucked up not finding the weapons."

Grant clamped his jaw, then finally answered, "We'll talk later." He went to the cockpit to call Mullins.

When he had finished the conversation, and had given the destination to Garrett, he asked, "How's the fuel?"

Garrett tapped the fuel gauge. "We'll be okay."

Adler walked to the cockpit. "Where we making the delivery?"

"Where they were going in the first place--Indian Head. Fewer eyes, fewer questions by outside sources. Scott confirmed with the President. A special team will be waiting."

"Think we're gonna need a replacement for Frank?" Adler asked.

"For the rest of this mission, I don't think we'll have time to call in anybody else, Joe. We're gonna have to go with six. . .plus Matt, unless he doesn't want the job."

Garrett shot a quick look at Grant. "Remember when you guys left me at Atsugi?" Grant nodded. "I was not a happy camper. This is what I've been waiting for! Fucking 'A!'"

*

Aboard the *Igor Brobov*

Confusion reigned supreme. Seamen were ordered to check all cargo holds, winches, any equipment or machinery that could have been tampered with. Inexperienced in any type of combat, they raced around almost frantically, shouting to one another, unbelieving what happened. Two crewmen were in sickbay with bullet wounds, one was dead with the back of his head blown out. His body was wrapped in a tarp, and stowed in the galley's walk-in refrigerator.

Captain Ivanov was inspecting the deck where the body had fallen. Two seamen were on their knees trying to scrub away blood, brain matter and leaked urine, stopping often to puke.

He stepped back in order to see overhead, where the man had been shot. Another seaman was washing down that section of bulkhead.

Ivanov lowered his head, then turned and walked toward the helipad. He climbed the steel steps, then walked to the middle of the pad, standing on a large white X. He glanced out across the darkness of the Atlantic.

Questions arose: Who were those men? How did they know about the crate being onboard? Was it possible they were the same men who made the delivery, and for whatever reason. . .? No. That was a ridiculous option to even consider.

These men acted like a team of professionals. They didn't permanently destroy equipment or machines. The radio and Morse Code key would eventually be repaired. And then there was the helmsman, who was given limited steerage of the ship.

Even though he and his crew were manhandled and threatened, they all survived, except for Officer Yeltzin. But it was Yeltzin who opened fire first. If he hadn't, would he still be alive? Having those AK-47s on board may have been a curse.

But the attackers seemed to be experts, firing their weapons from a moving chopper, managing to kill one, and injuring two.

He was relieved the incident was over. He no longer had responsibility for the crate and its unknown contents. Now he could concentrate on getting his ship and its cargo to Russia.

Walking from the helipad, he remembered the message: no further contact was to be made until he heard from the carrier. He was fully aware the U.S. was always listening to transmissions. He would obey the instructions given to him, and wait for the *Minsk*.

Chapter 13

Safe House
Alexandria
0500 Hours

Laying on the couch, Nicolai Kalinin slowly opened his eyes, then rubbed his hands briskly over his face. The past hours hadn't been restful ones. His sleep was constantly interrupted as he reviewed his plan for part two of the operation.

It was time to begin the same process he had done at the rental house. . .wiping down everything, taking no chances. Even though this place was only known to Russians, leaving fingerprints behind was too risky. He couldn't depend on Vikulin or Zelesky.

His suitcases were already in the truck, stamped as diplomatic pouches. The pilot waiting at Dulles had been notified. All documents were in order, along with his Russian diplomatic passport. His American passport was concealed in the lining of his suitcase.

He finally sat up, holding his hand against his stomach, feeling the "rumble." *No time to eat,* he thought. He'd wait till he was aboard the plane. He went to the fridge and grabbed one of the bottles of Coke he bought last night. He started drinking as he went upstairs to the main bedroom.

Blinds on both windows were closed. He started cleaning from the opposite side of the room and worked his way backwards until he got to the closet, panel and equipment. Time-consuming, but essential.

*

Russian Embassy
0600 Hours

KGB Zelesky rushed into the embassy, then ran to the elevator, pounding the button with a knuckle. Finally, the doors parted and he stepped inside, staying within a few inches of the doors. The elevator stopped with a jolt, and as the doors started opening, he jammed his heavy hands between them, forcing them apart.

A door to the ambassador's residence was just ahead, off a small entryway. Zelesky rang the bell then rapped his knuckles against the door. "Ambassador!"

"Yes?!" Vazov called, as he sat up in bed.

"I must see you!"

Vazov put on a robe. As he started opening the door, Zelesky hurried past him. Vazov closed the door, then tied his robe. "What is so important, Misha?!"

Zelesky held a manila envelope toward him. "You must look at this! I found it at one of the American's drop sites."

Vazov grabbed the envelope as he watched Zelesky through narrowed eyes. What he removed from the envelope shocked him. "This cannot be! I will not believe it is. . ."

"Look more closely!"

Vazov drew the official-looking color photograph

closer, finally noticing brown eyes, not hazel. "Who is this?!"

"Turn it over."

On the back, printed in black ink, was a name: Captain Grant Stevens, U.S. Navy.

Vazov walked slowly to the dining room table, all the while staring at the photograph. He pulled a chair out then sat down heavily. "The resemblance is remarkable."

A number of questions ran through Vazov's mind, mostly worrisome ones. Why would the American traitor suddenly release this photograph? He still had not asked for anything in exchange for the information. Did this person have something to do with the weapons?

Continuing to look at the picture, Vazov said, "Misha, see if there is a dossier on this 'Stevens.'" Zelesky left for the records room in the basement.

Vazov dropped the picture on the table. It was most imperative he contact the defense minister in Moscow, and Kalinin. He went to his bedroom to dress.

*

Heavy footsteps pounded against the tile, echoing in the long, second floor hallway, as Vazov hurried to the comm room. He wasn't about to wait until this evening.

Corporal Brusinsky spun around in his chair, as the ambassador burst into the room.

"Send this coded messages immediately," Vazov said, stepping near the counter holding the comm equipment. Brusinsky grabbed a pad and pen. "To Captain Ivanov aboard the *Igor Brobov*. 'Reconfirm package is aboard and you are proceeding as instructed. Immediate response required.'" Without hesitation, he began dictating the second message. "This goes to Defense Minister Andrei Troski. 'Merchandise being shipped today. Notify receiver.'"

Vazov left the room, then went to the opposite end of the hallway to his office. He unlocked the door, then turned on an overhead florescent light. No matter how early it was, he had to make the call to the FCD. Since he, Vazov, was the only person to know the identity, he'd have to privately communicate with him by phone.

He had his hand on the scrambler, when he decided to call Kalinin, hoping he hadn't left for Dulles. He dialed.

*

Kalinin was wiping down blinds, when the phone rang. He rushed to the side table, and picked up the receiver with the cloth. "Mr. Ambassador?"

"Nicolai! Good. You are still there."

"What is it, sir?"

"Misha found an envelope at one of the American's drop sites."

"More information or directions?"

"No. A photograph of an American naval officer."

Kalinin sat on the couch. "Not him, I assume."

"No, Nicolai, it is someone who looks just like you, except for the color of eyes."

Kalinin never expected that response. "Like me?!

Who is it?!"

"A name on the photograph was 'Captain Grant Stevens.' Does that sound familiar?"

Kalinin was quiet, thinking about his time in the Navy and the defense contractor he worked for. "I do not recall that name, nor do I remember seeing anyone who looked like me, sir!"

Vazov leaned back, shaking his head slowly. "Misha is looking through our files to see if we have a dossier on him. I do not understand why the photo was given. . ." A sudden knocking at the office door made Vazov break off the conversation. "Enter!"

Corporal Brusinsky walked to the desk, handed Vazov a paper, then immediately left.

"Sir?" Kalinin said.

"A moment, Nicolai. I have a message from Captain Ivanov." As he scanned the communication, sweat formed on his brow. His heart thumped against his chest. "No!" he shouted, pounding a fist on the desk.

Kalinin abruptly stood, concerned. "Mr. Ambassador! What is wrong?!"

Vazov didn't immediately respond as he reread the message. He finally answered Kalinin. "A team of men boarded the *Igor Brobov* during the night and stole the weapons."

Kalinin was stunned. "But I received a message from him earlier in the evening saying the weapons were safely onboard!"

"Apparently this happened after midnight." Both men were quiet, trying to assimilate the incident.

Kalinin finally broke the silence. "Sir?" No

response. "Mr. Ambassador! Was there any further information?! Does he have any idea who those men were?!"

Vazov perused the message again. "He said there were six onboard. Two spoke Russian. They left the ship by helicopter. One of the ship's crew was killed, two injured."

Kalinin paced the room. "We must get more information from him. What kind of weapons did they use? Were there markings on the helicopter? Anything, sir! It is vital we find out!"

"Yes. Yes. Of course."

"Should I still prepare to leave for Moscow with the remaining weapons?"

"I have sent a message to Defense Minister Troski, advising him shipment will be today. He should confirm soon. I will phone you."

Vazov put the phone down, just as there was a knock at the door, and the communication corporal rushed in again. "Mr. Ambassador, a message from Moscow!" Vazov ripped the paper from his hand, then waved him away.

Vazov read the message, and immediately phoned Kalinin. "Nicolai."

"Yes, sir."

"Moscow is notifying the base. Do you have everything ready?"

"Not quite. I have just started downstairs. The radio and Morse key are cleaned and secured again. Weapons are in the truck. I will call the pilot to file a flight plan."

"And what about a flight time?"

"I will wait until I am positive things here are completely cleaned, then I will call."

"Be sure to give me your exact departure time, Nicolai. I may want to send Comrade Vikulin with you for additional security."

"Yes, sir, I will. Have you received further information on those six men?"

"Not yet. I will try to contact the *Brobov* before you depart."

Kalinin hung up. *Six men,* he thought. But how? How could they have discovered his plan, and know the exact cargo ship? And what does Stevens have to do with anything? Kalinin slapped the cleaning cloth against his thigh as he paced the room. Then, he abruptly stopped, remembering the men who followed him that day. He closed his eyes, trying to picture them. Were they part of the team that boarded the ship? He could never understand how they knew he'd show up that morning. Unless it was pure luck. Coincidences were always possible, but not this many. Yet, all of them affected him.

*

The door swung open. Zelesky came in carrying a folder. He dropped it in front of Vazov, pointing to a name along the side.

Vazov scanned the papers inside. Certain areas were highlighted, catching his attention: Navy SEAL; Naval Investigative Service; speaks Russian and Japanese. He turned to the next page, but it was blank. The last entry was nearly a year ago, when Ambassador

Balicov died.

"Misha, find Petya. The two of you may have work to do." Zelesky immediately left. Vazov pressed the intercom, calling for the communication corporal. When Brusinsky arrived, Vazov dictated a message to be sent to Kabul, advising weapons would not be delivered. No explanation was given.

Then, holding the dossier, he called Kalinin. "Nicolai, I have very interesting information on 'Stevens.' He is fluent in Russian and he is a Navy SEAL. His dossier is. . ." Vazov looked up as Zelesky walked in with Vikulin. "Nicolai, I must go."

Kalinin wondered about the ambassador's report. "Navy SEAL," he said out loud. It had to be. A team of Navy SEALs boarded the cargo ship. And the two men outside the embassy were part of that team.

His worry now was finishing his work at the house, then getting to the airport. Too much had gone wrong in a short expanse of time. And if he was right about the men being SEALs, they were the reason.

*

Russian Embassy

"Has Misha explained the situation, Petya?" the ambassador asked.

"Only briefly."

"Here. Look at this," Vazov said, picking up the photograph.

Vikulin walked closer to the desk and reached for

the photo. He stared at the face, remembering his meeting with Kalinin. Everything suddenly became clear. Everything explained completely. He threw the photograph on the desk, then turned away. He should have known, with all the specific questions asked of him. How could he have been fooled? He brushed beads of sweat from his forehead as he debated how much, if anything, he should tell Vazov.

Vazov was obviously curious. "Do you know this man?!" Vikulin didn't respond. "Petya!"

Vikulin saw Zelesky out of the corner of his eye, watching him closely. He made a mistake in his over-reaction to the photograph. There wasn't any way to make a denial. "Mr. Ambassador, I had a meeting with someone who I thought was Comrade Kalinin, but. . ."

"You had a meeting with this man?! A private meeting?!"

"I am afraid so."

Vazov angrily shoved his chair away from the desk, and abruptly stood. "You?! A KGB officer?! Explain!" Vikulin proceeded to relay full details of the meeting. The longer he talked, the redder Vazov's face became.

He asked Zelesky, "Did you have knowledge of this?"

Zelesky shook his head. "No."

Vazov turned his attention again to Vikulin. "Confirm you did not discuss anything about the weapons."

"I did not! They were never brought up."

Vazov continued staring at the KGB officer. "Do you expect me to believe it is completely coincidental that you talked with this man, then the weapons were taken from the ship, and then we get this photograph?!"

"We did not discuss the weapons!"

"I will have to report this to Director Antolov (Mikhail Antolov, KGB). But I am making the decision to send you back to Moscow. You will report immediately to the director once you arrive. He will be expecting you."

Vikulin started to leave when Vazov called. "Wait!" He picked up the phone and called Kalinin. "Nicolai, Comrade Vikulin will be joining you on the flight. He has an 'appointment' with Director Antolov in Moscow."

"All right, sir. I will call you and verify a time." Kalinin had to wonder about the so-called 'appointment.' He still did not completely understand the inner workings of the KGB, but he imagined this was out of the ordinary.

After Vikulin and Zelesky left the office, Vazov sat quietly for several moments, then he went to the front window. Street lights were still on. Out of the corner of his eye he saw yellow flashing lights as a street sweeping truck turned the corner on M Street.

Standing there with his arms behind his back, he decided he'd had enough of the foolish game. As soon as Zelesky returned he would have him take a message to a drop site, offering to meet "Primex." There had to be more explanation why the American turned against his country. Unless he found out why, he would never feel comfortable, wondering if he himself would become a "victim" of this man. Maybe he was being foolish with these thoughts, but traitors were always unpredictable.

*

Eagle 8
Virginia

After all gear had been offloaded from the chopper then put in the SUVs, Grant returned to the cockpit. "You sure you don't need any more help, Matt?"

"No. I've just got a few more items on the checklist."

"Okay. See you at the house."

Garrett checked off the last items on his sheet, then secured the chopper. A decision still hadn't been made when or if the Team would be leaving anytime soon, but the plane would be ready. As he ran to the Gulfstream, in the distance he could see red taillights through a dusty haze.

Adler was driving the first vehicle, with Grant in the passenger seat. The console phone rang. "Stevens."

"Grant, it's Scott."

"What've you got for me?"

"My contact at Dulles just called. Your 'boy' hasn't showed up yet but a flight plan was filed--D.C. to Moscow; no refueling location yet."

"Dammit!" Grant beat a fist against the armrest. "What about a flight time?"

"Nothing."

"How many passengers?"

"That can change at any time, but for now only

one's been listed. I needn't tell you his name."

"'Kalinin.'"

"To be more specific, 'Nicolai Kalinin.' He's traveling on a diplomatic courier passport."

"Still no dossier on him?" Grant asked, but not expecting anything.

"Not a damn thing. That guy's cover must be deeper than the depths of hell."

Grant glanced at his submariner. "We're almost home. Call me there if anything changes."

"Will do." Call ended.

"Doesn't sound good," Adler said, giving a quick glance at Grant.

"A flight plan from D.C. to Moscow's been filed. Only one passenger registered--Kalinin."

"Now what?"

"Have to wait for Scott. Don't know what else we can do."

"What if we fly the Gulfstream to Dulles, then wait?"

Grant mulled over the suggestion. "Might work, but we'd probably be better off leaving from here, instead of getting caught up in Dulles flight control and air traffic. Besides, we've still got prep work to do."

Adler slowed the SUV as it approached the security gate. Within a couple of seconds, the automatic gate swung back. Both SUVs raced through.

The vehicles parked in front of the three-car garage, and the Zodiac was offloaded. Grant hurried into the house. Adler announced, "Listen up! If you want to clean up now then come back, do it--and fast!"

Slade responded for everyone, "We'll take care of

gear first, LT."

Working quickly under time constraints, the men hosed down all gear touched by seawater, finally storing everything in a section of the garage. The Zodiac was carried in then lined up directly behind the other rubber boat.

Adler walked into the brightly lit space, then knelt next to a door embedded in the concrete. The metal door was similar to one on an armored truck. He dialed the combination. Underneath the garage was a storage room. "Okay, guys," he said standing. "Get extra ammo, clips, and anything we need to refresh, then come into the house. We'll clean weapons inside. Secure this when you're through."

Garrett pulled up to the garage, then followed Adler into the house.

*

Coming out of the bedroom carrying his black boots, his "boondockers," Grant was now wearing black sweater, black pants. He called Bethesda for an update on Diaz. The Team hadn't had time to wait after getting an initial report from the emergency room doctor. Diaz would be kept overnight, on antibiotics and lactated ringer's. Stitches would remain for about ten days. Latest patient information reported he was resting and in stable condition.

"How's he doin'?" Adler asked, pulling a black turtleneck sweater over his head.

Grant sat on the couch and tied his boots. "He's doing good, Joe. Listen, I'm gonna get stuff from the safe. I'll start the coffee when I get back."

"I'll start breakfast." Adler opened the refrigerator,

and pulled out three dozen eggs, bacon, bread.

"What can I do, Joe?" Garrett asked, leaning on the counter.

Adler handed him the loaf of bread. "Toast."

Coming back to the kitchen, Grant dropped a zippered black bag on the counter. Cash, passports, credit card. Any extra money needed, they'd have to withdraw from the offshore account. He and Adler had the number memorized.

The garage door slammed. The four men came into the room, laying rucksacks and weapons by the table, then they hustled to the baths and bedrooms.

Grant shouted after them, "Coffee and breakfast ready in under ten!" He made the coffee then went to the table and started spreading layers of newspapers on top, preparing to clean weapons. He picked up individual weapons, laying each on the table as he thought about what was ahead for A.T.

Soon they'd be on the move again. This time possibly Russia, his "home away from home." A major problem loomed ahead. How the hell would they get to Moscow? They sure as hell couldn't just fly into the country. The Gulfstream had been modified for parachute drops, but without a second "seat," it was out of the question. He shook his head, frustrated.

They had to stop the Russian plane before it crossed into Communist territory. Sounded good, but how? *A 'sidewinder' would do it,* he smiled to himself. The most reasonable would be at a refueling stop. All they had to do was find out which one. He was depending on Mullins and the NSA.

Adler announced, "Breakfast's served!" as he

snatched a crispy piece of bacon off the plate.

Grant took a jar of Jif peanut butter from the cabinet, put it on the counter, then started pouring coffee into mugs as the men lined up, almost like in a Navy chow line. Instead of metal serving trays, they grabbed paper plates, plastic utensils. While they were gathered around the counter eating, Grant relayed the report from the hospital on Diaz's condition.

Adler asked, "You're worried about our next trip, aren't you?" as he slid a plate of bacon, eggs, and toast toward Grant.

"And it's not just about getting there. What happens if those weapons are 'distributed' to different locations? We wouldn't have a snowball's chance in hell tracking all of them."

Grant picked up a piece of toast, then smeared on peanut butter, as he looked at each of his men. Even though there were a couple of fuck-ups before and during the first part of the op, these men were the best he and Adler could've chosen. The mission to China proved their worth. He respected them, trusted them. And he had a feeling those fuck-ups would be the last. Lessons learned.

"Chow down quick, guys," he finally said. "And you might want to put away some extra caffeine. FYI, I've got your passports. Matt, you have all official papers in the plane?"

"Yeah. Just need a flight plan. Plus, I need to throw a few extra 'Lurps' in my car." (LRPs: Food Packet, Long Range Patrol, also called "long rats.")

"And take more of those MREs we've been asked to sample," Adler requested.

Refreshing their coffee, they all carried the coffee mugs to the dining room table. MP5s, .45s, K-bars were spread out on the table. Stalley had his medical bag next to his chair. Once he finished with his weapons, he'd check supplies, sorting, counting, refilling bottles, adding more tape, more battle dressings, and a couple extra syringes.

The phone rang. "Stevens."

"Grant, Scott here."

"Any changes?"

"No."

"I assume you notified the President about the cargo ship."

"Yeah. That's why I'm calling. Made him somewhat relieved, but . . ."

"I know. Look, Scott, he wanted to keep us and the investigation 'under the radar,' but we may need more help besides NSA. CIA always has its 'ears' on. Maybe they already have something but don't know it."

"Do you wanna talk with him?"

"Not necessary, but I'll leave that up to him."

"It might take awhile before I can reach him again."

"Do your best." Expecting another call, Grant carried the phone to the table, stretching the cord to its max, then repeated his conversation with Mullins to everyone. For the time being, Team A.T. was "dead in the water." Grant was beyond impatient.

Adler started cleaning up his kitchen mess, plunging his hands into hot, soapy dishwater.

"Joe, forget that for now," Grant said over his shoulder.

Clips were ejected, and weapons were

systematically broken down, a process each man could do with his eyes closed.

Grant was wiping down the gun with a cloth rag, when his motion slowed.

"Uh-oh," Adler said quietly to himself, as he sat across from him, seeing the clenched jaw. "Why are those 'wheels' spinning? Look, we're ready whenever you are. But you've gotta tell us what, where, and concerns. Out with it."

"If that plane gets too far ahead of us, we may never catch it or the weapons. We can't fuck this up."

"You still plan on waiting here?"

Grant nodded. "It'll take less time, Joe." The phone rang again. "Scott?"

"NSA boys are working their asses off for you!"

"And?"

"Intercepted a couple of messages from the embassy to the cargo ship and one to Moscow."

"They know about us 'lifting' the weapons, I assume."

"You can say that. Plus, Moscow still wants its half of the weapons. So for now, the Afghans are out of the picture."

"Is that it?"

"All for now!"

Grant loaded ammo into new clips. Not much was said by anyone, as they worked quickly, efficiently, waiting for the phone to ring again.

It did. Grant rammed a clip 'home' then answered, "Scott?"

"Grant! Flight time's 0830! They've scheduled Shannon as the fuel stop." (Shannon, Ireland was the westernmost non-NATO airport.)

Grant checked his watch. "We can do it!"

"Do what?!"

"Scott, thanks, but we've gotta move! I'll call you on the way to the airfield!"

This might be their last chance. He slammed down the phone, then swung around toward Garrett. "Matt, we'll take your gear. You head out now. Set a flight plan for Shannon, Ireland. We'll be right behind you!"

Grant turned to the others. "Listen up! Get what you need from in here, maybe a change of clothes." He asked Stalley, "Doc, is your medical bag. . .?"

"Yes, sir!"

"Okay! Let's go!"

Boots pounded against the wood floor as they hightailed it to the bedrooms. Adler unplugged the coffee pot, confirmed stove was off, then made a quick detour to the pantry and grabbed a few packages of Oreos.

Within five minutes, with gear and weapons in hand, they were out the door.

*

Dulles International Airport
0815 Hours

The pilot and co-pilot were in the cockpit, going through the final checklist before departure of the embassy's private jet, an *Antonov I,* similar to a Gulfstream in size, but lower to the ground like a 737.

The jet, with a modified cabin, had become standard equipment for most of Russia's embassies.

The co-pilot noticed a vehicle approaching, then left the cockpit, and waited at the top of the stairs for his passenger.

Kalinin backed the pickup truck close to the open cargo hold. He got out then lowered the tailgate, as he noticed a U.S. Customs agent walking toward him with a clipboard in hand.

Leaning slightly in order to read the name tag on the agent's green jacket, he greeted him in broken English. "Good morning. . .Agent Davison."

"Morning. Can I see your passport and documents for any diplomatic pouches you're carrying?"

"Of course." Kalinin removed his passport and papers from the inside pocket of his leather jacket, and handed them to Davison.

The agent laid everything on the clipboard, opened the passport and compared the picture to the man in front of him, examined all pertinent information, then date stamped one of the pages. He gave the passport back to Kalinin, and unfolded the documentation. He pointed to the truck. "Would you remove anything that's going with you?"

Kalinin put his suitcases on the ground, each one marked appropriately. As the agent examined them, Kalinin pulled out the canvas bags. Even though he knew the agent couldn't inspect the contents, he felt his heart pounding.

An approaching vehicle made both men turn. The Mercedes was within twenty feet of them when it stopped, and the driver shut off the engine. Zelesky got out then stood by the car, looking toward Kalinin.

Petya Vikulin let himself out from the passenger side, then removed a single suitcase from the back seat. He draped a suit bag over his shoulder, then walked toward Kalinin, with Zelesky following close.

The customs agent eyed the new passenger, then the manifest. "The manifest doesn't show any additional passengers."

Kalinin turned toward Vikulin, spoke in Russian, then answered the agent. "I am sorry, sir, that you were not informed in time, but Comrade Vikulin said he received an emergency message from Moscow, requesting he return home."

"Passport," Davison said, holding his hand toward the Russian. The passport was handed over, reviewed, and stamped. Then he pointed to Zelesky. "Is he going, too?"

Kalinin spoke to Zelesky, then responded, "He is not. He is here only to park the truck." Kalinin handed Zelesky the keys. Once the tailgate was closed, Zelesky drove the pickup truck to the embassy's assigned area. He returned to the Mercedes, and waited.

Davison stamped and signed official papers, then gave Kalinin a copy. "Have a nice flight," he said over his shoulder as he walked away, then disappeared inside the building. Taking one last look at the plane, he ducked into a side room and quietly made a call.

Kalinin reached for one of the pouches, saying to Vikulin, "Help me put these in the cargo hold."

Fifteen minutes later, with cargo loaded, exit door secured, and two passengers in their seats, the pilot received authorization to taxi to Runway 01R. Kalinin looked out the window, seeing the Mercedes being driven away.

Just as the *Antonov* began traveling parallel to Runway 01R, the engines of a BOAC 747 roared, the jumbo jet rumbling down the runway, its wheels finally lifting off concrete.

Kalinin leaned back against the seat. With the incident aboard the cargo ship still fresh in his mind, he couldn't help but worry. *Come on! Come on!* he repeated silently, slapping a hand on the armrest, anxious for takeoff.

Petya Vikulin sat two rows behind Kalinin, still speculating about two men who looked so very much alike. But were there two? Eye color could be changed easily with contact lenses. Could that be why the American traitor sent the photograph, to set them on a path looking for one man? Kalinin's cover story seemed accurate enough. Then again, any story could be cleverly created by the CIA or FBI, a ploy used by the KGB itself over the years.

He sat up straighter, as he began formulating a plan. For the next several hours, it would just be him and Kalinin. The pilots would be too preoccupied. Perhaps he could find a way to make Kalinin talk, and if not, the stop in Shannon might be to his advantage.

Vikulin had given himself much to think about, much to consider. By the time they landed in Moscow, perhaps he would have found a way to clear himself from his dire situation.

The aircraft slowly came to a stop, as a TWA 707 began its takeoff. The *Antonov* taxied into position, lined up on Runway 01R, then waited for clearance. Noises increased as flap motors, hydraulics, electric valves adjusted, then the engines wound up. Brakes were released, and the plane began its takeoff roll.

Once airborne, Nicolai Kalinin breathed a heavy sigh of relief, while he watched the city of Washington, D.C. pass below. His first mission as a Russian operative was almost completed, even though it had not gone entirely as planned. Whether or not he was allowed to return to the U.S. rested in the hands of officials in Moscow.

*

Building of the First Directorate
Kabul, Afghanistan

Sounds of automatic weapons and explosions outside the compound couldn't distract the two men. Farhad Hashimi angrily turned away from Major Viktor Zubarev. The news just delivered was not what Hashimi expected. Keeping his back to Zubarev, he asked, "You are certain you read the message correctly?"

"Yes. As I already told you, the weapons were stolen from the cargo ship. It was confirmed by the captain and the embassy in Washington."

"I am finding this very difficult to believe." Hashimi spun around. Standing close to the Russian, he questioned, "During the night, while that ship was underway, in the Atlantic Ocean, the weapons were taken?!"

Zubarev nodded. "They weren't just taken! They were stolen!"

"What is being done to find those weapons, weapons promised to me?!"

"I do not know. I am not in charge of any investigation. How could I be?!"

"You must be in contact with someone!"

"Communication between the U.S. and here has been difficult. We may never. . ."

Hashimi cut Zubarev off. "If those weapons were as top secret as you claimed, they could have had an impact on our fight against the rebels. Now we must continue to use old weapons?! Will you be supplying us with anything?! Old?! New?! Anything?!"

Zubarev had delivered the message. Any further information or conversation was unnecessary. "That is all I have to report. You will not be getting weapons." He gave a quick bow of his head, then turned and walked out of the building.

Hashimi's hands balled up into tight fists. He took short, quick strides toward the entry. Zubarev was already in his vehicle. As it turned past the building, he completely ignored the Afghan. Leaning toward his driver, he made a motion with his hand, as if pointing ahead of them.

Two of Hashimi's guards, with RPGs slung over their shoulders, stood on either side of the entry, waiting for him to give them an order. All it took was a short nod. They ran down the steps, jumped into an overused, beat up UAZ, then sped across the compound. Ten minutes later, an explosion destroyed

Zubarev's vehicle, along with him and his driver.

For a few moments, Hashimi's eyes followed a billowing cloud of black smoke beyond the north side of the compound. Rubbing his fingers continuously over his mustache and short beard, he turned and walked to his office. Standing by the window, he wondered if there was a way to obtain more sophisticated weapons.

He never saw it coming, only heard the telltale sound as he looked overhead, but by that time it was too late to take cover. Shells fired from two M-47, 152mm field guns, destroyed the entire section of building. Two more landed in the compound. Rebels? Russians? Was it immediate retribution for Zubarev?

No one was alive to question.

Chapter 14

Eagle 8
In the Lead Chevy

Dust and dirt flew out from beneath the wide tires of both SUVs, as they sped along the one lane dirt road. None of the passengers bothered looking at watches. They were already committed to their mission.

Grant phoned Mullins. "Scott! We're heading to the airfield. Any updates?!"

"Report is the plane left just about on time."

"Looks like we've got a chase on our hands."

"Listen, I also got word your 'boy' wasn't the only person making the trip."

"Who?!" Grant asked with surprise. He pressed his back against the seat, steadying himself because Adler wasn't about to let up on the gas.

"Does the last name 'Vikulin' sound familiar?"

"You're shittin' me!"

"So you do know him."

"He gave me the address of the safe house."

"Oh, shit! I'm gonna need that story, too!"

Adler started slowing the SUV. The Gulfstream was straight ahead, navigation lights blinking, cabin and cockpit lights glowing.

"We're at the Gulfstream. Hey! Do you have any markings for that plane?"

"Just so happens I do. It's an *Antonov I,* number RA-42624."

"RA-42624. Got it. Try to call me if you have urgent shit to report. Gotta go. We're here."

"Godspeed, buddy."

"Thanks, Scott."

Adler and Novak drove the SUVs close to the plane's steps. Doors slammed as the men jumped from the vehicles, then immediately unloaded all the gear, putting everything near the plane. Adler and Novak drove the SUVs closer to the tree line, locked them, then ran back to the Gulfstream.

Garrett was in the cockpit, checking gauges, flipping switches. He heard the Team coming aboard. "Evenly distribute the weight of that gear!" he shouted over his shoulder.

Grant and Adler boarded last, with Adler stowing both rucksacks.

Grant put on his aviator sunglasses, then went to the cockpit and climbed into the co-pilot's seat, slipping his arms through the shoulder harness. The Team had been on the "hunt" for a new co-pilot ever since Paul Butner, the co-pilot for their mission to China, declined the offer due to family responsibilities. They had to find someone who knew the C-130, too.

Grant was the only one with any flying experience, even though it had been in props. He and Garrett had already been through the basics aboard the Gulfstream, taking it up more than once.

"We're clear back here," Adler reported. Grant hit the switch to pull in the steps and secure the door.

"Shit!" Novak said, leaning over the back of Stalley's seat. "Doesn't look like we'll have a flight attendant on this trip either!"

"Buckle up!" Grant said over his shoulder, as he put on a set of headphones and adjusted the mouthpiece. He picked up the clipboard. "Okay. Ready for pre-flight check." He called out the takeoff procedures, as Garrett verified each was complete. Finally, the last three: landing, taxi, strobe lights on, transponder on, engine instruments checked.

Garrett taxied out to the grass and dirt runway. The engines started winding up. He advanced the throttles close to fifty percent. As the Gulfstream started down the runway, Grant kept his eyes on the speed indicator, calling out the speed. If there were any major problems, such as engine failure or fire, they'd have to abort takeoff before reaching V1. But once past that speed, takeoff was the only option, no matter what happened afterward.

When the engines stabilized at forty-five percent, Garrett accelerated them to takeoff thrust. Reaching Vr (rotation speed), he raised the nose gear off the runway, then finally, the landing gear.

Both men were quiet, concentrating, watching gauges, watching for air traffic, adjusting controls.

Light from a brilliant morning sun spread throughout the interior of the Gulfstream, as the plane continued its climb. Garrett brought the aircraft to a northeast heading. They'd travel close to the eastern seaboard until Nova Scotia, then begin the Great Circle Route over Newfoundland, on a course for Shannon, Ireland, on the trail of a Russian mole.

Grant pulled back a side of the headphones. "Listen, Matt, you haven't had any sleep for over two days. Once we're over the Atlantic, maybe I can takeover for a while, with autopilot on!"

"Thanks, Grant. I should be okay. You guys haven't had any either."

"Yeah, but we're used to it." Turning for a better view of the cabin, he tilted his head toward it. "Maybe I spoke too soon. Two of them are already cutting Zs! But you've been out of the habit for a while. Well, I'll leave it up to you."

Grant took off the headphones, then released the seatbelt harness. "Want something to drink?"

"Anything with caffeine."

Grant walked slowly down the aisle. Novak and James were asleep, Slade was reading the latest issue of SI, Stalley and Diaz were playing cards. Adler was making coffee, and munching on a peanut butter sandwich.

"Got anything for me?" Grant asked, as he got a Pepsi from the fridge.

Adler opened a drawer. "Well, what have we here?"

Grant laughed, immediately grabbing a handful of Snickers candy bars. "Think these'll last?"

"What you see, is all you get!"

Grant bumped a fist against his friend's shoulder. "Thanks, Joe." He put one on seat trays and table as he went back to the cockpit.

He handed Garrett a Pepsi, then held an open hand toward him, with two Snickers. "Not for me," Garrett said.

Grant climbed into the seat, and unwrapped the candy. "Shannon Airport can be a real bitch for landings and takeoffs."

"Yeah. The winds coming across the runway are

wicked sometimes."

"Tell me about it. Made a couple of landings hard enough to blow out tires."

"Promise I'll be careful."

"Confirm something about refueling."

"Shoot," Garrett said, before taking a drink.

"Private jets are refueled away from the terminal, right?"

Garrett wiped a hand across his mouth. "Yeah. They're kept out of the way of bigger commercials. The airport usually provides small buses to take passengers to and from the terminal."

Even with his sunglasses on, Grant shielded his eyes as he glanced out the windshield. "Looks like good weather. Think we'll pick up a tail wind?"

"Maybe. We've got clearance for thirty-three thousand feet. You've flown this route enough to know if we pick up the jet stream, we've gotta be prepared for CAT winds." (Clear air turbulence is caused by vertical and horizontal wind shear associated with jet streams.)

"We'll stay on alert," Grant replied, seeing nothing but blue sky and a couple of jet trails. He pointed toward one. "Think that might be our 'boy' up ahead?"

"Possible," Garret answered, as he leaned forward trying to get a better view.

"Kick this 'baby' into high, Matt," Grant said, giving the jet trail one more glance. "I'm gonna go sit with the guys. Give a shout if you need anything." As he left the cockpit, he detected a change in engine noise, feeling the aircraft surge forward.

*

Grant sat in an aft facing seat across from Adler, who was chowing down on a freshly prepared MRE of beef stew. Grant wrinkled his nose. "You really enjoying that?"

"I know. I know. They've already been labeled 'Meals Rejected by the Enemy' but it's hard to get good food at thirty thousand feet. I brought you that."

"Thanks." Grant picked up a wrapped peanut butter sandwich. "But don't eat all those Oreos," he said, pointing to the open package.

Stalley called out, "Anybody want a drink?"

"Bring me a Coke, Doc!" Grant said.

As Stalley handed him the drink, Grant asked, "Did you eat?"

Stalley swallowed orange soda. "Besides the Snickers, tried a package of those franks and beans earlier."

"Ohhh, Doc! Why'd you do that?"

"Sir?"

"Doc! We're in an aircraft. You know--no windows to open!"

It finally dawned on the young corpsman. "Oh shit!"

"We'd prefer you didn't, Doc!" James said standing two rows away.

When the laughter died down, Grant called everyone. "Gather 'round, guys. Let's talk about what we've got ahead of us. Speak up if you've got any feedback. Matt, you listening?"

"Affirmative!"

Any plans the Team made all hinged on the

Russians still being at Shannon Airport. If they already departed for Moscow, that would mean a whole different ballgame. Time wasn't in their favor.

But there was one other possibility--the last option. It would mean NSA having on its best "ears." If they could find out the specific location those weapons were going, then A.T. might have the time to get into Russia undetected. But retrieving the weapons would be out of the question. They'd have to be destroyed. President Carr had given "his blessings" to make it happen.

*

Preparing for their mission, they reviewed call signs, hand signals. Weapons were ready. They discussed the airport, location of buildings, color of fuel trucks, distance from the terminal to private aircraft area, anything and everything that would give them a heads-up.

Grant sat back, and stretched his arms overhead. "You guys try and get some rest." No one protested. He leaned over the armrest. "Matt! You awake?!" No answer. "Matt?!" Grant bolted from his seat and went to the cockpit, seeing Garrett greeting him with a wide smile.

"Shit! I won't make that mistake again." He went back to the cabin.

Adler changed seats. "Well, what are you gonna do when you finally see him?"

"Kalinin?" Adler nodded. "He's just another 'asset,' Joe. Part of another op."

"You still haven't remembered where you saw him?"

Grant rested his elbows on his knees, squeezing one

fist then the other. "No."

Since the first time they all saw Kalinin's picture, Adler wondered if he should even broach the subject. But knowing Grant the way he did, Grant had already thought about it.

He leaned closer. "Can I talk to you about something?"

"Sure."

"Let's go aft."

They walked to the rear of the plane, where engine noise was a little louder, helping to drown out some of their conversation.

Sitting opposite one another, Adler leaned forward. "Look, I'll find it hard to believe if you tell me you haven't thought that your. . ."

Grant tried keeping his voice low. "What, Joe? That maybe my dad had a fling? That he cheated on my mom? That that guy could be my half-brother?!"

"That's what's been bugging you, not that you couldn't remember where you saw him." Grant lowered his head, staring at his balled up fists. Adler waited briefly, then said, "You knew your dad, the kind of man he was, the relationship the two of you had. And you know how much he loved your mom and you . . and being a corpsman. Come on! Do you really believe that could've happened?!"

Grant raised his head, locking his eyes onto Adler's. "You said it yourself, Joe. We look like brothers."

"And just where the hell do you think that, uh, liaison could've happened? Was he in Europe during the war?"

"Right after."

"Oh. Well, I still say bullshit. Look, for as long as we've known each other, you've been the one who could process information until you reached a reasonable explanation. You're just hung up on the guy looking like you." He poked an index finger against Grant's forehead. "Get that brain working."

Grant flopped back against the seat, knowing Adler was right. Before he could give any response, his friend added, "Hey, you know it's said each of us has a twin somewhere in the world. You just happened to find yours. Too damn bad he's a goddamn communist!"

Grant finally laughed. "Guess you haven't found yours. I'm positive you would've spread the word by now."

"Uh-uh. Mine's still in hiding."

"C'mon," Grant said, giving Adler's knee a light bump with his fist. "I'll treat you to a cup of java, then we'll go keep Matt company."

*

Russian Embassy
0915 Hours

Zelesky knocked on the door, but didn't wait for Vazov to respond. He opened it, then slammed it behind him. His jacket flapped open as he took hurried steps toward the ambassador's desk. He dropped two envelopes on the blotter.

"Two envelopes?" Vazov asked, puzzled.

"One is yours, with the note offering to meet him.

The second was already at the drop site, so there was no need to leave yours."

Vazov turned the envelope over, seeing it had already been opened. "Should I even look, Misha, or perhaps you would care to tell me what is inside."

Zelesky didn't respond.

Vazov removed a single sheet of paper. Only three brief sentences had been written:

"I've accomplished what I set out to do. I will expect you to leave fifteen thousand American dollars at this drop site by midnight tomorrow. Don't expect further contact." Signed, "Primex."

Vazov angrily crumbled the paper, then threw it toward Zelesky. "You had a chance to follow him that day at the train station! You and Petya should have done more to find him!"

"And what would have been the point?! He gave us something of great importance! Those weapons will be in Moscow before the day is through." Zelesky took a step closer to the desk. "It is over. It is worth the money. Do you have that much on hand?"

Vazov merely nodded. "You will make the drop."

"Are you going to contact Moscow, or should I?"

"It is best if I make the call." Zelesky left. Vazov lifted the phone receiver, then he hesitated. He put the receiver back in its cradle, then he went to the window. The sky was perfectly blue, making him think of Nicolai Kalinin on an aircraft headed to his homeland. He remembered the conversation the two of them had the evening they met.

Rocking back on his heels, he wondered if his own return to Russia might be sooner than expected.

Chapter 15

Shannon Airport
2100 Hours - Local Time

Shannon Airport was located approximately forty miles east of Ireland's west coast and the North Atlantic. Situated along the River Shannon, the small airport had one asphalt runway, 10,500 feet long. Even though it had become the first transatlantic gateway between Ireland and the U.S., very rarely were planes waiting to takeoff or land.

Sunset had been at nineteen thirty hours. Ground temperature was hovering around forty-two degrees and dropping. Winds remained constant at twenty knots.

Grant switched on landing lights, and lowered cabin lights, before he lowered the landing gear. Garrett communicated with the control tower, then he adjusted the plane's heading, speed, and altitude.

Team A.T. looked out windows, trying to get a glimpse of their destination. Adler called out, "Get your glasses! Be ready to look for that plane!"

Terminal, control tower, parking lots, and hangars were all on the starboard side of the runway. If the Russian jet already landed, it'd be parked away from the terminal.

The controller in the tower checked that runway and flight path were clear, updated the Gulfstream with weather and wind conditions, then gave clearance for it to land on Runway 06. Winds buffeted the aircraft as it began its final approach.

"Lot of lights out there," Adler reported, as he kept scanning the area. "Hope they won't be a problem."

"Get ready for touchdown!" Grant warned.

A gust of wind caught the Gulfstream, just as tires were about to meet runway, slamming it hard against asphalt. Tires didn't blow. Garrett kept it under control, gradually slowing to taxiing speed.

"Target acquired!" Novak shouted. "Three o'clock! Tail numbers confirmed!"

"Is it refueling?!" Grant asked, as he doused all cabin lights.

"Can't see it anymore, boss! Have to wait till we come around!" Everybody shifted to the port side, with glasses poised.

Following the controller's instructions, Garrett proceeded to a designated parking site. He made a right off the runway, then headed in the direction of the terminal. Approaching the concrete section of the airfield, he made a slight turn left, following a curving, painted yellow line.

"There it is!" Adler confirmed. "Still no sign of a fuel truck."

"They must've just landed," Grant commented quietly. "Nice job, Matt!"

Stalley swung the glasses to another area. "Think I see fuel trucks, LT! Eleven o'clock!"

"Moving?"

"Static!"

An airport marshaller, wearing headphones and a reflective orange vest, came from around the *Antonov* then waited for the Gulfstream. Placing himself near the yellow line, he stood far enough away in order for Garrett to see him at all times, head-on with Garrett's left shoulder. Using illuminated wands, he signaled the plane forward. Garrett kept the nose wheel on the yellow line, rolling forward, until the marshaller held both wands overhead, then immediately crossed them. Garrett brought the plane to a stop and gave a quick salute to the marshaller, who immediately walked toward the airfield. The Gulfstream was fifty feet from the Russian plane, nose to tail, and about five hundred feet from the terminal, located at its four o'clock.

Grant and Garrett ran through the final checklist, then Grant went to the cabin and leaned toward a window. They may have lucked out. This section of the airfield had fewer lights, giving them more shadows they could take advantage of. "Seen any civilians in the immediate area?"

Novak checked starboard side, Stalley, port. Both answered, "Negative." Novak added, "But looks like maintenance workers are coming and going around the terminal."

"Doc, keep watch from the cockpit. Mike, starboard window." Grant said, as he sat across from Adler, Slade and James. "Any sign of the crew, Doc?"

"Negative," Stalley reported. "Wait! Both of 'em are coming out of the plane now. A fuel truck's driving across the airfield."

They waited. "Update, Doc."

"Truck's within range. Parking starboard side now, maybe twelve to fifteen feet from the plane. That's where those two guys are heading."

"We can't delay," Grant said, adjusting his throat

mike and earpiece.

"Hate to 'rain on your parade'," Adler said, "but what about the passengers?"

The right side of Grant's mouth curved up. "When have we ever let small details get in our way?"

"Pretty much never. So we go with a diversion?" Adler asked, knowing the answer.

"Just like we planned, Joe." He turned toward the cockpit. "Hey, Matt. You finished with the fuel paperwork?"

Garrett checked the fuel gauge, making a mental note of remaining fuel. "Done," he replied walking into the cabin. He dropped the paper on a seat then opened an overhead storage bin, taking out a shoulder holster holding his .45. Once he'd adjusted the holster, he put on a windbreaker and zipped it up to his throat, concealing the mike. He had to chance it that the earpiece wire wouldn't be noticed.

"Okay, you know what to do," Grant said. "Give us a couple of minutes first." He leaned toward the cockpit. "Doc, you stay aboard. Keep those updates coming."

"Yes, sir."

Grant turned toward the Team and nodded. Almost in unison, five men pulled down black one-hole masks, readjusted earpieces and throat mikes. Silencers were retightened, then a sound of clips being ejected, rammed back in, slides being jacked back. Alpha Tango was ready.

"Okay, Matt."

Garrett went to the cockpit and hit the switch, lowering the door and steps. When he returned, Grant said, "Time to do your thing."

Garrett stopped at the bottom of the steps, then put on a plain cover (cap), similar to a commercial pilot's. As he walked around the nose of the Gulfstream, a blast of wind nearly took his cover. He grabbed the brim, then kept walking. It was up to him to stall the refueling of the Russian plane, keeping the pilots preoccupied as long as possible, giving the men enough time to take their positions.

Stalley reported, "He's about halfway to the fuel truck. Doesn't look like he's been noticed yet."

"Any time now," Grant said softly. The Team gathered closer to the open door.

A sound of jet engines. Stalley swung the glasses toward the terminal. "A 707's getting ready to taxi."

"Should keep everyone busy for a while," Grant said.

Stalley moved the glasses, focusing again on the Russian plane. "Okay. Matt's at the truck. He got somebody's attention. Go!"

Alpha Tango moved almost as quickly as a heartbeat, getting out then lining up alongside the plane. Grant eased himself closer to the nose, then held up a fist. Taking a quick look around, he motioned with a hand, signaling Novak, Slade and James. Crouching low, they ran at an angle away from the plane, heading toward a row of parked maintenance vehicles. While Slade covered their backs, Novak and James kept their eyes on the plane, Grant and Adler.

James verified the three were ready, then he pressed the PTT. "Zero-Niner. Six-Eight. All in position. Copy?"

As he continued scanning the immediate area, Grant quietly responded, "Copy that." From his position, he was unable to see the fuel truck or Garrett. He pressed the PTT. "Five-Two, still clear?"

"Clear."

Grant and Adler took off, running to the Russian plane's port side. Staying low, and close to the fuselage, they ducked under the wing. Adler tapped Grant's shoulder, pointing to a closed cargo door. Taking it slowly, they stopped by the stairs, immediately hearing voices inside. The conversation seemed more one-sided. Grant recognized the voice-- KGB Vikulin.

On the starboard side of the plane, Matt Garrett glanced at his watch, then turned to see another fuel truck driving across the airfield. In his earpiece he heard Stalley, "Eight-Four, everyone in position."

Time to get refueling underway, Garrett thought. He walked toward the Gulfstream, waiting for the approaching truck.

The two Russian crewmen were obviously perturbed over the delay the American had caused. They handed over their paperwork, then backed away, as the driver began the refueling procedure.

The driver hopped out of the second truck, and Garrett handed him the paper, showing gallons and type of fuel. Following safety procedures, the driver attached a ground wire, and hooked up the fuel hose. Fuel started flowing almost immediately.

Stalley heard another sound, and focused the glasses on a small passenger bus coming toward the planes. Two men jumped out. The bus pulled away.

As Grant and Adler were about to make a move up the steps, they heard in their earpieces, "Zero-Niner! Five-Two! Eyes on deuce, possible UFs! Take cover!" (UFs, unfriendlies) Hearing Stalley's warning in their earpieces, James and Novak took aim, directing their weapons toward the UFs.

Without hesitating, Grant and Adler rolled under the plane, staying in its shadow, and the shadow of the fuel truck, looking aft, waiting, not moving.

Garrett backed away from the fuel truck, keeping an eye on the two UFs. Then he inconspicuously adjusted his earpiece.

Spotting the two men as they ran around the tail of the plane, Grant and Adler slowly crabbed their way aft, taking shelter next to the starboard wheels. They were able to see both UFs, wearing long, black leather coats. Then they heard someone stomping through the cabin.

The two men stopped near the steps, then dropped two suitcases. One of them shouted in Russian, "Open it!" He pointed to the cargo hold.

Vikulin stood at the top of the steps. "Who are you!"

"We were ordered here from East Berlin by Comrade Director Antolov! Now, open the compartment!" Orders also dictated they verified weapons were onboard.

Vikulin wasn't satisfied. No mention of these two men had been made by the ambassador, unless he had not been informed either. With everything that had happened recently, Vikulin wasn't about to trust two strangers.

"I must see your credentials!" he ordered. His

shoes pounded on each step as he came down.

Kalinin stood in the doorway, with his hand gripping his Makarov behind his back.

The two men opened their coats, showing their KGB badges pinned to their suit jackets.

The sound of the fuel truck's engine caught everyone off guard. Then hearing the sound of voices, all three Russians reached for weapons in shoulder holsters. The crew came around from the nose of the plane, and stopped dead in their tracks.

Vikulin stepped aside, motioning for them to board. They hurried into the cabin, stepping in front of Kalinin, then went to the cockpit, trying to avoid the situation by beginning their takeoff checklist.

One of the strangers took a step closer to Vikulin, as he removed a folded red ID card with the KGB symbol on front, and "KGB CCCP" printed across the bottom. He held it near Vikulin's face. "Comrade Vikulin, you are one of the reasons we are here."

Vikulin had no choice. He said to Kalinin, "Have them open the cargo door." Kalinin remained where he was, giving the order to the crew.

Grant and Adler held their breaths. Whatever was going to happen, they were going to be involved.

*

Refueling of the Gulfstream was completed. As the truck drove away, Garrett ran down the starboard side toward the tail, then stopped. He knew where Slade and the other two men were, but, as expected, he couldn't see them. He pressed the PTT, and whispered,

"Eight-Four heading into plane." The Team now knew where he was. No response was necessary.

As he slowly made his way around to the port side, he had to act nonchalant. He was just another pilot, making a cursory inspection of his aircraft, checking under the wings, looking at tires, looking in the cargo area. He stopped briefly near the steps. The Russians were partially hidden by the *Antonov's* wing, but seemed to be checking inside the cargo hold. No one was paying attention to him.

He climbed the steps slowly, whispering into his throat mike, "Coming in, Doc." Once aboard, he rushed to the cockpit, and climbed into the pilot's seat. "Do you see Grant and Joe?"

"They're near the starboard side tires."

Garrett brought the binoculars close, finally spotting Grant and Adler. Holding the glasses with his left hand, he drew his .45 from the shoulder holster. "Doc, watch for Grant's signal to fire up the engines."

"Roger." All they could do was wait, watch and prepare for anything.

*

Vikulin stood motionless, with his eyes going from one KGB man to the next. He finally said, "I have done nothing wrong. You need to question him!" he said pointing to Kalinin.

Kalinin stood in the doorway, not moving, not replying, the grip on his weapon remaining firm.

Across the airfield, a small vehicle was towing a BOAC 737 toward a hangar, while engines roared as a

707 landed on Runway 06. Grant had enough. He motioned to Adler. They crawled out from under the plane on the starboard side just behind the wing. Getting up into a crouch, they silently went to the tail end. The Russians were still in confrontation mode.

Grant spotted Garrett in the cockpit with glasses on him and Adler. He held an arm up and twirled two fingers in the air, then held one finger. Garrett laid the glasses down, ready to start the engines in one minute. All lights would remain off until the Team was onboard. Only then would he notify the control tower they were ready for an airport marshaller.

Grant pressed the PTT, whispering, "Seven-Three, Zero-Niner. Confirm sights on targets."

"Sights on targets," Novak responded as he and James eased forward, staying hidden near the machinery. Slade waited for Grant's signal. Novak got down on the tarmac and stretched out on his belly with his weapon ready.

"Zero-Niner and Two-Seven going in." The entire Team heard Grant in their earpieces.

Grant gave Adler a nod. Adler took off, hustling along the starboard side of the plane, then positioned himself near the nose. Once he was in place, he pressed the PTT. "On three. One. Two. Three."

The timing was perfect. As Garrett started the Gulfstream's engines, the Russians were distracted just long enough. Grant and Adler came from opposite directions, with weapons pointed straight ahead.

The three men spotted Adler, started to react, when Grant came from behind, shouting in Russian, "Hands up! Hands up!" The Russians spun around, with their hands still on their holstered weapons. Again Grant shouted, "Hands up! I will shoot!" Hands slowly raised. He pointed to Kalinin, "You too! Hands up!" Kalinin brought his hand from behind his back, then he raised both hands, still holding his Makarov.

"Drop it! Now!" Grant ordered.

Kalinin leaned forward and dropped the weapon on the ground. "Down here!" Grant motioned with a hand. Kalinin slowly came down the steps. Seeing the Russian up close and personal gave Grant a brief, unsettling moment.

Suddenly, Slade came out of nowhere, rushing toward the plane, aiming his weapon. Surprised again, the Russians snapped their heads around, watching Slade run behind them. Without stopping, he ran up the steps, taking charge of the crew.

Grant ordered again, "Drop your weapons. Now!" The three KGB men remained defiant, angered, focusing their stare on Grant, until seeing Adler move into position just beyond them. Still, no one budged.

Enough of this shit! Grant thought. He backed up a step, held up his left fist, raised one finger, then he immediately made another tight fist.

An instantaneous sound of a loud *clap* in the distance. One of the KGB men shouted in pain, grabbing his right arm where the bone had shattered. He collapsed on the tarmac, with blood running down his arm.

Again, Grant shouted, "Now! Drop them!" Vikulin and his KGB counterpart finally removed weapons from shoulder holsters, letting them fall to the ground.

Mike Novak readied himself again, waiting for

Grant to signal.

Kalinin was standing near Vikulin, not taking his eyes from Grant. He knew without a doubt that these were the same men who were on the cargo ship. Suddenly, the connection was made. The man in the photograph he'd been informed of. The American who looked like him. Although all he could see were brown eyes because of the mask, he thought, *It's got to be him!*

Grant continued in Russian. "Now, the three of you, transfer those pouches to that aircraft," he indicated with a quick movement of his weapon. "As a warning, I have more men ready. Move!"

Reluctantly, slowly, the three Russians pulled the pouches from the cargo hold, dragged them to the Gulfstream, and shoved them in. Kalinin's head throbbed. What was happening felt surreal.

Grant heard Stalley in his earpiece, "All clear."

"Back to the plane," Grant ordered. It was time to make a decision. What to do with the Russians, especially Kalinin?

The three Russians walked toward the plane, with Grant and Adler covering them. They were just beyond the cargo hold when, without warning, Vikulin fell to his knees, pulled another weapon from an ankle holster, then turned, and aimed it directly at Kalinin. In a split second, Grant reacted, tackling Kalinin from behind. Both men landed hard on the tarmac. The stray bullet from Vikulin's weapon punctured the fuselage under the passenger compartment. Three rapid, muffled shots rang out, all finding Vikulin's chest, all from Adler's . 45. Slade rushed from the cockpit. Standing in the open doorway, he kept his weapon aimed toward the cockpit.

The sound of the Gulfstream's engine may have masked the gunfire, but the Team couldn't count on it and had to act fast.

Adler immediately aimed his weapon at the remaining KGB man. Grant jumped up, grabbed Kalinin's arm and jerked him to his feet.

Novak and James stayed in place, waiting for Grant's orders. Stalley left the cockpit, then he ran down the stairs, and immediately took up a defensive position near the nose.

Grant made his decision. He pointed to the uninjured Russian, then to the man laying on the tarmac. "You! Get him onboard!" He looked up at Slade and pointed to Vikulin's body. "Get the crew!" Within a couple of minutes, all Russians were onboard. . . except for Kalinin.

Kalinin was astounded, part from Vikulin wanting him dead, and part from the efficiency with which this team of men carried out the operation. All he could do was wonder who they were. . . and what were their plans for him?

Grant pressed the PTT. "Five-Two, are we clear?"

"Clear."

Grant signaled for Novak and James to come in, then he turned his attention to Kalinin, and said to Adler, "He's coming with us. Put him onboard. I've gotta finish here. Tell Matt to hold off on final takeoff procedures." Kalinin was led away. Once he was onboard, Adler came out of the plane, standing watch with Stalley.

Novak shoved Kalinin toward the rear of the plane, then motioned with his weapon for him to sit.

"I speak English," Kalinin stated.

Novak laughed. "Well, of course you do! Silly me!" He backed up, but continued keeping his weapon aimed at the Russian.

Grant hustled into the Russian plane, taking a quick look at Vikulin's bloody body laying in the aisle, aft. The injured Russian was laying on a bench seat, looking pale and in obvious pain.

Grant walked closer to the cockpit, making sure the two men were paying attention. "You will start takeoff procedures in exactly five minutes. We will be waiting until you have departed. But, be aware that we have the ability to monitor your transmissions, so you should be careful what you say and who you say it to." He made eye contact with each man, before looking at KGB, then moving slowly toward the exit door, he said, "And in case you are wondering why. . . there is a device planted under this aircraft." He went quiet for a moment. "Once you have reached fifteen thousand feet, we will no longer have the ability to activate it. Need I say more?" Absolute silence. "Idti (go)," he said to Slade. They rushed down the steps, one behind the other, then picked up the Russians' weapons that were laying on the ground.

As they ran to the Gulfstream, Slade laughed. "Monitor transmission? Activation? Christ, boss! You sure as hell know how to weave a tale!"

"Worth a shot!"

Without saying a word to anyone, or looking at Kalinin, Grant headed to the cockpit. Climbing into the co-pilot's seat, he put his .45 on his lap, then pulled the face mask over his head, brushing a hand quickly over his hair.

"What now?" Garrett asked.

Grant glanced at his submariner then refocused again on the plane. "Gave them five minutes to start takeoff procedures. Once they're rolling, contact the tower. I'll fill you all in once we're underway." He hit the switch, securing the steps and door.

He and Garrett went through the checklist for takeoff procedures. They were almost through the list, when the *Antonov's* lights came on, engines wound up. A marshaller posted himself at the front, then signaled with lighted wands. The plane began rolling, passing along the starboard side of the Gulfstream.

As it made the turn toward the runway, Grant breathed a sigh. "Okay, Matt. Our turn."

Garrett adjusted his headphones and mike, set the frequency, then contacted the control tower for permission to taxi. Takeoff was from Runway 024, right behind the Russians. Garrett received heading and altitude. Following the airport marshaller's signals to proceed toward the runway, Garrett gave a quick salute.

Grant glanced over his shoulder, into the darkened cabin. Kalinin paid no attention to the aircraft leaving without him, but stayed focused on the cockpit.

"They're underway," Garrett said. The *Antonov* lifted off the runway. It began a slow, wide turn, putting it back on an easterly heading. Before long, its navigation lights were no longer visible.

Garrett contacted the tower. "Shannon Tower, Mike 581 (M581) ready for takeoff."

"Mike 581. Cleared for takeoff Runway 024."
"Cleared takeoff Runway 024. Mike 581."

*

Over the North Atlantic

The Gulfstream was at cruising altitude twenty-nine thousand feet. Head winds were strong. Flight time to D.C. was estimated to be close to eight hours.

"Matt, do you need anything to eat or drink?"

"Maybe a Pepsi. I'll eat something later."

Grant came out of the cockpit. "Hey, DJ. Get Matt a Pepsi."

James came forward with the drink and Grant said, "Stay with him for a while, okay?"

"Sure, boss."

The rest of the Team knew it was time for Grant to meet Kalinin. They remained quiet, but heads turned as he started down the aisle. Adler stopped him, saying softly, "Listen, Skipper, back there. . . I should've searched that guy."

Grant just nodded, laying a hand on Adler's shoulder, then he continued toward Kalinin.

Stopping by the compact refrigerator, Grant took out two Cokes. He turned, seeing the Russian sitting on the edge of a seat, leaning forward with his head hanging down.

"How about something to drink?" Grant asked, as he held the can toward Kalinin. The Russian reached for it, but didn't look up. Grant popped the top on the can, then sat opposite him.

The only intelligent, non-combative conversations Grant ever had with a Russian were with Moshenko. That friendship started when Grant rescued his now very good friend from a sinking chopper. This was going to be a helluva lot different.

As he downed a good portion of soda, Grant told himself he had to get into the guy's head. Even without speaking to him, he had a feeling they were on the same level playing field.

Kalinin finally looked up. He had to agree. They did resemble one another, except the American had brown eyes, more scars, and maybe was a few years older. His eyes dropped to Grant's hands, scarred and obviously strong.

The silence between the two men was about to be broken. "Why'd you save me back there?" Kalinin asked.

Grant put the can in a cup holder, then scooted closer to the edge of the leather seat. "Because it's my job to take you back to the States. . .alive." He locked eyes with Kalinin's, then added, "Or maybe it was pure reaction to protect a defenseless. . ."

"Don't consider me 'defenseless.'"

"Okay. Maybe poor choice of words, but you didn't have a weapon, did you? And you sure as hell weren't diving for cover."

Kalinin rolled the cold can between his palms. "You're Grant Stevens, aren't you?"

Grant tried to conceal his surprise. "And I'll bet you're Nicolai Kalinin. Or would you prefer I call you by your American name?" He didn't have a clue what that was, but bluffed anyway.

Kalinin wasn't falling for it. "'Comrade Kalinin' will be fine."

Adler had been leaning on the armrest, straining to hear over the engine noise. He whispered to Novak, "This is getting good."

Grant gave somewhat of a smile. "'Comrade Kalinin.' Just doesn't roll off the tongue easily. Think I'll call you 'Nick.'" Kalinin opened the Coke and took a long drink.

Grant pointed to scrape marks on Kalinin's face. "Do you need something for that? We've got. . ."

"Not necessary."

Grant pushed himself back, then put his hands behind his head. "I've gotta tell you something." Kalinin appeared to finally relax somewhat, as Grant continued. "I've seen you before. It was years ago, but I'm pretty damn positive."

"I don't know where that could've been."

"Well, we both know you're what we call a 'sleeper' which means you've been in the States for a helluva long time, probably since you were a little kid." Grant sat forward again, staring straight on at the Russian. "And I'll bet you were either in the U.S. Navy or at least worked for a defense contractor aboard one of our ships."

Kalinin's expression never changed. "Interesting idea, but still just a guess."

Grant knew he had him. "No," he said slowly shaking his head. "I think I'm right on the money."

Sudden slight air turbulence caught them by surprise. Grant stood, balancing himself against a seat. "Buckle up. Be right back."

Adler got up and followed him toward the cockpit, then waited. Grant leaned forward between the seats, looking for possible storm clouds. "What's up, Matt?"

"Caught some CAT winds. I've received clearance to thirty-four thousand feet. We should have a smoother ride from there."

"You need me?"

"Should be okay." As Grant started to leave, Garrett asked, "How's the meeting?"

Grant glanced at Kalinin. "Think I'll reserve my comments for the time being. Oh, listen, Matt. Let me know when I can contact Scott." Garrett gave a thumb's up. Grant left the cockpit, then leaned against the bulkhead, preparing to talk with Adler, who was sitting on an armrest.

"Well, did you get your answer, or are you still allowing that foolish thought to cloud your brain?"

"All clear, Joe."

"And?"

"I told him I'd seen him before."

"Did you tell him where?"

"Yeah. Gave him something to think about, but I still can't get his American name."

Adler slapped Grant's shoulder. "Give it time!"

Grant glanced toward the rear of the plane, seeing Kalinin drinking Coke. He looked like any other guy, wearing black slacks, a white shirt under a dark blue pullover sweater, now slightly soiled from rolling on filthy tarmac. He could be a ballplayer, a teacher--even a U.S. Navy officer. Lowering his voice, he said to Adler, "Joe, between you and me, if things were different, my gut tells me we could be friends."

"Then what you've gotta do when we land, sure as hell will be damn unpleasant."

"Tell me about it," Grant responded. "Say. . .why don't you go talk with him for a while. You know how to make friends and influence people."

"I've tried teaching you the secret, but. . .," Adler said over his shoulder.

Off and on during the remainder of the flight, Grant Stevens and Nicolai Kalinin conversed, with Grant trying to put Kalinin more at ease, hoping he'd spill information. Not an easy task, considering Kalinin was on his way back to the States, with a "welcoming committee" of special agents ready to assume control.

Chapter 16

Washington, D.C.
Russian Embassy
2230 Hours - Local Time

Ambassador Vazov reread the message from Moscow. Twice he ordered the embassy's communication corporal to confirm that the message was authentic and correct. Twice it was confirmed.

He slumped in his chair, with an arm hanging over the side, his hand gripping the piece of paper. "Nicolai. No. No."

Defense Minister Andrei Troski's message stated the aircraft carrying the weapons had been reported missing somewhere off the eastern coast of England, apparently crashing into the sea. The British Navy and Coast Guard had vessels and planes searching. Two Russian ships were headed to the area. Reports were coming in slowly, but so far the plane nor its black box had been found. Hope had diminished for finding any survivors.

A knock at the office door didn't take Vazov's attention away from his thoughts. Zelesky came in and went directly to the desk, prepared for business and nothing else.

"Mr. Ambassador."

Vazov slowly raised his head. "What is it, Misha?"

"Will we be giving the American his money as planned?"

Even with his thoughts on Kalinin, Vazov realized he had to move forward. He still hadn't been able to "shake" his concern about the traitor, concerned he'd want more money, or perhaps he'd notify the American authorities, or he was a double agent. Vazov decided he couldn't take the risk. "You will make the drop tomorrow night. But I have decided not to give this American his money. I will prepare a message instead."

"You are sure this is what you want to do?"

"We do not have weapons that were promised. Our men have died and still we do not have weapons. For all we know, the American could have been involved in taking the weapons from the cargo ship. Are you sure you want to question my motive for denying him, Misha?!" Zelesky remained quiet. Vazov continued, giving Zelesky new orders. "I do not care how long you must wait, but you will follow him. Find out where he lives, if he meets anyone else, what car he drives. Do not harm him, do not approach him, just report your findings to me. . .only me. Do you understand?"

"I do."

"He expects a package by midnight. I will have it ready for you at six."

Zelesky started to turn then asked, "And what about the Navy SEAL Stevens?"

Vazov hadn't even thought about him, with his main focus centered on the traitor. "Right now, Misha, concentrate on 'Primex.'"

Zelesky left the office. As he walked toward his office, he glanced over his shoulder at the ambassador's door. Once this matter was completed, he would be

making a full report to Director Antolov. He was
keeping explicit notes.

*

White House
Thursday - Day 4
0900 Hours

Grant rubbed a hand across his clean-shaven face,
finally free of stubble. His hair was a bit longer than
his usual military cut, but it was neat and squared off
across the back. Wearing a dark, charcoal gray business
suit, a white, long sleeve shirt, with a diagonally-striped
gray and white tie, he stood in front of a bank of tall
windows, looking out across the West Colonnade. On
his mind was an upcoming meeting with President Carr.

On one hand the mission was a success, but on the
other, they hadn't uncovered the traitor. Clues or trails
leading to his identity were non-existent or they'd been
covered very well. Maybe it was time for the President
to turn the matter over to the FBI or Naval Intelligence.

Grant slid his hands into his trouser pockets as he
thought about Nicolai Kalinin. Four special agents had
been waiting for him when the Team landed at
Andrews. Grant had walked with him down the steps
of the Gulfstream. An agent immediately handcuffed
him, then led him away. Grant remembered the
moment vividly with mixed emotions. But he reminded
himself Kalinin was a communist, who stole top secret

weapons, was probably responsible for the destruction of a chopper and the men aboard, and somehow, for the deaths of four American Navy men.

A door opened, and he heard a pleasant voice. "Captain Stevens?"

He turned, seeing Claudia Stockwell, one of the President's office assistants. She was in her mid-thirties, about 5'5", hazel eyes, chin-length brown hair, and what could only be described as picture-perfect features.

She held the door open. "The President will see you now."

He paused briefly in front of her. The light fragrance of her perfume drifted into his senses. "See you on my way out, okay?"

"All right," she smiled, looking up into his handsome face and warm brown eyes.

She closed the door and gave a brief sigh as she walked to her desk. It wasn't the first time they'd seen one another in the White House, and there were always pleasantries spoken between them. But this time was somewhat different. "See you on my way out," she repeated quietly, as she sat behind her desk with a smile on her face.

*

"Mr. President," Grant said walking toward Carr.

Carr dropped a pen on his desk then came around it with an outstretched arm. "Grant! Good to see you!" He held onto Grant's hand with a firm grip.

"And you, sir."

"Come on! Have a seat!" Carr lead the way toward the middle of the room. "Sit," he said pointing to one of two beige-striped couches. An oval silver tray, on a glass-top coffee table, held glasses, a silver ice bucket, and several cans of Coke.

"Before we begin, Grant, mind if I tell you that you look good in that civilian suit?"

"Uh. . .thank you, sir."

"How'd you like a job on my staff?" Carr had a huge smile on his face.

Grant cleared his throat. "That's one heck of an offer, Mr. President, and I'm flattered. But. . ."

"I know. I know," Carr responded, waving a hand. "It wouldn't compare to your active lifestyle. Right?"

Grant laughed, with his head bobbing up and down. "Something like that."

"When did you get back?"

"Plane landed at Andrews around 0300. Flight was longer than expected."

"Guess none of you have had much sleep these past few days," Carr commented, noticing dark circles under Grant's eyes.

"Not much."

Carr handed Grant a can of Coke, then immediately asked, "How's your man, the one who was injured?"

"Frank's doing okay. A couple of the men were going to stop by and see him at his apartment."

"Glad to hear it. Will he be ready when Alpha Tango is needed again?"

"Affirmative, sir." Grant's eyebrow raised. "Do you have another job for us?"

"Not as of this moment."

Carr got up and went to his desk, then returned with a piece of paper, handing it to Grant. "This came in earlier."

Grant read the report, then handed it back to Carr. "I saw it on the news this morning. That's gotta be the plane 'our' Russians were aboard. They took off just before us. The timeframe looks about right."

"Straight up, Grant. Did you or any of your Team place any type of device in, under, or on top of that aircraft?"

"Negative, sir! We had nothing to do with that plane going down. I'll take an oath on that. So will my men."

Carr folded the paper and laid it on the coffee table, then he popped the top on the can and took a drink. "All right, Grant. You're on."

Grant started from the first time Kalinin was spotted at the embassy, to Grant's meeting with Vikulin, to the op aboard the cargo ship, and finally Shannon Airport.

Carr had very few questions during the entire two and a half hours Grant spoke, managing to down three full cans of Coke.

Grant moved toward the front of the cushion. "Mr. President, I'm sorry we haven't uncovered our traitor. As I said before, Nick. . ."

"Whoa, Grant! Nick?"

Grant laughed. "Yes, sir. That's what I called him on the trip home, when he wasn't being too talkative."

"Well, why not," Carr responded with a slight shake of his head.

"He didn't offer up any intel to us."

"Understandable."

"I have a feeling that whoever's questioning him will find he's got fingerprints on file, along with his

American name."

"I've thought along those same lines, Grant, especially after remembering your mission aboard the *Bronson.*"

Grant nodded, then said, "Mr. President, the Team's ready to offer its services in finding 'Primex' if you need additional assistance. We sure would like to know who the. . . uh, who he is."

"We all would, Grant. I appreciate your offer, but I think it's time to turn the investigation over to the FBI."

"Will NIS still be involved ?"

"They're moving forward with the chopper incident, trying to determine who those men were, etc." Carr put the Coke can on the table, then leaned back. "Now, tell me what you think about the Russian."

Grant had to be careful with his response, and not give away his true thoughts on Kalinin, as in the word 'friends.' "Well, he's intelligent, personable, quick to respond, and even has a sense of humor. Although our conversation was pretty much one-sided, mostly my side, I felt there was a 'connection' between us. You know what I mean, sir?"

"Yes, I do, Grant. I've had those same feelings during many of my one-on-one meetings with dignitaries and world leaders."

"I don't know how long it took him to plan his mission, but there was a helluva lot of work and thought put into it."

"A helluva lot of work you and your Team tore apart, Grant."

"Yes, sir. We did."

"You know, Grant, I'd like to convince him to

'come over' to our side."

"If you don't mind my saying so, Mr. President, I'm not sure the odds would be in our favor."

"Well, look what happened with Colonel Moshenko."

"That's true. But Grigori's older, and he spent his whole life in Russia. He had to face some really harsh times, went through a lot of horrendous conflicts. His final decision was based on what was best for him and Alexandra at this time in their life.

"But Nick grew up here. I guess what he learned about Russia was what his folks told him, being brainwashed with negative remarks about us, and overly positive statements about the 'Motherland.' And by the time he learned about his heritage, he was probably at a very impressionable age. That's not to say he didn't like living in the States, and didn't form his own opinions. But I can't imagine what it'd be like learning that your whole life was preplanned, dictating that you'd be working for a foreign government, and working against the only country you'd ever known." Grant shook his head slowly. "Hard to imagine." He went quiet, then said, "Sorry, Mr. President. Hope I didn't get too carried away."

"Not at all."

"I guess it wouldn't hurt to try and convince him, though."

Carr started to respond when the intercom buzzed. "Excuse me a minute." Carr went to the desk. "Yes, Theresa?"

"Mr. President, Secretary Williams is here for his appointment."

"I'll be with him shortly."

Grant stood and re-buttoned his suit jacket, as Carr walked toward him. "Well, Grant. It's been a very interesting meeting." He extended a hand.

Grant reached for it with a firm grip. "Yes, sir. If we can do anything to help with the remaining investigation, let us know. We'd be more than happy to."

Continuing to shake Grant's hand, Carr said, "The Team did a remarkable job on the mission, Grant. I thank you all."

"Our pleasure, Mr. President. I'll be sure to tell them."

As Grant stepped into the outer office, Carr said with a smile, "Keep my offer in mind!"

"I will."

Carr gave a slight wave, then motioned Treasury Secretary Williams to come into the office.

Grant gave a quick look at his submariner. Then, he started walking, seeing her sitting behind her desk, busily sorting through a stack of file folders.

He stood next to her desk, and said quietly, "Hi."

She looked up. "Oh! Captain Stevens."

"No formalities, okay? Just call me 'Grant.'"

"All right. Grant it is," she smiled.

"I know this is kind of sudden, but how'd you like to have dinner with me, say, Sunday?"

She couldn't take her eyes away from his. "That sounds lovely."

He reached for a pencil and notepad, and handed them to her. "Would you mind giving me a home phone number? I don't want to bother you here--like

I'm doing right now."

"You aren't bothering me at all," she replied, as she wrote down the number, tore the paper from the pad, and handed it to him.

He gave the number a quick glance, then put it in his jacket pocket. "I've gotta go. We're still trying to catch up since we've been back. I'll call you in a couple of days, then we can set up a time for me to pick you up. How's that sound?"

"Sounds perfect. I'm looking forward to it," she smiled.

He started backing away. "Yeah. Me, too." Then, he turned and headed to the main door.

Once he was out of sight, she returned to filing, when another assistant laughed, "Wow! Way to go, Claudia!"

*

State Department
Office of Scott Mullins
1600 Hours

"Permission to come aboard, **sir**!"

Mullins swung his chair around. "Hey, Grant! Welcome back!"

Grant went to the desk with his arm outstretched, grabbing hold of Mullins' hand. "As always, it's good to be back!"

"Sit!" Mullins said. "How about something to drink?"

"No, thanks. Had a Coke with the President

earlier."

"Well, listen to you! 'Mr. Name Dropper'!"

"Guilty," Grant laughed.

Mullins rocked back and forth in his swivel chair. "So, what's he like?"

"Who, the President?"

"You know who I mean."

"Oh, you mean 'Nick.'"

"Who the hell's 'Nick'? I meant Kalinin."

"Nick Kalinin. You know. 'Nicolai'?"

"Oh, fuck. Don't tell me you two are buddies already?"

"Not exactly." Grant proceeded to fill Mullins in on the whole op. When he finished he asked, "Do you know where they're holding him, Scott?"

Mullins shook his head. "Haven't been able to find out. But the FBI's most likely got him in one of their 'hideaways' which means there's a good possibility he'll be moved to another location, and probably soon."

"Think you could do some investigating for me?"

"You won't be able to have any contact with him, Grant."

"I know. I know." He locked onto Mullins' brown eyes. "C'mon, Scott. That's not much to ask for. A few phone calls."

"I'll see what I can do."

"Thanks."

The phone rang. "Let me get this. Mullins." The call was one-sided, until Mullins said, "Okay, Phil. Thanks for the info." He slowly replaced the receiver. "Seems that a Russian private jet went down, not far off the coast of England."

"Yeah. I heard."

"Did you have anything to do with it?"

"Excuse me?!"

"You heard me."

"Jesus, Scott! I'll tell you the same thing I told the President. No! We didn't plant any device on that plane. We had nothing to do with it going down. Anything could've gone wrong. Listen, those pilots were fuckin' freaked. Maybe they weren't paying attention to their instruments. Hell! Why'd you even ask?!"

"Oh, maybe I just like getting your blood boiling once in a while," Mullins finally laughed.

Grant leaned across desk, shaking a finger in Mullins' face. "Bad agent! No more donuts!" He cracked a smile, then stood. "It's been fun, but I've gotta meet the Team at Eagle 8. We're still taking inventory."

Mullins came from behind the desk. "How are the supplies holding up?"

"Off the top of my head, we'll need jet fuel. Think we can get it today?"

"Don't see why not."

"I'll call after inventory." Grant reached for Mullins' hand. "We've gotta do this again sometime."

"Roger that, buddy."

*

Northeast D.C.
Deanwood Section
2330 Hours

Misha Zelesky parked the Mercedes two blocks from the intended drop site, then shut off the engine and headlights. As long as he left the package by midnight, they would still be in compliance the American's request.

He removed the envelope from the glovebox. The thickness was about right, as was the weight for large bills that would total fifteen thousand American dollars. The plain pieces of paper, cut to size, were held together with tape, then put inside an envelope and sealed. That envelope was inside a larger one with the note Ambassador Vazov had written.

He got out, and quietly closed the door. Feeling a light rain, he tucked the envelope under his jacket, then pulled up his collar. Taking one more survey of the area, he began walking.

Most of the buildings were abandoned, windows were broken, street lights were few. He swiveled his head occasionally, never knowing if the American--or possibly a second conspirator--could be watching.

He stopped. Up ahead was the drop site at the base of a partially dismantled railroad trestle. Resuming his steady pace, he stayed on alert until reaching the wooden structure. The farther under the structure he walked, the darker it got. Squinting, trying to see the exact location, he edged forward. Taking one last look left then right, he got down on a knee, and shoved the envelope across soft dirt, pushing it as far back as possible.

Hurrying to the Mercedes, he got in and drove

away. Only he wasn't going to the embassy. Driving three blocks past the trestle, he shut off the lights, then turned a corner, and parked again. This time, when he got out, he took his Makarov.

Skirting around buildings, he chose one where he'd have a good view, and one that was close enough if he had to take chase. A second floor window would work.

*

An hour later, Zelesky leaned closer to a window. "There he is," he whispered, looking through spider web cracks.

A man was walking at the base of the embankment, heading toward the trestle. He turned his head, looking to see if he was being followed, then he kept walking. He stopped, put his back against the embankment, then appeared to be scanning the darkened area across from him. Finally, he ran to the opposite side.

Zelesky lost sight of him for a moment, then he suddenly reappeared, only this time he was running back the way he came. Zelesky hurried down the interior steps of the building, then ran to his vehicle. The American could have only parked in a certain area, and that's what Zelesky was counting on.

As much as he wanted to hit the gas, Zelesky took it slow with headlights off, until he spotted taillights ahead. He swiveled his head quickly, looking for any other lights but didn't see any. His hunch was right. He dropped back, continuing to keep the red taillights in sight.

Traffic was sparse, but it was finally safe for him to

turn on headlights. The American was still in sight, easy to follow. *Inexperienced fool,* Zelesky thought.

Twenty minutes later, the vehicle turned off the main road and into a neighborhood. Zelesky shut off the headlights and slowly drove forward, seeing brake lights flash, as the car turned left into a driveway. He immediately pulled to the side of the road, and killed the engine. An overhead light came on in the American's car, just before the car door slammed. Zelesky had a very limited glimpse, but it didn't matter at this point. He got out of the Mercedes, closed the door quietly, then cautiously hustled toward the target house, four houses away.

He scurried behind the vehicle, then peered through the car windows. Lights came on in the house. Crouching low, he slid his back along plastic siding, then ducked beneath a large picture window. Hearing the American shouting and swearing, Zelesky slowly stood just enough to peer into the window. The American was on the phone.

Zelesky wasn't able to pick up every word, but what he did hear was more than enough. As the American slammed down the phone, Zelesky took off for his car.

On his drive to the embassy, he had a thought. What if the person the American was talking to was the man in the photograph? The Navy SEAL. The one who looked like Kalinin. He'd report his idea to Vazov, wishing there was more time to investigate.

Chapter 17

Grant's Apartment
Washington, D.C.
Friday - Day 5
0530 Hours

Standing by the living room window in his old, blue Navy jogging shorts, Grant opened the blinds, then sipped on his hot, black coffee. It had been awhile since he'd slept a solid eight hours. It sure as hell felt good. Turning his head slightly, he was able to see running lights on a private yacht, heading south along the Potomac. He had to admit there were still moments when he missed the sounds and feels of a ship, the smell of seawater, an overwhelming feeling of wonder when looking at a million stars against a pitch black evening sky from the middle of an ocean. Luckily, those moments didn't last long.

He turned away from the window, downing the last few mouthfuls of coffee, then went to the kitchen, and rinsed the cup. He started walking to the bathroom, looking forward to a hot shower. Besides driving his Vette, a shower helped him think, sort things out.

Hot water beat against his head and shoulders. He lowered his head, when his thoughts were interrupted by one question that stuck in his craw: Who the hell was 'Primex' and would he ever be found?

*

Eagle 8
Noon

Today the Team tasked itself in finding a co-pilot for future flights. They compiled a list of names, the same way Grant and Adler made selections for Alpha Tango.

Adler pushed aside a sheet of paper. "Feels like deja vu all over again," he said seriously, stretching his arms overhead.

"Hey! I know that one!" Stalley said, pointing his finger in the air. "Yogi Berra, New York Yankees, right?"

Grant was leaning against the kitchen counter, with one foot crossed over the other. "And you can associate that with what, Doc?"

Stalley swung around. "Huh?"

Grant pressed a finger against his ear. "Come in Yankee Five-Two."

"Really?! That's where you came up with our call sign?!"

"Not really," Grant answered, grinning. "It just sounded good."

"Shit, boss. You guys are always jerkin' my chain."

Novak put an arm around Stalley's shoulders. "That's because we love you, Doc!"

Laughs died down just as the phone rang. "I'll get it," Slade said. "Slade here. Yeah. Hold on. Boss, it's Scott." Slade covered the mouthpiece. "He sounds hyper."

"Scott?"

"Grant! I just got word! Kalinin got away!"

Grant jerked to attention. "What?! How?!"

"He was being transferred to another holding facility. The van got T-boned!"

"Oh Christ! Anybody hurt?"

"Word was a couple of agents had broken bones but that van's 'toast.' A witness on scene said he ran to help. Two men in the back were unconscious, but a third was crawling around, trying to get out. He seemed disoriented.

"Two witnesses helped that guy out of the van, then turned their attention to the driver and a passenger. By the time cops and rescue vehicles arrived, Kalinin was gone."

"Where'd it happen?!"

"They were heading south outta D.C., somewhere along Glebe Road. I think that's 120."

Grant was pacing. "I think I know where he's headed! If you've got updates, call Joe's car phone!"

"Where's he go. . .?!" Too late. Connection broken.

"What happened, Skipper?" Adler asked with concern.

"There was a car accident. Nick got away."

"Holy shit!" was voiced by more than one of the men.

"Everybody hang here. Joe and I are gonna try and find him. He may be headed to the safe house. C'mon, Joe! You drive!"

*

Twenty-five minutes later, Adler turned his red '67 Mustang off the main road leading into the neighborhood. "You realize we'll be in a world of shit if anybody finds out what we're doing, don't you?"

"Take the next left," Grant said. He folded a map and shoved it under the seat. "The next street on the left should be Aless. Drive past it so I can get a look." Grant raised binoculars, turning in the seat, trying to get a better view. "Don't see any cars in the first two driveways. Think 'our' house is the second one, left side of the street, if I'm reading the numbers on the mailbox correctly. Go to the street behind it."

Adler made a K-turn, then headed back. "You really think he's here?"

"Closest place to where the accident happened, Joe, but it's still just a guess. Don't even know how he would've gotten here, unless he hitched. The agents would've taken all his personal stuff, so he wouldn't have any money on him."

Adler turned the Mustang at the next street. "Okay. Guess this is good enough," Grant said.

They tucked the weapons into their front waistbands, zipped up their jackets, then got out.

"Joe, get that emergency medical bag. He could've gotten pretty banged up in the accident." Adler got the bag from the trunk, hooking the strap on his left shoulder.

They perused the neighborhood. So far, not much activity, except for a gray-haired older man across the street digging flower beds behind a chain link fence. A small black poodle yapped and jumped at every shovel of dirt tossed. Most driveways were clear of vehicles.

Who and how many were inside the homes was a different story. But at least homes were few, spread out, with enough property between them.

"Let's go," Grant said as he started walking.

Adler continued watching their backs, scanning the whole area, until Grant said, "This is it."

They were behind a rundown, single car garage. Getting as close as they could to the structure, then easing toward the corner, Grant slowly leaned his head forward until he saw the house. Windows were closed, shades and blinds were drawn. No one was in sight.

"Looks clear. You take the door's port side. Ready?"

"Go!" Adler whispered.

Crouching low, they hustled across the property, taking positions next to the door. They waited and listened, but it was quiet. Grant eased closer to the door. It was closed but not secured. Part of the framework was splintered.

He slowly pushed it open, just enough so he could get close. "Nick! It's Grant!" Nothing. "C'mon, Nick! Open up. Joe and I are here to help you." They waited. There was a possibility Kalinin had passed out from a head injury, or he was very suspicious, or he wasn't here. Grant was ready to enter, when the door opened.

Kalinin had obvious surprise on his face. "What the hell are you doing here?" A S&W .38, taken from an agent, was gripped in his hand.

Grant pushed his way past him. "I told you. We're here to help."

Small cuts from broken glass, bruises and scrapes

were on his face and hands. Blood from a cut above his eyebrow had dripped on his shirt. Spots of blood had already dried on his clothes. He rubbed a shoulder as he went into the living room, walking past both men. He continued holding the gun. "How'd you know about this place? I mean, its location?"

"Uh, information was turned over to me by a certain party member." Grant unzipped his jacket, making sure Kalinin knew he was armed, too.

Kalinin's eyes narrowed. "Comrade Vikulin, right?"

"He's the one."

Now Kalinin understood the KGB officer's line of questioning and suspicions toward him. "But how'd you know I was here?"

"Part guess," Grant answered. "C'mon. Sit down. Let Joe take a look at those cuts."

Adler knelt next to the couch and opened the bag. "Guess there aren't any broken bones, right?" he asked as he dabbed antiseptic on the cuts.

Kalinin shook his head. "Doesn't feel like it, mostly muscle soreness."

Grant sat at the opposite end of the couch. "How'd you get here?"

"Hitched a ride on trucks."

"Nobody questioned your injuries?!"

Kalinin managed a brief smile. "I wasn't always riding in the cab." He turned his head to look at Grant. "I can't believe you're taking the risk in coming here. Why?"

"Don't know. Just felt we had to." It was the only answer he could think of. "Weren't you in cuffs?"

"Found the key in one of their pockets."

Adler put the last of the Band-Aids on Kalinin. "Okay. That'll have to do." He closed the bag then stood.

Kalinin touched above his eye. "Thanks." He got up and went to the front window, with Grant watching him. He finally turned around. "You don't expect me to 'come over,' do you?"

"That'd be your decision."

"So, you're going to turn me in."

"No."

Kalinin was shocked, confused, but asking for a reason hardly mattered for now. "Then, what happens next?" He put the gun in his front waistband.

Grant finally stood. "There's probably a shitload of folks looking for you. The best we can do is take you to the embassy."

"Which one?" Kalinin asked with somewhat of a smile.

"Don't think you wanna come to ours." Grant started walking the room with his head down, hands thrust into his pockets. "We can't hold off until dark. We've gotta get you to the embassy, without your being seen."

"Or us," Adler quipped.

"Right, Joe." He swiveled his head, searching the room with his eyes. "Is there a scrambler installed?"

"There was, but that was the first thing I looked for. The phone's been disconnected. Everything was removed."

"Everything?" Grant said with a slight smile.

"Everything, but I can't figure out why."

Grant turned away, rubbing his chin. "The parking garage on L Street."

"You know about that, too?!"

Grant continued his train of thought. "We'll take you there, then you can call the embassy to have someone pick you up."

"Uh, Skipper. What about the plane? You know?"

Grant looked directly at Kalinin. "Hate to tell you, but there was some kind of accident. The *Antonov* went down in the North Sea."

Kalinin sucked in a lungful of air, shocked. "Any survivors?"

"Last we heard, no."

The Russian ran his hands over his disheveled hair. "They think I'm dead, don't they?"

"Afraid so."

He looked around the room. "That's why the equipment was removed." He was quiet for a brief moment. "Guess when I make that call it'll have to be brief." He planned on using his code name: Antares.

"And you'll probably want to use your code name," Grant said.

"I'd like to know you better, Grant Stevens!"

"Wish we had the time. Are you ready?"

"Let's go."

"Joe, get the car, bring it behind the garage." Adler left.

*

Twenty-five minutes later they were in the parking garage, on the top level. Cars were coming and going, doors were slamming, people were rushing to and from elevators. Exhaust fumes permeated the air.

Adler drove slowly down the outer aisle. "There," Grant pointed. "A phone booth."

Adler pulled behind a parked vehicle. Grant got out then Kalinin. Grant reached into his pocket and pulled out some change. Sorting through the coins, he gave Kalinin a quarter. "I know it's not secured, but you've got no choice. We'll wait."

Grant leaned against the car, with a hand resting on the handle of his .45. Keeping an eye on Kalinin, he questioned what he and Adler had just done. Aiding and abetting a foreign spy. A Russian. "Christ!" he whispered between clenched teeth. His motives were unclear. Maybe this was finally the time when his instincts would be his demise.

"Someone will be here shortly," Kalinin said.

Everyone turned as a white Pontiac LeMans drove past them, heading for the down ramp.

"We'll pull over there until you're safe." Grant pointed toward a darkened area at the end of the aisle.

Kalinin leaned toward the open window, giving a slight wave to Adler. "Thanks."

Then he extended a hand to Grant, who latched onto it firmly. The two just looked at one another.

Kalinin said, "This sure is . . ."

"Strange?" Grant asked.

"Yeah. Strange. Listen, saying thanks just doesn't seem to be enough," Kalinin finally said.

"It's enough. Do svidaniya, Nick."

"Do svidaniya, Grant."

Grant got in the car, and Adler drove to the far end of the aisle, then pulled into a hatch-marked, no-parking space. They both turned sideways, watching out the rearview window.

Headlights appeared, and a black Mercedes pulled in front of Kalinin. He got in the front seat, closed the door, and the Mercedes immediately headed for the exit.

"Well, Skipper, another fine ending, except, I wonder what Leavenworth's like this time of year?" He backed the Mustang up, then shifted into first.

As Adler turned left onto L Street, he asked, "What about Nick? Do you think he'll let the 'cat outta the bag' that it was us who helped him?"

"My gut?"

"What else?"

"Don't think so. C'mon. Let's head back to Eagle 8. We've gotta report to the guys, and I'll have to call Scott."

"Maybe I shouldn't ask, but what about the President? Think he should know?"

"That's the tough one, Joe. Really tough."

Chapter 18

Russian Embassy
1530 Hours
Friday - Day 5

Ambassador Vazov stood by the desk in the lobby, still unbelieving Kalinin was alive. He was more than curious, though, to hear the entire story.

Zelesky drove the Mercedes close to the entrance, trying to give Kalinin some cover, allowing him to stay in the shadow of trees. A black van was parked across the street, undoubtedly FBI.

Kalinin walked into the lobby, looking tired and obviously injured. Vazov reached for Kalinin's extended hand, but immediately put a finger to his own lips, then pointed to the elevator.

Once the elevator motor started, Vazov said, "Nicolai, we thought you were dead!"

"I am sorry that I was unable to contact you."

"You are hurt."

"Nothing serious, sir."

"We will go to my residence. I will give you food and drink."

As they rode the elevator, Kalinin felt it strange to be inside the Russian Embassy. The closest he'd been was the morning he left the newspaper, the start of his mission, a mission that ended in failure. It was not easy for him to face the ambassador now, a man who had expressed such confidence in him, depended on him to get the weapons to their intended destinations. But Grant Stevens and his team of specialists derailed the entire plan.

Vazov interrupted Kalinin's thoughts as he opened the door to the residence. "Go in, Nicolai." Kalinin entered the apartment. The lavishness of the decor surprised him. Red velvet-covered sofas, chairs, expensive mirrors, paintings, crystal chandeliers, heavy red drapes. He remembered his parents telling him about the harsh conditions most Russians had to deal with, then seeing this. . . But perhaps that was part of what made Russians such a strong, proud people. . . the little they did have.

"Nicolai, sit over here," Vazov said, indicating an ornate wooden chair by the ten-foot rectangular dining room table. "I am having hot food prepared."

Kalinin pulled the chair from under the table, then sat down.

Vazov reached for a bottle of Stolis Vodka. He poured the clear liquid into his glass, then Kalinin's. He raised his glass. "A toast, Nicolai, for your return to us." Kalinin raised his glass, then drank a small mouthful.

Vazov sat at the head of the table. "Now, Nicolai, do you want to talk about what happened?"

Kalinin leaned back, and began. When he finished, Vazov asked, "And those men were the same who took the weapons from the cargo vessel?"

"While I am not positive, it seems to be the most logical."

"And Comrade Vikulin. Was his body left at the

airfield in Shannon?"

"No, sir. His body was put onboard. Oh, Mr. Ambassador, my American passport was on the aircraft, and the agents confiscated my Russian one. I. . ."

"Do not worry. I will see that a new diplomatic passport is ready." Vazov took another sip of his drink, wondering if it was the right time. He needed to know more. "Did the agents identify themselves when you landed?"

"No, sir. I didn't see any badges, and they remained quiet during the whole trip."

"Hmm. They must have been FBI. Do you know what airport?"

"The airport didn't look familiar, and as soon as I was turned over to them, I was immediately put in a paneled van."

"Do you remember where you were held?"

"Not specifically. I just remember the sound of traffic on the way. We stopped at, what I assume, were a lot of traffic lights. When we arrived at the destination, the van was parked in a garage, but it wasn't a typical garage, more like a large, empty, concrete room. We took an elevator to a lower lever, then I was taken to a room and left there for hours."

"Were you tortured, Nicolai?"

"No. Not at all, sir."

Vazov sounded relieved, as he asked, "And what about interrogation?"

"Two agents questioned me, but they seemed to be pretty standard questions. I was fingerprinted, and had my picture taken." He rubbed a hand over his face, then commented, "It was all very strange, Mr.

Ambassador. It was as if they already knew. . . everything."

"Do you know where they were taking you when you escaped?"

"No. They used the same type van. We had traveled perhaps twenty minutes when the accident happened. I remember seeing a road sign for Route 27 when I escaped." Kalinin finally gave a very slight smile. "Is there a special place where they take 'sleepers' like me?"

Before Vazov could respond, a door from the kitchen opened, and two women, wearing housekeeper-type clothes, walked into the dining room carrying silver trays. Two serving plates each held shashlik, marinated lamb on skewers; pelmeni, dumplings with meat filling wrapped in thin pasta dough, and knish, a baked potato dumpling. For dessert, lymmonyk, a type of lemon pie.

A dinner plate was placed in front of Vazov who sniffed the aromas. "Ahh, Nicolai. Now you will experience good Russian food. How long has it been since you have eaten our food?"

"When my mother was alive, she would occasionally prepare my father's favorite meals. But I have not eaten any since they died." Kalinin glanced at the plate of food. His appetite was practically nil. The past couple of days had drained his mind and body. But, he ate slowly and what he could manage, if only to please the ambassador.

*

As they ate, Vazov continued asking Kalinin questions, and Kalinin answered as honestly as possible. . . for the most part.

"Nicolai, you are remarkable."

"Sir?" Kalinin asked with eyebrows raised.

"Your escape from the Americans, then managing to come all the way into the city. Tell me how you managed to get here?"

"I rode with truckers. It was easy to stay out of sight riding with them. And with the possibility of the Americans watching the embassy, I felt the safest place to call from was the parking garage."

"I see," Vazov nodded, then pointed to the cuts on Kalinin's face. "How did you manage to care for your wounds?"

"A trucker made a fuel stop at one of those large facilities. I was able to, uh, 'lift' a package of Band-Aids then cleaned up in the restroom."

"Well, we will have our doctor check you over. You must relax, Nicolai. You are safe. Your country will protect you."

"Sir, may I ask you something?" Vazov nodded. "Have you discovered the identity of the American traitor?"

Vazov wiped his mouth with a white linen napkin, then dropped it next to his plate. "As a matter of fact, we have."

"Who? Who is he?"

"While we do not yet know his name, Misha followed him to his place of residence last night. Do you know, Nicolai, he actually demanded fifteen thousand American dollars for his information?"

"Am I to assume you refused?"

"Yes. Instead of money in the envelope, I left a note, telling him--as the Americans would say--to go to hell! We did not get our weapons, our brave comrades died. No! He would not get the money. And since we know where he lives, I am considering contacting him, making him aware we have damning information, with the threat of turning it over to the CIA or FBI, or maybe both."

The two men continued talking throughout the meal, each surprising the other with news and information. Vazov leaned toward the table. "Nicolai, you are not looking well."

"Just very tired. Is there a place in one of the offices where I could get some sleep?"

"Nonsense! There are four extra bedrooms here. Come. I will show you." Vazov laid a hand on Kalinin's back, noticing the soiled, blood-splattered clothes. "I will see that Comrade Yudin gets you new clothes tomorrow. Then perhaps we can discuss your ordeal further."

*

Washington, D.C.
Friday
2225 Hours

Grant pulled his blue sweatshirt over his head, picked up his gym bag, then walked into the lobby of the Y. "Night, Charlie," he waved to the manager.

"See ya, Mr. Stevens. I'll lock up right behind you."

Grant jogged down the steps then walked across the parking lot, digging his keys from his sweatpants. It wasn't unusual for him to "help" close the facility. Friday and Saturday nights meant time for partying for thousands of D.C. workers, relieved the week was over. Tonight he had the entire pool to himself.

Lap after lap, his strong arms and legs had propelled him forward in the fifty meter pool. Clear, cool water streamed over his shoulders. His mind was free of worries. He wasn't going for any record, and kept his breathing controlled, steady, as he swam thirty continuous laps. It wasn't even close to his days in BUD/S, but he was a helluva lot younger then.

He tossed his gym bag on the passenger seat, then slid behind the wheel, glancing at his watch under the overhead light. He promised to call Adler when he got back, planning to discuss an upcoming meeting with President Carr. They wanted to be prepared for a serious G2.

He turned the key in the ignition, and the 'big block' engine roared to life. Shifting into first, he drove out of the parking lot and headed for his apartment. With the current traffic, it was going to take at least twenty-minutes. He reached for the radio dial, then put his hand back on the steering wheel, with the day's events creeping back into his mind.

Twenty minutes later he pulled in front of the apartment garage gate, punched in a code on the box, then waited for the gate to lift. Parking was also available to non-residents, but they were required to deposit dollar bills into a slot, then park on the second level and above. Once parked, they had to leave through the entrance or back exit door. The elevator to the apartments required a code.

He drove slowly to the end slot, his assigned space, then turned in next to a Ford wagon, belonging to a family on the third floor. In his rearview mirror he saw the elevator doors closing.

Getting out, he stretched his arms high overhead, then reached for his gym bag. Slinging it over his shoulder, he walked to the elevator, and punched in the code. The elevator light showed floor number seven.

He heard footsteps and turned seeing a man hurrying toward the elevator. The man was middle aged, brown short hair, with streaks of gray.

"Evening," Grant said.

"How are ya?"

"I'm good, thanks. How 'bout yourself?"

"Fine. Fine." He glanced up at the lighted number, then turned again to Grant. "I'm visiting my daughter and grandkids. Got here from Ohio this morning."

"Sounds like you're going to have a busy stay. Hope you have a good visit," Grant smiled. He looked up. The light showed "six."

"Say, you don't think my daughter will get in trouble for giving me the code to this place, do you?"

"It shouldn't be a problem, sir."

As Grant looked up at the lighted numbers, a blow to the back of his head knocked him unconscious. The "visitor" grabbed him before he hit the deck. Lifting Grant's arm over a shoulder, he struggled walking to the exit door, as "Primex" held it open, carrying Grant's gym bag. Keeping in the shadow of the alley, he backed up near the brick wall, trying to keep Grant upright, who was a good six inches taller.

"Primex" ran to the next street. Within a minute, he'd started the engine, then turned a corner, driving toward the alley. He threw the gearshift into park, then rushed to open the back passenger door, throwing the gym bag on the floor. Suddenly, a glare of headlights, and a sound of an engine made him duck. The other car kept moving toward Virginia Avenue.

When it was clear, he ran back to the alley, helping to get Grant to the car. They shoved him in the back seat, and working quickly, "Primex" removed a syringe from inside his jacket pocket, and took off the protective plastic cover. Pushing up Grant's sleeve, he injected the solution.

"Let's go!"

Doors slammed, and they drove away.

*

Grant's Apartment
Saturday - Day 6
0030 Hours

Adler punched in the code numbers, shoved the heavy glass door open, then walked through the brightly lit lobby, going directly to the elevator. It was already on ground level, but his impatience was obvious, as he stepped in then constantly kept pressing the button for the fifth floor. Keeping his eyes on the lighted numbers, he worried. He'd tried repeatedly to call Grant's apartment and his car phone. Then, deciding enough was enough, he drove to the apartment building.

When the doors parted, he cautiously stepped into the hallway, glancing in both directions. Somewhere down the hall, he heard voices. *Only a TV,* he thought, letting out a breath.

As he went toward Grant's door, he pulled a key from his pocket. Looking around one more time, he inserted the key in the lock, then turned it slowly, feeling the deadbolt beginning to give. Grabbing hold of the doorknob with one hand, he pulled his weapon from the holster, then he opened the door just wide enough to slide around. He immediately closed it. Just enough light filtered through slats in the blinds, but still, he waited as a precaution.

The apartment was eerily quiet. The only sound came from the steady drone of the refrigerator in the galley-style kitchen. Holding his weapon close, he began walking toward the living room, then stopped, turning his head to peer down a hallway leading to the only bedroom and bath. He went just beyond it, swiveling his head, trying to see any telltale signs of a struggle--or body. Nothing. Nobody. His mind was telling him Grant wasn't here, but he needed to check the bedroom anyway. Again, nothing. He put the weapon back in the holster, then flipped on the hall overhead light.

Standing near the front door, he scanned the room again. Nothing was out of place, but there was definitely something wrong. "Goddammit," he said through clenched teeth.

He shut off the light, locked the door, then took the elevator to the garage. Pulling his jacket down over his holster, he kept watching the lighted floor numbers above the doors. The elevator lurched to a stop. "C'mon!" he said, impatiently waiting for the doors to open. He rushed off, taking a quick look around. Nobody was in sight, no engines running. He spotted the Vette, parked in its usual space. "Oh fuck!" he said quietly. In a way he'd hoped the car hadn't been there, but this reinforced the fact--something had happened to Grant.

He made a visual inspection around the car. No signs of forced entry. He rubbed a hand over his head. "Maybe his keys, or maybe he dropped something," he said quietly. Getting on his hands and knees, he started crawling on filthy concrete, looking around the tires, feeling behind them. Nothing. He rolled on his back, frustrated and extremely worried. A sound of a car coming into the garage made him scoot sideways under the Vette. Tires screeched as the unknown vehicle rounded the curve going to the second level. It grew quiet again.

Suddenly, a thought hit him. "Can't be!" He squirmed under the frame, then began reaching, feeling along and behind door sills. His fingers touched something just behind the passenger door sill. He yanked it off. A homing device. He sat up, staring at the small black box. "What the fuck?"

It didn't answer the question where Grant was, but now it confirmed the fact that whatever happened to him, he didn't go voluntarily. It also brought up another disturbing question? Who and why was someone following him? The Russians were a real possibility. But why?

He got up slowly, checked it was clear, then he ran down the ramp, heading for the Mustang. Tires squealed as he pulled away from the curb. He had to get to his apartment and contact the whole Team, maybe even Mullins. There wasn't any use to call the cops. They'd just tell him he'd have to wait twenty-four hours to report Grant missing. He wasn't about to wait. But where the hell would he start?

"C'mon, Adler, get your fuckin' brain working!"

A traffic light turned red, and he hit the brakes. The car skidded on the blacktop, coming to a stop in the crosswalk. He squeezed the steering wheel, then started talking to himself. "Is it possible?! Did 'Primex' have something to do with it?" No matter who was involved, there wasn't a fucking clue to go on. Grant was out there somewhere. How the hell were they going to find him?

The light turned green. He stomped on the gas. The Mustang's tires smoked and screeched, before grabbing hold of blacktop, leaving a black trail of rubber.

He hadn't experienced it often, but the sick feeling in the pit of his stomach was not a good sign.

*

Washington, D.C.
Saturday - Day 6
0115 Hours

Grant started regaining consciousness, unaware of the cold, hard, rough concrete under him. His head throbbed. His body ached. He felt nauseous, dizzy. Just trying to open his eyes was difficult, and when he did, the room would spin wildly. Keeping them closed didn't help much. Somewhere in the distance a horn blared, the sound penetrating his brain like a knife, and he clamped his hands over his ears, waiting for the sound and pain to stop.

Just as it subsided, he let out a moan, crossing his arms over his stomach, as sudden, excruciating pains made him ball up and roll on his side. He couldn't prevent the vomit creeping up into his throat, then spewing out his mouth. Gagging, choking, he swiped a hand over his mouth and rolled on his back again. Sprawled out, he looked through half-opened eyes, trying to focus on the overhead, but dizziness prevented that. Even with his sweatsuit, low blood pressure caused chills to shake his weakened body.

Pure instinct made him attempt to get up, to move. Struggling, he rolled on his side again, then using every ounce of strength he could muster, he managed to get on his hands and knees. He wasn't able to focus through the dizziness, but he thought he detected something ahead. A wall. He started crawling, barely able to stay in a straight line. But he had to get close, needing it for support, or else he'd never be able to stand. Beginning to feel nauseous again, he stopped and took some breaths.

The crawl seemed to take hours, but finally he reached out and touched the damp, rough, cinder block surface. He swallowed hard, trying to prevent puking. Pressing both palms against the wall, with his head hanging and eyes closed, he slowly, unsteadily started to stand, but his legs wanted to buckle. He leaned his forehead against the blocks, waited, then rolled on his back, spreading his legs apart for balance. Resting his head back, and keeping his eyes closed, he took short, slow breaths. Between the dizziness, constant puking, and low blood pressure, he wasn't able to think clearly.

Then the pain picked up where it left off. He held his head with his hands, trying to stop the throbbing. Nauseousness struck, and he vomited again. His legs started giving way. Even before his body hit the floor, his world went dark.

Off and on during the next two hours he'd become semi-consciousness. The vomiting had all but stopped, when bouts of dry heaves picked up where they left off. With each attempt to stand, his legs would give out. He was weak, dehydrated, but at least the dizziness wasn't as intense.

His conscious moments were brief, hardly long enough for him to figure out where he was. His brain captured distorted snapshots of pipes, ductwork, and wires hanging high above. Lights came and went, shining through an overhead window. Gradually, those lights no longer caused eye pain.

But he was still too disoriented to question, nor did he understand that everything he was going through was from the drugs wreaking havoc on his mind and body.

*

Basement of House in D.C.
Saturday - Day 6
0500 Hours

Slowly, he started coming around. The dizziness and nauseousness had begun to subside. He took long, deep breaths, trying to clear his brain, but instead, he inhaled a sickening, acrid odor. Dried vomit on his sweatshirt, on the concrete. He immediately rolled on his back, but his arms were caught under him. Struggling was getting him nowhere. Then his brain finally registered. . . his wrists were tied.

"What the. . . ?!" His voice was hoarse, his throat raw, both caused by the vomiting and dehydration. He laid still, running his tongue over dried, cracked lips. Swallowing was nearly impossible due to lack of saliva.

A noise off to his left. Then a small light came on, nearly blinding him. He squeezed his eyes shut, when he heard a voice. "Well, finally awake, I see."

Squinting, he turned his head left then right, but he couldn't see anyone. A moment of dizziness, and he went still. Then, he tried sitting up, without success. A sound of footsteps coming closer, then something scraping against the floor.

"Need some help?"

Grant blinked, trying to clear his vision. When he

looked to the side, who he saw left him dumbfounded. "Jack?!"

Without responding, Jack Henley reached under Grant's arm, helped him up, then held onto him until he sat unsteadily in the wooden chair. Immediately getting down on a knee, Henley picked up a piece of rope, then quickly lashed Grant's legs to the chair.

Henley came around to the front, staring down at Grant. "Yeah, it's me."

Dizziness overtook Grant, and his head rolled back. He opened his eyes wide, and he looked again at Henley, trying to understand. "What . . .?"

"Here. You look like you need a drink." Henley unhooked a canteen from his belt, then unscrewed the top, letting it hang from a small chain. He held the canteen to Grant's mouth.

Grant swallowed enough water, then coughed, but even plain water sent his stomach churning. His brain started functioning better, but it didn't clear his total confusion or answer the question: why the hell didn't Henley untie him?

Henley screwed the top back on the canteen, then dropped it on the concrete. Grant flinched from the sound.

"Jack, what. . . what's goin' on?!" His voice sounded gravely, but he answered his own question when his eyes fell on a Beretta tucked in Henley's waistband. "Jesus Christ, Jack! You're. . .'Primex'?!" He nodded to himself, as he understood the code name: Primary explosive. EOD. Henley was in charge of the EOD team at St. Mawgan, England.

Henley drew the weapon from his waistband, then

held it behind his back. "Finally pulled one over on the 'great' Grant Stevens."

Grant was beyond surprised, trying to understand Jack Henley. When they met in England, after all the years that had passed since they graduated from the Naval Academy, Henley made some statements to Grant with a hint of jealousy attached. But this. . . this was beyond reason. There had to be more to it. "Why, Jack?!"

Henley started his story. After resigning his commission, he returned to the States from England. Even though he was angry, lonely, and discontented, he took a job with the Department of the Navy as a paper-pusher, but a job. He had access to top secret information and was responsible for signing off on paperwork for the development of new weapons.

After a few months on the job, someone in his office approached him, probably from hearing his disgruntled comments on procedures, the Navy, and government in general. The two met several times before his new "friend" made a proposal: help provide information to the Russians on the upcoming delivery of top secret rifles.

Grant found it difficult to take in what Henley was telling him, part from the drugs and part from total disbelief. Apparently, Henley hadn't even questioned the motives of the individual, nor did he even wonder if it could be a setup. The guy could've been FBI, CIA, Naval Intelligence. Instead, Henley jumped at the offer.

Then Henley added more to the unbelievable story. "Rumors started circulating about an 'off the books' team who made a daring rescue of two SEALs captured by the ChiComs. And you know what? Your name kept cropping up." He waited, expecting some kind of response or reaction from Grant. Nothing. "I've been waiting for this moment for a long time."

Grant tried focusing on Henley through squinted eyes. "You must've had a million chances. Why not sooner, Jack? Just me! Four. . . four good men died because of this fuckin' deal you made!" He coughed, and forced a swallow.

"You're so fuckin' right! And if it wasn't for my 'associate,' I would've. Believe me. But he insisted I wait until the operation was completed."

"Who. . .who was the asshole?"

"Wouldn't you like to know?"

"Yeah. I would. What difference does it make? I have a feeling it won't matter."

Henley didn't answer immediately. Grant was correct in his assumption. It wouldn't matter, not for what he had planned. "Easton. Fred Easton."

Grant had a blurry picture of someone in his mind. A man. "The little bastard by the elevator?"

"Correct."

A moment of dizziness caught Grant by surprise. He squeezed his eyes shut, tilting his head back, waiting for it to stop, as nauseousness crept over him. "What the . . .?"

"Still not feeling so hot?"

Only then did Grant make the connection. Drugs. "Jesus! What the. . hell. . did you. . . give me?"

"Couldn't pronounce them if I tried."

The dizziness slowly subsided. He kept trying to untie the rope, but his fingers just wouldn't work.

"How'd you manage to find me tonight? How'd you know where I'd be? You couldn't have posted surveill . . ." His eyes narrowed as he answered his own question. "A homing device."

Henley nodded. "Even that didn't make it easy. You kept 'disappearing,' sometimes for days at a time. Your precious Vette would stay parked in the garage. Of course, with my full-time job, I couldn't always track you. I'm assuming that's when you got most of your 'work' done."

Grant still couldn't imagine why the hell Jack Henley had become a traitor, and why he wanted him dead. "Why, Jack? A big fucking why'd you do it?"

"Doesn't your current situation remind you of anything?"

"My current. . . situation?"

"The night you and Joe found me and Vicky at the old airfield in England. Isn't this how you found us? Tied, beaten?"

Grant's shoulders went slack. "This is about your wife?"

Henley waved the gun in front of him. "You're goddamned right it's about Vicky! Isn't that reason enough?! She died because of you!"

Grant was stunned. He was still weak from low blood pressure, and his voice kept giving out. But he couldn't let it go, and he verbally struck back. "Vicky took her life because she couldn't come to terms with what she did! She betrayed you, Brits, Americans, and herself! And you know that's the. . . fucking truth, Jack!"

Henley stepped directly in front of him, leaning

close. "No!" he shouted. "You and Joe took your fuckin' time trying to find her even when I asked you to! All you could think about was tracking down that sonofabitch Labeaux or talking to Torrinson, when you could've been looking for her!"

Grant suddenly realized Henley had "gone off the deep end" months ago. If he could only convince him he needed help. . . before he pulled the trigger.

"Jack, look, right now we both need to calm down. C'mon. Untie me. Once we're outta here, we'll find. . ."

"Bullshit!"

Grant took a deep breath. Okay. Different approach. "Listen, Joe and I made our decision to retire in part because of what happened to Vicky."

Henley slowly lowered the Beretta, trying to make sense of Grant's statement. "You. . ."

"That's right! Don't you think for one goddamn minute her death didn't weigh heavy on us, too, Jack! Why do you feel so goddamn sorry for yourself?"

"What the fuck do you mean?"

Grant closed his eyes, as dizziness swept over him again. His voice was getting more hoarse. "What?"

"I said, what the fuck do you mean?!"

"Oh, yeah. Do you believe you're the only one who's lost somebody close?"

"What does that have to do with you and me?!"

Grant took a deep breath. His brain was telling him to keep talking, bide for extra time. But he didn't know why. "I lost my wife, too." Henley's eyes narrowed, and he shook his head. Grant continued, "I'm. . .I'm pretty sure I told you. . . that night we ran into each other at that pub. My wife Jenny died while I was in Nam. I couldn't get home in time to be with her. She died, all alone. I never forgave myself," he added quietly. A longer moment of coherency and Grant struck back. "But you were the only one who could've stopped your wife, gotten her help. Why didn't you, Jack? Because you're nothin' but a weak 'dick!'" *Uh-oh,* Grant thought.

"You sonofabitch!" Henley lunged forward, swinging his weapon, the barrel striking just above Grant's temple.

Grant's body rocked sideways, the chair nearly tipped over. Dazed, he felt warm blood dripping down the side of his head. His vision blurred, but he could tell Henley was backing up with his Beretta held at arm's length. Even if he could somehow move out of the line of fire, turn, fall over, anything, Henley would take more than one shot.

Grant lowered his head. He pushed too far. He had to face the fact--he was a dead man. He exhaled almost all the breath left in him. After all the combat missions, Vietnam, the death traps, hell holes, all the risks taken, yet here he was about to die in a dark, damp basement, at the hands of a former Navy commander.

Henley kept backing up until he was ten to twelve feet away, making sure he had an easy, accurate shot.

Grant was powerless to do anything. "Jack, don't. . do . . this." But he knew it was going to happen. "Jack!!"

Henley took aim, and pulled the trigger.

Two bullets found their mark. One struck Grant in the right shoulder, just missing his collarbone, the jolt sending him and the chair backwards. His head hit hard on the concrete, knocking him out.

The second round penetrated Henley's chest. The impact from the hollow point slammed his body against the wall, with the round fragmenting, maximizing tissue damage, causing rapid blood loss. He fell forward. His body landed on the concrete with a sickening *thud*.

Fred Easton walked past Grant, verifying he was unconscious, then he stood over Henley's body. He knelt on one knee, with his S&W .357 Magnum held tightly. With the size of the wound, and the amount of blood loss, Henley should've been dead, but Easton checked for a pulse anyway, surprised to find one, weak, but still beating. Standing up, he kept looking at the man who had mentally lost it.

In the beginning, he was confident they could pull it off. He also believed he would never come under suspicion for the theft of top secret documents. Henley had assumed full control. But then Henley found his chance to turn the theft into a personal vendetta, telling him he planned to kidnap, then kill Grant.

They could have ended it right after they drove away from the garage, in some deserted field, or alley, or even the river. Instead, they brought Stevens here, to suffer, as Henley put it. Easton saw there was only one way to end it, to protect himself. He'd get rid of Henley.

He checked for a pulse again. Nothing. Turning away, he walked back toward Grant. He debated. Should he finish what Henley started? Stevens not only knew his face, but his name as well. He'd just answered his own question. He moved his arm forward, aiming the weapon at Grant's head.

An explosion of sound erupted within the confined space, as Adler and Novak came rushing in, firing simultaneously. Rounds struck Easton in center mass, with more penetrating the upper chest. His body spasmed as each round hit him. He stumbled backwards, falling against the cinder block. Staring down, unbelieving at blood pouring from his chest, he slowly slid down the wall, his body crumbling.

Adler and Novak cautiously moved forward, keeping their weapons aimed. Adler knelt near Grant, but kept his eyes on Easton.

Novak moved closer, kicked away the .357, then got down on a knee, and checked the carotid artery. "Deceased," he said as he crawled over to Henley's body. "Ditto."

They holstered their weapons. Novak crawled next to Grant, as Adler's knife sliced through the ropes binding his wrists and legs. Then they lifted him off the chair and laid him on the floor.

Adler crawled behind him, then sat on his own haunches before gently lifting Grant's upper body off the concrete. He scooted closer, enough for Grant to rest against him, keeping his shoulders above his heart. Novak pressed his hand over the wound. Blood flowed more swiftly then they expected.

"Mike, I'll take over," Adler said, trying to quell the amount of blood flowing. "You call for an ambulance. And bring in that medical bag!" Novak ran from the basement. As he got outside, in the distance he heard a faint sound of sirens--cops! Someone had called 911.

Grant started coming around, beginning to feel the

pain in his shoulder, and again in his head. Somewhere in his subconscious he heard a voice.

"Skipper! Come on! Look at me." Adler was really worried. Grant's face was drained of all color. Then, his eyelids started opening, and he blinked a couple of times. He was feeling pressure against his shoulder, then the voice called again, "Come on! Open your eyes!"

He slowly rolled his eyes toward the sound. The person wasn't quite in focus. He closed his eyes, thinking he was hallucinating again.

Adler unscrewed the canteen top, then held it close to Grant's mouth. "See if you can drink."

Cool water dripped on his dried, cracked lips, and he managed a small mouthful. He opened his eyes and looked overhead as the face finally came into focus. "Joe?"

Adler smiled. "None other." Grant tried sitting up, but Adler gently pulled him back. "Stay where you are."

Novak came rushing in. "Ambulance is on the way." He knelt down, pulled out a battle dressing, then tore it open. He took over for Adler and pressed it against Grant's shoulder. "How ya doin', boss?"

"Bastards shot me full of. . . something."

"You mean other than a bullet?" Novak chuckled.

Grant managed a nod, then focused on Adler. "I thought I was dead, Joe."

"You came pretty damn close."

Confused, Grant asked with a raspy voice, "What happened?"

"Don't you remember?"

Grant forced his brain to work. "Jack. Where's. . . Jack?"

"He's dead."

"You?"

Adler shook his head. "Don't know who the guy was, but I assume Jack was shot by his 'associate.' And, yes. He's pretty much dead, too."

"Easton."

"What?"

"I. . . I think his name's Easton." Grant let out a short grunt. "I'm gonna puke."

Adler immediately reacted. "Mike, keep holding that dressing. I wanna get him on his side." He succeeded just in time. He poured some water in his palm, then washed around Grant's mouth. "Feeling better?"

"Not much."

"Here. Rinse your mouth, then spit."

Two different sounds of sirens started growing louder. Ambulance and cops. "Mike, go wait for them. I'll take over. And Mike! Call Scott!" Novak took off.

Adler kept a hand on the battle dressing. "Help's here, Skipper. Hang in there."

As he waited, Adler started worrying, and not just about Grant. Two dead men, one with multiple bullet holes in him, all fired from his and Novak's weapons. Overkill? Maybe. But not in Adler's mind, not when the bastard had a .357 pointed at his friend's head, who was unconscious. One saving grace was that forensics would determine the caliber bullet that killed Henley was from the Magnum. Eventually, the cops would get their answers.

"And then there's the President," he said under his breath. "It just keeps getting better and better."

Chapter 19

Russian Embassy
0830 Hours

A small double charcoal burner, called a "samovar," was on a credenza behind the desk. A teapot warmed on one, with a very concentrated infusion of tea, while the other pot held plain hot water. Vazov poured tea into a traditional tulip-shaped glass then diluted it slightly with hot water.

"Misha?" he asked, offering tea to Zelesky, who declined.

A knock at the door. "Enter," Vazov said, barely speaking loud enough. The sound of opera music was playing in the background.

Kalinin opened the door, surprised to see Zelesky sitting in front of the ambassador's desk. He closed the door.

"Nicolai, you are looking better this morning," Vazov commented.

Kalinin stood by a chair, until Vazov motioned for him to sit. "I feel better, sir. And thank you for the new clothes."

Vazov eyed the black slacks and white pullover sweater, saying, "Comrade Yudin made good choices." Kalinin nodded. "Tea, Nicolai?" Kalinin declined, then Vazov said, "I thought you might be interested in what happened early this morning. Misha was just about to tell me."

"Does it have to do with the American traitor?"

"Indeed it has to do with him. Misha, begin."

Zelesky began his story, from when he followed Henley after leaving the envelope by the trestle, to the actual shootout at Henley's house.

Vazov and Kalinin remained quiet, until Kalinin finally asked, "Did you see anybody come out of the house, Comrade Zelesky--dead or alive?"

"Someone was loaded into an ambulance. I can only assume it was Stevens, because two men walked near the gurney until he was loaded inside, then they ran off, possibly to a vehicle.

"By the time the medical examiner showed up, neighbors were crowded around, more police arrived, and I believe one or two reporters. I remained in the car, and it was somewhat difficult to see, but I believe two body bags were carried out."

Kalinin shifted his eyes back to Vazov. "Has there been any report on television?"

"Yes. It was reported that a home invasion left two dead and one injured." Vazov picked up a sheet of paper where he'd made notes. "The two dead men were identified as Jack Henley and Fred Easton, who both worked for the Department of Defense." He dropped the paper on the desk. "The injured man was still not identified."

Zelesky commented, "The Americans are just as devious as KGB when it comes to imaginative stories."

"I have asked Comrade Yudin to bring the newspapers as soon as they are delivered," Vazov said, "but it is probably still too soon for there to be any published article."

Kalinin stood. "I will go see if any have arrived." He left the office. Riding in the elevator, he could only wonder if he made the call in time. *One injured, two dead.* Whatever the outcome, he had done his best, and what he thought was the right decision at the time.

The elevator lurched to a stop, and he rushed off, walking toward the front desk. "Comrade Yudin! I see the newspapers have arrived. I will take them to the ambassador." He started to walk away, then turned. "Thank you for buying the clothes, Comrade." She smiled then sat down behind her desk.

He got in the elevator, let the doors close automatically, then pressed the button. He quickly scanned the front page of three of the five papers, reading the top half, then flipped them over and read the bottom. But he didn't see anything about the incident. He got off the elevator, and looked at the last two papers. Still nothing. But the ambassador was probably correct in saying it was too early.

*

"Put the papers here," Vazov said, pointing to the corner of his desk. "We will look at them later. He sipped his hot tea, before saying, "Well, Nicolai, it looks as if Stevens survived the assassination attempt."

"It appears to be the case."

Zelesky picked up a folder. "Comrade, do you believe it was Stevens who led those teams on the ship and at Shannon?"

Kalinin kept his eyes straight ahead, watching Vazov. "It was very possible, Comrade Zelesky. As I told the ambassador, the men were very efficient, very organized, the same way Captain Ivanov described their actions."

Zelesky handed the photo to Kalinin, then walked behind his chair. "Can you identify that man, Comrade?"

Kalinin briefly looked at the photo, then handed it back to Zelesky. "The men at Shannon wore black masks the entire time."

"Even during the long flight to the U.S.?"

"Not entirely. But the interior lights on the plane were kept low. I was made to sit at the rear of the plane, and they usually kept their backs to me." Kalinin stood, and moved the chair aside. Keeping his eyes on Zelesky, he asked Vazov, "Mr. Ambassador, would it be possible to speak with you. . . alone, sir?"

Vazov motioned with a hand. "Leave us, Misha."

Zelesky kept his eyes locked on Kalinin's, until he heard Vazov again. "Leave us."

Once the two men were alone, Kalinin stood in front of the desk. "Mr. Ambassador, Comrade Zelesky seemed to imply that I am withholding information, that I am being deceptive. . ."

Vazov interrupted. "That is his job, Nicolai. He is KGB. You do not yet fully understand the inner workings of that organization."

"That is true, sir, but. . ."

"Do not let it concern you. Now, is there anything else?"

"I apologize for disappointing you and our comrades in Russia."

"I would be lying if I said we were not

disappointed. I am waiting for Defense Minister Troski to contact me." Vazov stood and turned toward the credenza, refreshing his tea. "If you are directed to Moscow, Nicolai, it will not be for punishment. Moscow wants you to explain in your own words how you prepared your mission and possibly why it went wrong." He sat down, then looked over the top of his glass. "Do you know why it went wrong?"

"Because of an experienced, intelligent team of men, sir."

Vazov gave an almost indiscernible smile. "But how did they learn of your plan?"

"I think we must look again at the traitor. While he never knew directly what was planned, he could have notified the Americans--anonymously, of course. That should have put the NSA, CIA, and FBI on alert, and any other 'alphabet' agency the Americans have. They may have intercepted one or more of our transmissions." He cleared his throat. "That is my opinion."

"I will tell you, Nicolai, that I never trusted him. I still believe he was a double agent, in a loose sense of the word." A knock at the door. "Enter."

The communications corporal walked in, barely acknowledging Kalinin, then passed a sheet of paper to Vazov. He immediately left the office.

Vazov read the message, then held it toward Kalinin. "It is from the defense minister."

*

Grant's Apartment
Monday - Day 7
1330 Hours

Grant unlocked the apartment door, and swung it open, with Alder following him. He flipped on a wall switch, then turned on an overhead light. As he tossed his key on a small side table, he caught his reflection in the mirror hanging above it. His hair was disheveled, his eyes were bloodshot, he still hadn't gotten all his color back. He leaned closer, touching the bandage near his left temple, then he turned his head. "Well, at least they match," he said under his breath, referring to another scar.

"What'd you say?"

"Nothing, Joe. But you were right."

"About what?!"

"I'm a mess."

"Would I lie?" Adler laughed. "Listen, maybe I'd better stay overnight, just in case you need anything or if you want to make a return trip to the hospital since you can't drive."

"That's not gonna happen, but, sure, stay if you want. You know where everything is, including the fridge. I'll get you sheets and a pillow." He turned down the hallway. "I'm gonna go wash off and put on some clean clothes. Then I want you to fill in all the blanks from the other night."

Adler went to the fridge and called after him, "Want anything to drink?"

"Just water."

"I believe I'll have a root beer." He dumped ice cubes in a tall glass, then filled it with fresh water. As he carried both to the living room, he said over his shoulder, "I left a message with the President's secretary, confirming our meeting with him tomorrow morning at 1030 hours." No answer. The water in the bathroom sink was running full blast.

Several minutes later, and wearing gray sweatpants, Grant walked barefoot into the living room. He dropped the sheets and pillow on the couch. "Thanks," he said taking the glass, just as the phone rang. "Stevens."

"My friend, you are home!"

"Hey, Grigori. Yeah, Joe and I just got here."

"How are you feeling, Grant?"

"I'll live."

"Alexandra and I would like to see you tomorrow, if you are up to it."

"Sure. You wanna come here?"

"No. You and Joe come for lunch. Alexandra insists."

"We'll be there! I'll call you before we leave."

"All right, my friend."

"See ya, Grigori." He turned to Adler. "Lunch with the Moshenkos tomorrow."

"No problem here! Hey, you realize we still keep calling them by their real names?"

"Yeah, I know. Just can't get used to 'Leonov.' As long as we don't slip up around anybody else, they should be okay." ("Leonov" was the cover name given to the Moshenkos when they defected.)

Adler opened the root beer, took a gulp, then

noticed blood trickling from under Grant's bandage. "Whoa! You need that dressing changed. Come into the bathroom and I'll take care of it."

Grant leaned back against the edge of the sink, as Adler started removing the old bandage. "My brain's still not working right, Joe."

"Do you think maybe it's because you've been bashed in the head one too many times these past couple of years?" He opened the medicine cabinet door, took out a bottle of antiseptic, then dabbed the wound with a piece of gauze. "Doc did a good job with the stitches. You'll be pretty as new in no time." He taped a new dressing in place. "You've got one thing going in your favor."

Grant looked up through squinted eyes. "What's that?"

"Well, it could be worse. You could still be in la-la-land."

Grant finally smiled. "And that's supposed to make me feel better?"

"I can only do so much."

"Guess I had my 'head up my ass' thinking this shit would be over once we left the Navy."

"It'll never be over until we're rocking on a porch somewhere, and keeping our teeth in a bedside glass."

"Remind me about that next time! C'mon," he said, leading the way into the living room. "Fill me in."

"I was hoping you could fill me in. You must've had a conversation with Jack. I'd like to hear about it."

Grant sat on the couch, with Adler opposite him. "It's starting to come back, Joe. But my question to you is how the hell did you find me?"

"You don't remember me telling you?" Grant shook his head. "After I discovered you weren't in your apartment, I got on a conference call with the guys and Scott. We hashed out ever possible scenario, every location. I ruled out you were with Grigori. So, I hung out at my place while Scott made inquiries. Everybody but Mike took off in their cars, trying to pick up a trail, hoping they'd find. . ."

"What? My body?"

Adler shook his head. "No, but we didn't have squat to go on, Skipper. I had Mike come to my apartment just in case we got a lead, so I'd have backup."

"Then you found me, but how, Joe?"

"Your new friend. Nick."

"Nick?! But, how? That doesn't make sense! I mean. . . Jesus! He was at the embassy! What. . ."

Adler held up his hand. "Will you let me answer?!"

"Sure. Sure."

"For obvious reasons, he couldn't give me complete details, and was talking kinda fast, but the other KGB guy at the embassy followed Jack home, overheard a very heated phone conversation with someone. Jack said he was planning to kidnap you the following night, take you to his house, and then. . ." He pointed two fingers at Grant. "Boom."

"How'd he do it, Joe? How'd Nick contact you?"

"He let his 'fingers do the walking' and looked me up in the phone book."

"No shit?!"

"No shit. Plus, he used an embassy phone. And in case you're wondering why it took so long for us to get to you, he'd fallen asleep."

Grant massaged his arm. "Understandable. He probably hadn't slept since well before we got him in Shannon. Plus the interrogation. Plus the accident."

Adler continued. "Again, he didn't relay complete details, he only said when he woke up, it was already past 0430. He took a chance in staying on the phone as long as he did."

Grant finally smiled. "Guess I was lucky this time."

"You're damn straight you were lucky! And if all that surprised the shit out of you, you'll love this. When he called, he said--and these were his exact words--'This is James Broyce.'"

"He told you?!"

"Swear on 'Sammy's' nose!" (Sammy the SEAL, the SEALs' mascot.)

Grant took another drink of water, then stared into the glass, as he swirled around the liquid. "Why the hell would he give it up?"

"Don't know. Does it ring any bells?"

"No. That's why I think the first time I saw him was just in passing, aboard ship." He put his glass on the coffee table. "Christ, Joe! He saved my life! How can I just let that go?"

"You aren't planning on trying to make contact, are you? Hell! That was two days ago. For all we know, they could've put him on another diplomatic flight."

"But he could still be in the embassy."

"Hold it! Just hold it! We can hash out whatever it is you have in mind while we eat." He went to the kitchen and opened the refrigerator. "All you've got is roast beef." He took out the platter and sniffed the meat. "Smells okay. Want some?"

"Yeah, that's fine." Grant reached into the fridge for a jar of dill pickles, sliced Swiss cheese and horseradish, and put them near Adler. He leaned back against the counter. "Joe, we've talked about fate, and whether or not it plays any part in life."

"Yeah. What about it?"

"Think about this. If we hadn't brought Nick back to the States, if he hadn't escaped from the agents, if we never got him to the embassy--I'd be dead."

"That's pretty damn deep--but probably true. So, let me see if I understand this," Adler said, shaking a knife in Grant's direction. "What you're saying is, it was you, who helped you, save your life?!"

Grant smiled. "Well, I can't take all the credit, but, yeah. Something like that."

"Makes about as much sense as any other explanation, I guess." Adler spread horseradish on the bread, then slapped a couple slices of cheese on the meat.

A knock at the door, and Grant opened it. "Hey, Scott! C'mon in."

"Called the hospital and they said you'd checked out." He saw Adler. "Joe, how are ya?"

"Good to see you, Scott. We're just getting ready to eat. How about a roast beef sandwich?" Adler asked, already taking two more slices of bread from the wrapper.

"Sure. Never turn down food."

"Now you're sounding like Joe," Grant said, slapping his friend's arm. "Help yourself to something to drink."

Mullins got a beer, then pulled out a chair. "So, how's that shoulder, and your head?"

"Both improving. Thanks."

The three sat at the table, eating and discussing the incident at Henley's. Mullins asked, "You're not seriously thinking about contacting him, are you?"

"See. I'm not the only one who thinks that's a bad idea," Adler said, before drinking some root beer.

"So, he's still there?" Grant asked.

"Last we knew." Mullins' beeper went off. "Can I use your phone?"

"You know where it is," Grant said, crumbling up his napkin, then tossing it toward the trash can with his left hand. Adler went and picked it up.

"Well," Mullins said, walking back to the table, "that Russian replacement plane. . ."

"It left," Grant interrupted.

"Twenty minutes ago, and . . ."

"Nick was onboard."

"Why the hell do you do that?!" Mullins laughed, smacking the table with his palm.

"Well, Skipper, guess a decision's been made for you," Adler commented, with relief in his voice.

Chapter 20

White House
Tuesday - Day 8
1015 Hours

President Carr's secretary, Rachel, stood in front of her desk with an open calendar day book, going over the afternoon schedule with the secretaries and assistants. Her attention shifted and she glanced past the women. "Claudia, look behind you," she whispered.

Everyone turned around, seeing Grant and Adler walking into the room, both dressed in dark blue business suits.

"Oh, no," Claudia whispered. She laid her steno pad and her pen on the edge of the desk, then started toward the two men.

"I'll be over there, Skipper," Adler said, pointing to a couch near the Oval Office door. He nodded and smiled as Claudia passed him.

She stood in front of Grant, reached to touch the bandage on his head, then pulled her hand away. "What happened?"

"Uh, sorry, but it's classified," he winked, but she realized it was the truth. He moved closer to her, looking down into her hazel eyes. "Listen, I want to apologize for not calling."

"Not necessary," she said, lightly touching his arm

in its sling. "Will you be all right?"

"Affirmative! Hey, why don't we start over? How'd you like to have dinner with me?"

"I'd like that," she smiled broadly.

"Good. I've still got your home number. But you might have to give me a few extra days," he said, moving his arm slightly. "Unless you wouldn't mind Joe driving us."

"Either way," she laughed.

"Captain Stevens?" He looked toward the Oval Office door, seeing the secretary. "The President will see you and Lieutenant Adler now."

He started walking past Claudia. "I will call. Promise," he smiled. Then he met up with Adler and they went into the Oval Office.

Claudia rejoined the other women, and picked up her pad and pen. The meeting continued, but all she saw in her mind was Grant, his injuries. She wondered: Is this what happens? Is this what it's like for these men, and for anyone they become involved with? The classified missions to places unknown; separations; worry. She reminded herself they were just going to dinner. But still, she wondered.

*

Carr sat behind his desk, leaning back, with his hands folded on his stomach. His eyes went to Grant then Adler, then back to Grant. "Grant, what's the prognosis on that arm?"

"It'll be fine, sir. Doc's prescribed therapy. He doesn't see any future problems."

"Any leftover issues from the drugs?"

"Tests showed my system was clean, organs working properly."

"And the concussion?"

"Get an occasional headache, but that's all."

"You were lucky all the way around then, weren't you?"

"Yes, sir. And I'll be the first to admit it." Grant cleared his throat. "Mr. President, have you received any word on how the agents are, the ones who were in the accident?"

"Two broken arms, bumps and bruises, but I've been told they're all back to work."

"That's good to hear."

Carr rocked back and forth. His demeanor left both Grant and Adler uncomfortable, worrying about the upcoming G2.

"You want to tell me about that evening, Grant?"

"Well, sir, after 'meeting' Easton in the garage, not a whole lot has come completely into focus." He revealed all he could remember, with bits and pieces of actual conversation still missing. "What I do remember is Jack telling me why he did it." Grant shook his head slowly, still not believing. "I don't know when I've felt more shocked.

"But what I remember most clearly was a Beretta pointed at me, and the sound of the gun firing. I wish I could tell you more, sir, because I need answers, too."

"Joe," Carr said, "I'll get to you in a minute." Then, he returned his attention to Grant. "You knew Jack Henley at the Naval Academy?"

"I did, but after graduation, we never kept in touch, so when we met that night in England, both of us were surprised." Grant readjusted the sling. He looked away from Carr, momentarily. "I can't believe he turned traitor because of me."

"Us," Adler added, with Grant nodding in agreement.

"You both actually think that's why he did it?"

"Maybe we could've handled that op differently. Maybe we didn't put enough emphasis on finding Mrs. Henley."

"Look, the man was obviously deranged. I think his wanting to kill you, Grant, made that pretty damn clear."

Grant locked eyes with Carr. "Four good men died, Mr. President, because Jack wanted revenge. If he were alive, I'd see that he was charged with treason and murder, just as if he pulled the trigger himself."

"I'd have to agree with you there. But what about Kalinin? I'd say he was just as responsible, if not more so."

"Possibly, but maybe the men who were aboard that chopper took it upon themselves to kill those four men, so there wouldn't be any witnesses. Men for hire have not been known to have scruples. And again, it still started with Jack."

"Speaking of that chopper, Grant, do you think Kalinin had anything to do with it going down?"

"I. . .I don't know. The initial report was some kind of an explosion. Agent Mullins is staying in contact with the Coast Guard. Do you know if NIS has found anything?"

"I'm still waiting for their report." Carr turned to Adler. "Joe, how about you tell me your part of the story?"

Adler kept his eyes on the President during the entire time he relayed the facts of Grant's rescue. "Once we were on scene, sir, it was over pretty quick. The cops questioned Mike and me, but I'm sure their investigation will be on-going."

Grant interjected, "They came to the hospital and questioned me, too, sir."

"I assume both of you have seen the newspaper article?"

"We have." Enough was said.

Carr rolled his chair away from the desk, then stood and went to the window. Grant and Adler shot brief glances at each other, expecting what was coming next.

Carr slowly walked to the front of his desk, then sat on the edge, directly in front of the two men. "Joe, how'd you find out where Grant was being held?"

"A phone call, sir."

"A phone call."

"That's correct."

"And you believed this. . . caller."

"Mr. President, we were desperate. We didn't have a clue where he was, and didn't know where to begin. But after finding the homing device under his car, we knew it was a planned kidnapping. To tell you the truth, the Team believed that considering the overall time he'd been missing, our chances of finding him alive were pretty slim." Adler cleared his throat. "Whoever that caller was, we felt we had to put our trust in him."

"'Him?'"

"Most definitely."

"This caller didn't happen to identify himself, say, with the name 'Nicolai Kalinin,' did he, Joe? Or maybe he used the name 'Nick?'"

"No, sir! I'd definitely remember that! But as soon as he gave me Jack's address, the phone went dead. Mike and I hauled ass right after. . . oh, excuse me, sir."

Dead silence in the Oval Office, until Carr asked, "Grant, what if that was Kalinin? Why do you suppose he would have helped you--hypothetically speaking, of course."

"Hypothetically?" Carr nodded. "Well, sir, it may have been possible he felt some kind of obligation because I saved him from possibly being killed."

"I'd hardly expect an adversary to think like that, Grant, especially after you brought him back to the States, and turned him over to the FBI."

"He was nearly shot by a 'comrade,' Mr. President. That had to give him something to think about, something to question, along with the 'connection' I mentioned the other day."

"You know, gentlemen, everybody, and I mean everybody, was looking for that Russian."

"Agent Mullins notified us the Russian plane departed Dulles yesterday, and . . ."

"Kalinin was onboard. Yes, I know, Grant."

Silence again, until Carr said, "I'm sure you heard that the other Russian plane had been located in the North Sea, along with the black box."

"We have."

"I've contacted the Russian premier and offered America's condolences."

"I hope they find answers soon."

"Is there anything else you gentlemen need to add-- or want to add?"

Grant looked at Adler, who gave a slight shake of his head. Grant responded, "No, sir."

Carr stood, immediately followed by the two men. The meeting was over.

Carr offered a hand to Adler. "Joe, thanks for your help in finding those weapons, and finding your buddy."

"Mr. President."

Carr then extended his left hand to Grant. "Take care of that arm."

"I will, sir."

"Oh, by the way. Have your sniper--'Mike' is it?"

"Yes, sir."

"Have him report to Indian Head next week. I've arranged for him to do some of his own testing with one of those prototypes."

"Be happy to! Does he get to keep it?"

Carr smiled. "We'll see, Grant."

"I'll guarantee that weapon will never fall into the wrong hands, Mr. President."

"One final word, gentlemen. You both need to lose that guilt you're carrying around for Mrs. Henley."

"We'll work on it, sir," Grant answered, then turned to leave.

Adler opened the door, and took a step into the outer office, when he heard Grant call quietly, "Joe, wait up."

He saw the expression on Grant's face. Shaking his head slowly, he whispered, "No. Don't do it."

Grant kept his eyes locked on Adler's, and without

replying, he closed the door. No matter what the outcome, he knew he couldn't live with himself unless he cleared up the facts.

Carr stood by his desk, watching Grant, waiting, when the intercom buzzed. "Yes, Rachel."

"Mr. President, there's . . ."

"Give me a few minutes, Rachel."

"All right, Mr. President."

Carr switched off the intercom, then looked at Grant, who was still by the door. "Grant?"

Grant exhaled a long breath, then turned and walked to the desk, standing in front of Carr. "Mr. President, I have a feeling you know what happened, how Nick got to the embassy. It was my decision, mine alone, and I take full responsibility for my actions."

"Why, Grant? Why the hell did you do it?"

Grant rubbed a hand across his forehead. "I. . . I just had a feeling in me. Something told me I had to."

"That gut of yours?"

"Maybe, but maybe there was more to it."

Carr looked at Grant through narrowing eyes. He'd seen the pictures of Kalinin. Suddenly, a thought registered, a thought almost too hard to comprehend. "Grant, you don't seriously believe Kalinin's . . ."

"I thought I'd shaken the idea, but apparently not. And it wasn't just our appearance. We seemed to think alike, too."

"But. . . how in the hell could it even be possible?!"

"My dad was stationed in Europe."

Carr turned away, then walked behind his desk, analyzing an explanation he never expected. "And did you discuss this with Kalinin?"

"Negative, sir."

Glancing down at an open folder, Carr finally asked, "It was Kalinin that called Joe, wasn't it?"

"I believe Joe when he said the caller didn't identify himself as 'Nick.'"

"I believe him, too, Grant. But what name did he use?"

"'James Broyce.' He called himself 'James Broyce.'"

Carr gave somewhat of a smile. "So, Joe only gave me part of the truth then."

"Not really, sir. Neither one of us knew his American name."

Carr picked up a paper and handed it to Grant. "Take a look at this."

The report confirmed what Grant had suspected all along: fingerprints on file with the Department of the Navy, a 'Secret' security clearance, a copy of an official Navy ID card for 'James Broyce.'

"You were right on target with your assumption," Carr commented.

Grant didn't feel a need to respond and handed the paper to Carr who put it back in the folder. He tapped a finger against it before looking up at Grant's pained expression.

"Mr. President, I apologize, and again, I assume full responsibility. I'm prepared to accept any punishment you deem fitting."

Carr came around the desk, stood less than an arm's length away from Grant, then with a low, stern voice, he said the words slowly. "You aided and abetted a Russian operative, Grant."

Grant was quiet, and then, "Yes, sir. I did." Even though he'd said the same words to himself, hearing them from the President cut into him like a jagged knife.

"Can I just let that go?"

"No, sir. You can't."

Carr's eyes met Grant's. "Once again you risked your life, you recovered top secret weapons, you saved a life, and you were instrumental in uncovering two traitors, although probably not in a manner you would have preferred."

Grant's brow furrowed. He was having difficulty comprehending what Carr was implying. Maybe those damn drugs were still in his system!

"I. . . I don't understand, Mr. President."

"Listen, Grant, in this case, I believe the good definitely outweighed the bad." He patted Grant's good arm, and offered a smile. "Relax. I'll delay my decision about Leavenworth for the time being." Obvious surprise showed on Grant's face, then Carr laughed, "Bet your gut didn't see that coming!"

"Sure didn't, Mr. President."

"C'mon. I'll walk you to the door." Carr had a hand on the doorknob, but before turning it, he offered a suggestion. "You know, Grant, there's a way for you to resolve your issue."

Grant nodded. "DNA testing."

"Think about it."

*

Grant closed the Oval Office door, seeing Adler

pacing in front of the windows. "Joe, let's go."

Adler spun around, wiping beads of sweat from his forehead. He caught up to Grant. "No handcuffs?" he asked quietly.

"I'll talk to you outside." He didn't see Claudia, and assumed she'd gone to lunch.

On their walk to the car, Grant told Adler the entire conversation he had with the President. Adler unlocked the doors to his Mustang, then peered over the roof at Grant, who was putting on his aviator sunglasses. "Listen, Skipper, I'll admit you scared the hell outta me when you went back in the Oval Office. But, I guess you did the right thing all the way around."

"Couldn't keep it inside me, Joe."

Adler understood completely. Time to lighten up the conversation. "Lunch! What about lunch?!"

"Did you forget Grigori and Alexandra invited us over?"

"Oh, yeah! I'd never pass a chance to sample Alexandra's cooking! Hey! What say we contact the guys? Maybe we could all head up to the mountains for a couple of days of R&R, you know, the cabins you go to in the Blue Ridge."

"Sounds good, Joe. We sure as hell could use it."

They got in the car, and Adler asked, "Wanna invite Scott?"

"Sure. Wonder if he'd want to bring his girlfriend."

"They'll have to get their own cabin!"

"I'll call Grigori and let him know we're on our way. Then I'll call the guys."

Adler turned the key in the ignition, then shifted into first, noticing Grant's hand lingering on the phone.

The setting of the square jaw, grinding of teeth again. Adler shifted into neutral, and rested his arms on top of the steering wheel. "Well, what the hell are you thinking about? The DNA thing?"

"Yeah."

"You want my opinion?"

"You'll give it to me anyway, so, sure."

"Get it done."

"I'll think about it--seriously." He looked at his good friend over the top of his sunglasses. "Aren't you curious what sort of reception Nick might've gotten?"

"Well, sure."

"He failed his mission, Joe."

"Yeah, but not for lack of tryin'. You even admitted it was a helluva plan." He closed his eyes as if in thought. "I can just picture it now."

"What?"

"The next time the two of you meet up. I'll pay big bucks for tickets to that one!"

"I wouldn't hold my breath! C'mon!" Grant said, as he picked up the phone. "Let's get the hell outta here. I'm hungry!"

Epilogue

Moscow, Russia

After four days of near spring-like temperatures, the weather had taken a downturn, dropping well below freezing. Rain overnight left slick patches of ice on roads and sidewalks. Traffic had remained heavy, constant, but by noon, the sun broke through the cloud layer, melting most of the hazardous ice.

He sat in the car with the engine running, continually wiping a gloved hand in a circle against the windshield, waiting for the defrosters to kick in. An open window wasn't helping much.

Gradually, the fogged windshield cleared. He backed out of the parking space, then shifted into first, slowly driving around the circle.

Glancing in the rearview mirror, he noticed the building's yellow facade, mimicking gold bricks. Lubyanka. Headquarters of the KGB, with its notorious prison in the basement.

Where he'd just been, who he'd spoken with, and what was offered to him, left Nicolai Kalinin astounded. Director Mikhail Antolov, at the recommendation of Defense Minister Troski and Ambassador Vazov, told him he was to report in two days for training at the USSR KGB Krasnoznamennyi Institute (KI). Upon graduation, he'd take part in countering foreign intelligence services and conduct operational and combat activities. As honored as he was, learning he wouldn't be returning to the U.S. left him disappointed. But he understood the reason. Agencies would be on the lookout for him. . . again.

He turned his attention to finding his way through Moscow. It was like his first trip navigating through Washington, D.C. Except here he was surprised by the heavy traffic, and the number of private citizens who owned vehicles. Most were very used and beat up models, unlike Americans with their love of fancy cars. It was a far cry from what he pictured all those years growing up.

Crossing over the ring road, he started south on the M2 highway. As traffic thinned, he finally had a moment to think about the American. Grant Stevens, his nemesis. Grant Stevens, his. . . friend? Was it even possible? Perhaps that was part of his disappointment, not getting to learn more about him. Then again, one day soon he'd have access to KGB files, and probably files with more collected intelligence. A sound of a blaring car horn brought him back to the present.

He calculated the drive would take nearly seven hours, and tomorrow he'd repeat it on the way back to Moscow.

But today, Nicolai Kalinin was going to Kursk. He was finally going home.

Acknowledgements

For SPECOPS: We never know where you are, what your missions might be, but we do know you're protecting us and serving your country with honor. Hooyah!

BTF: Couldn't do without your advice, exceptional humor, encouragement. Spaseeba!

Made in the USA
San Bernardino, CA
17 September 2016